GERMAN NARRATIVE PROSE

GERMAN
NARRATIVE PROSE
VOLUME III

edited by
WERNER REHFELD

Dufour
1968

© 1968 OSWALD WOLFF (PUBLISHERS) LIMITED, LONDON

First published 1968

Library of Congress Catalog Card No.
66-13842

MADE AND PRINTED IN GREAT BRITAIN

CONTENTS

ACKNOWLEDGEMENTS

Acknowledgements are due for permission to print these stories in their English versions to the authors and to the following publishers :

Heliopolis Verlag, Tübingen, for "Ortner's Story" by Ernst Jünger;

Suhrkamp Verlag, Frankfurt/Main, for "Trip into the Blue, 1960" from "Karsch und Andere Prosa" by Uwe Johnson © 1964; for "The Andorran Jew" from "Tagebuch 1946–1949" by Max Frisch © 1950; and for "I Walked Behind Her" from "Ein Flugzeug Uber Dem Haus" by Martin Walser © 1955;

Dr. Jan van Loewen Ltd., London, for "Lucas, Gentle Servant" by Siegfried Lenz;

Verlag Klaus Wagenbach, Berlin, for "A Place for Chance Encounters" by Ingeborg Bachmann;

Die Arche, Zürich, for "The Theatre Manager" by Friedrich Dürrenmatt;

Prof. Dr. Walter Jens for "The Conquest of Troy" by Walter Jens;

Günter Grass for his story "The Lefthanders";

S. Fischer Verlag, Frankfurt/Main, for "The Photograph" from "Schwarze Geschichten" by Herbert Heckmann;

Verlag Kurst Desch GmbH, München, for "Footsteps in the Sand" by Hans Werner Richter.

Three of the stories have been published before in English, and acknowledgement is made to the publishers due to their version :

To Messrs. Martin Secker & Warburg Ltd., London, for the story "Angels in the Night" by Ilse Aichinger;

To Messrs. MacGibon & Kee Ltd., London, for the story taken from "Traveller, If You Come to Spa" by Heinrich Böll;

To Penguin Books Ltd., Harmondsworth/Middlesex, for the story taken from "German Writing Today" by Peter Weiss. © Christopher Middleton, 1967.

INTRODUCTION

1945—after six years there ended for the world a war, and for Germany twelve years of National Socialism. The extent of the catastrophe is even now hardly credible: cities and industrial plants were destroyed; there was not a single family which had not lost close relatives killed in the war; Germany itself was divided into four Zones of Occupation; almost the whole of the population of her Eastern territories was moving westwards.

Those were the conditions under which German writers after 1945 began to work again. The whole material world had collapsed. No intact external façade existed which might have been able to give shelter to and nourish crises of the spirit. This provided an almost perfect opportunity and field for critical minds.

Who, during the war and before it, had in Germany the opportunity to keep abreast of publications in France, England or America? What, in this deepest trough of human life and spirit, had these critical minds in the way of standards of comparison or sense of direction? For twelve years, since the beginnings of National Socialism in 1933, German writers had been cut off from the world, and had been forced to live on in national isolation. At that time German writers of any international standing had left Germany and had emigrated: Thomas Mann, Bertolt Brecht, Robert Musil, Hermann Broch, Franz Werfel, Carl Zuckmayer, to name but a few. Their novels and plays were published abroad and were thus inaccessible to the German reading public. Even more than this, the Nazis had systematically corrupted the language, to such an extent that the most important prerequisite for any literature, namely the feeling for linguistic quality, could no longer be guaranteed.

These, then, were the conditions under which literature began to flourish again in post-war Germany: without any material or spiritual stability, without the contact with foreign contemporaries, so necessary in any process of revitalisation and recovery; without even contemporary standards in the native language: such models were unknown or had to be imported. Add to this the existence of a language so bastardised by propoganda of an unparalleled extensiveness that it constituted no standard at all.

At first it was inevitable that traditional standards were sought. Expressionism and its language provided a starting point; foreign writers were belatedly studied: Hemingway, Wolfe, Faulkner, Wilder, Joyce Cary, Graham Greene, Giraudoux, Anouilh. At the same time the native language was thoroughly overhauled, and there set in a period of "deforestation"—no superfluous words and no unpondered phrases were tolerated. This process was easiest for the older writers.

In this collection there are examples of the work of writers of a wide range of age and style. Some of the authors in the collection come from East Germany and have settled in the West, and some have not settled in Germany at all, either East or West. Included are also examples of the work of Austrian and Swiss writers. The oldest writer represented here was born in the same year as Röntgen discovered X-rays and was old enough to serve in the First World War; the youngest was not even born when Hitler seized power, and was hardly out of his cradle when Otto Hahn succeeded in his experiments in the nuclear fission of uranium and thus made the manufacture of the atom bomb a possibility.

Ernst Jünger (1895), prostituted by the Nazis because of his early novels where war and battle were glorified and soldierly virtues extolled, published in 1949 his allegorical novel *Heliopolis*. Here political problems of the moment are veiled in poetry and paraphrased in symbolic language. Jünger had always had the ability to illumine the contemporary scene and to sense hidden powers behind it. With this he developed an ability to deduce from any present manifestation changes and coming events: what better "pathfinder" could German writing have than this almost Wellsian scientific utopian?

The younger generation, which began to write first after 1945, regarded such experiments with reserve. Hans Werner Richter (1908), is the founder of the "47 Group"—in 1947 there met for the first time a number of young German authors to read and discuss their most recent writings, inspired originally and guided by the vision of Hans Werner Richter. Richter begins his own novel *Footsteps in the Sand*, published in 1953, with these words:

"When I was born the Kaiser was still making his customary trips to the north, the men of the village where I came into the world still wore drill sergeant's waxed moustaches, and the 20 Mark gold coin was still legal tender"—a glance back at the past as one means of facing the future. A cool, matter-of-fact language, understatement became the rule. The prose-style of foreign literature, for example Hemingway's, becomes evident: it is no longer a language of symbols but of reality itself. Richter is a stout protagonist of the committed writer, and is thus more interested in content than in form. His own radicalism, and his urge to record and inform, are concentrated in a fine burst of writing covering only a few years and culminating in 1958. The story in this collection is a masterly example. He remains a mentor and guide, ever alert to provide encouragement to such writers and publicity for them.

The years from 1945–1950 were for post-war German writers a period of preparation for an international "come-back". Assurance and versatility come into their own, and there emerges a period of experiment in style. The age of "schools", dedicated to specific forms and content, is past. Memory of the 1933–1945 period and its horrors, remains nevertheless vivid. Dürrenmatt (1922) warns us all in his story "The Theatre Manager" of the demagogue who deceives and misleads the masses. As a matter of course we respect very much the views of a writer of Dürrenmatt's stature, a man who is at home in so many fields: in the drama, where he is best known, in the radio play, in the short story, and as a film script writer. He says of himself that he is fond particularly of the theatre, because "it obeys the rules", and, at the same time, like the detective story, leaves room for the miraculous and the surprising, a much longed-for but sadly overlooked drug of a great portion of the reading public. More than most writers represented in this selection Dürrenmatt seems to be in a direct line of a literary tradition, from Aristophanes and on through the Comedies of Shakespeare and of Nestroy.

In his "Andorran Jew", Max Frisch (1911) appeals to reason and conscience and calls on us all to learn from the past for the sake of the future of all mankind. Frisch is outstanding for his versatility as a man and for his refusal to be dragooned into any one system of thought. Prepared as are few writers to accept changes in this world, he is nevertheless critical of all he sees, and

never becomes ecstatic in his acceptance of progress for its own
sake. The writer, he wrote once, hears from inside what to many
other people is already audible, but . . . from outside. No interpretation, he maintains, is an order. The story included here is
a kind of rehearsal, a prelude, to his play "Andorra".

"My Place" by Peter Weiss (1916), because of its very lack of
commitment, its cool, objective style achieves the very opposite :
namely revulsion at the crimes perpetrated in Auschwitz. Here
we have an example of one who accepts shame for all or for the
many who are incapable of feeling shame or unwilling to accept
it. It is difficult to define Weiss' prose style in fiction (the piece
printed in this collection is autobiographical-typographical in its
conception). All his writing is characterised by an impressive and
powerful momentum and of word manipulation unparalleled in
European literature since James Joyce. (Weiss' "Parting from
Parents", for example, has not a single paragraph division in its
entire length of 140 pages.) The effect is to absorb the reader
entirely : mind, body, soul and spirit are swept up in an irresistible forward march. He says of himself that, so deeply has his
experience affected him since 1933 (he has lived outside Germany since 1936), whenever he uses German, all he is aware of
is a "monologue in vacuum". But his every word is an adventure,
and he deserves the very serious attention of all who value
literature.

The political situation in a divided Germany and the human
problems arising out of the resulting conditions is also one of the
themes of German writing since 1945. Ingeborg Bachmann
(1926), in "A Place for Chance Encounters" describes the fate of
Berlin : an interplay of associations which reveals the true condition of that city. The whole range of her writings covers a much
wider field, indicating in some way the progress of her own interests, which began with research in metaphysics and has included
a Visiting Professorship in Poetry, where her subject was "Utopia
in Literature". Throughout her work we note a predominant
lyrical element, even in her prose. Her own guide idea is: "the
people need poetry as they need bread." This questing Austrian
can sometimes almost alarm us with her unerring insight and
understanding.

The scene of Uwe Johnson's (1934) "Trip into the Blue, 1960"
is placed on both sides of the zonal frontier, in East and West

Germany. Here is an example of a writer who is almost taciturn and yet remarkably eloquent. He is a native of what is now East Germany, where he has spent the greater part of his life. He is not, he says, a refugee, as most West Germans would describe him, but one who has, quite simply, moved from one place to another. A large part of his major work, the novel *Suppositions concerning Jakob* deals with the movement of individuals, in mind and spirit, as well as physically.

Günter Grass (1927) in "The Lefthanders" writes: "There is nothing, no crime of which we have not reproached ourselves . . . it is the Bible which calls on us to root out all evil. But more acute is the burning, continual desire to see one's way clearly, to understand clearly one's own situation. . . ." This is the question facing the young generation, the thirty and forty year olds: they are "far from fouling their own nest" when they revert continually to the past; they feel a sense of responsibility towards present and future; they ask continually about those forces which caused the Second World War, in order that they may prevent a repetition. Grass writes in a style and manner which defies ordinary interpretation—graphic, abounding in metaphors and yet precise. This "enfant terrible" of literature (and politics) startles his reader by thrusting some reality at him, and giving him no chance of personal rumination or retrospection to check his impressions. The change of pace in his writing is at the same time stimulating and bewildering, with his immense range of allegory and in his progression and pause.

"Our doors must remain open, I said, no matter who may wander in from the street and with no matter what intentions. The Association must and should be strong enough to deal with such strangers." Thus Martin Walser (1927) in his story "I Walked Behind Her". This, too, is characteristic of post-war Germany. After years of impeded communication with one's neighbours and with the outside world, discussion and exchange of views are encouraged. The solution does not lie in a restricted-membership club, but only in the willingness to open one's heart and mind to the stranger. "Narration, relating, telling—all tantamount to admission . . .", such is Martin Walser's own definition of writing; and he continues: "while doing so, one must throw up a defence of calm and serene aloofness." And one really feels this when reading him. The reader is trying all the time to get nearer. We therefore find in his work not figures and characters in the conventional sense but voices, as in the poetry of Günter Eich. In Martin Walser the role of the speaker is all important : it is a world where language alone has meaning.

We have already established that a plurality of styles and themes characterises German writing since 1945. How difficult it is to classify or co-ordinate with the rest of the examples in this collection "The Photograph" by Herbert Heckmann (1930). Is it perhaps sick humour? Heckmann writes with pleasure and perhaps with ease, but he is concise and witty. We find in him and in his characters a wisdom well beyond their actual years. Even his child creations are precocious. It was once prophesied that Heckmann would, after his novel *Benjamin* (1962)—it is his only novel to date—write something better and certainly something unusually modern. The story in this collection is only one example of a statement which certainly looks like being true.

One can also find associations with antiquity and new, contemporary interpretations of its mythology and facts. Heinrich Böll (1917) "Wanderer, if you come to Spa . . .", Walter Jens (1923) "The Conquest of Troy", as well as elements of phantasy going back to the Romantics—Ilse Aichinger (1921) "Angels in the Night", and even attempts to comprehend one's own fate by exotic action, that is, by alienation : Siegfried Lenz (1926): "Lukas, Gentle Servant".

Heinrich Böll rose in ten years from complete obscurity to world fame. This is all the more remarkable since this fame is as great abroad as in Germany itself. Why is this? Is it because he seems to fulfil a *social* function, to have a social significance? For the Anglo-Saxon world he is the quintessence of post-war German writing. A Roman Catholic of unquestioned devoutness he nevertheless does not attempt to offer a Christian interpretation of events. There are signs that he has grown out of the stage of straightforward story-telling, based largely on his war experiences; these stories are masterpieces of the topical and of the short story as a form. What is his direction, now in this surfeited world so different from the one which inspired him so wonderfully hitherto?

Walter Jens has been in his time essayist, novelist, critic and university professor, and cannot make up his mind which to make his main field. To do so would denote for him limitation, and that he cannot accept. In his novels there is faint reminiscence of the milieu of Zola, but this is tautened by an Orwell-like urgency and a Kafka-like insistence.

Ilse Aichinger's main, indeed only theme is mankind in the bondage caused and nourished by his own lack of concern for his fellows. A fresh insight is needed, she says; traditional modes of thought fail now : we must get behind the façade of all human existence as we see it.

The Hemingway influence is stronger in Siegfried Lenz than in any contemporary German novelist. Lenz offers a cautious, pondered testimony, rather like that in Uwe Johnson's work, where the form, as to some extent with Lenz also, is that of a long series of rhetorical questions. There is in Lenz a definite alignment with legend, with parable and the symbolic.

The varied items in this anthology of German writing have not been assembled under any such heading as common theme, specific content or even according to a clearly defined form. They are deliberately so varied that they do not "fit together" (e.g. "The Photograph" and "My Place"). But therein lies the charm and purpose of an anthology.

Dr. W. Rehfeld
J. C. Alldridge

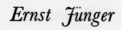

Ernst Jünger

Translated
by
Ivo Jarosy

ERNST JÜNGER

ORTNER'S STORY

IT happened long ago, and I shall not mention my name. It is unworthy of being recorded.

I was wretched, ruined in body and soul through my own fault. My parents had spared no expense to give me a good education. I had gone to the university and had not lacked the means for private travel and study. But I had destroyed myself through extravagance, vice and idleness. For a long time I had been penniless, homeless even, and my friends and acquaintances, tired of coming to my aid, were avoiding me. I did not mind that and kept out of their way, for I was devoured by a hatred of men and society. I felt at ease only in the hiding places of the outcast and rejected.

Lacking the means to indulge in select and expensive vices, I had to content myself with cheap and ugly forms of debauchery —with cheap liquor, the company of slum tarts and, above all, with gambling in the dens of the big city. Thus I lived trapped in a dark and terrible dream. My fate more and more resembled the dirty cards, moist with sweat and liquor and marked by card-sharpers—the aces, knaves, black and red queens and their con-stellations—towards which my drunken passion was directed. Low, greedy faces surrounded me at the round table, and hands that anxiously grasped hold of their cards. The mornings brought losses and savage quarrels.

Thus I dragged out my days, and their burden was made all the heavier by the memory of rich islands, of luxury and abun-dance. All this I had known and enjoyed, and I was haunted by the desire to return to those tables where money is not counted. Happiness and content appeared to me solely in the form of money, of vast sums. It seemed to me that there was no way to happiness except through the kind of calculations gamblers engage in.

One ought, so I frequently thought, to arrive at a relation to the world and its treasures analogous to that which gamblers call "a lucky strain". At times, while gambling, I had had an

17

inkling of a force that, like a subtle magnetism, grants us an insight into Fortuna's realm and endows us with a lucky hand. But I never managed to go beyond the law of series—suddenly the current failed and heavy losses followed. And yet, like all gamblers, I was convinced that one could arrive at a kind of nimble lightness not subject to the laws of chance. I believed that one's luck could be forced, that there exists a power within us that decides where the ball comes to rest, which is the winning card. During the long nights, I thought about these possibilities.

Like all such dreamers I was approaching magical realms, if not worse. The gambler's form of existence pushes him powerfully towards superstitions and then towards spiritual crimes, too grave to be recognised by human judgment and human law—whose very names do not figure in any legal code. Once we totally abandon ourselves to gambling, we soon enter into a world of talismans, of mantic places and hours, of cabbalistic systems. And if we are bold enough to penetrate into these labyrinths, where the walls glow with signs and numbers, we approach at every turn, every false move, more powerful bearers of magic power. They remain invisible, but exert their influence over our thoughts and deeds. When the corruption has gone sufficiently far, they have at all times appeared in visible form as well, repeating the eternal promise that we shall gain the world at the price of our salvation.

It is a strange fact that unbelief renders them particularly strong and effective. Since my earliest youth I had despised what is commonly called "sin" and "the other world". Now I had moved so far from those spheres that I did not even ridicule them any more. I regarded the world as a vast automaton; one's luck depended on the degree to which one was able to guess at its construction. The devil of the Middle Ages was a silly sot, a buffoon invented by childish fears and childish imaginings. He offered men treasures for a bill of exchange drawn on absurd realms, for a worthless signature. Not a bad wish dream, to imagine someone with whom one could do such splendid business.

"If I were the devil, I wouldn't give those lazy blighters a penny for their signatures. If he appeared to me, he could have mine for a farthing. He wouldn't have to offer me Fortuna's purse or a magic ring. All he'd have to do would be to re-fill this glass."

Thus I rambled on, in a state of drunken stupor, with my head resting on a rough wooden table. The place was a large waiting room, just before sunrise. I felt oppressed and giddy, as though in a ship on a rough sea. Around me I heard loud voices and the clinking of glasses. Drunks were quarrelling with waiters, with their girls, with policemen, for whom this was a good hunting-ground. All this ebbed and flowed in a swirling movement that made me feel seasick. Late revellers used to come here after the pubs had closed, and prostitutes lay in wait for their last clients. Those without a roof over their heads, like myself, waited for the next morning in this dreary hall.

Nowadays I could show myself only in dark places, since even my rags were beginning to fall apart. I presented a terrifying spectacle, and already had a good idea from which thicket my corpse would scare the children who had strayed there in the course of play. I felt that I had turned entirely into refuse, through a decay that, working outwards from within, had eaten through my shirt, shoes and clothes. It had become necessary, indeed inevitable, that I should do away with myself. But still I was pursued by a vague dream of happiness, as by a melody heard on a ship that is sinking fast.

My head seemed to be filled entirely with quicksilver. Swaying with the effort, I got to my feet. To my surprise I saw that my glass had been filled. I rubbed my eyes, but there was no room for doubt : a red elixir filled it to the rim.

*

"Blackberry Brandy; you must fortify yourself, my friend."

These words were uttered by a soft but penetrating voice close by. I turned round and saw that I was sharing the table with an unknown man, who was watching me attentively. He wore a grey lounge suit, inconspicuous but of exquisite cut. His face was inconspicuous too, of a type one encounters every day in our world. The sharp, attentive features show that their owner is accustomed to making important decisions on his own; the pale skin testifies to work continued after office hours. One finds such faces in ministries, universities and industry. But not in the most prominent places; they tend to exert their influence from hidden rooms. In business negotiations one wanders for a long time through a maze of corridors, until at last a servant takes one to the cell of one of these grey eminences. Here matters suddenly become transparent and, in two or three sentences, are clarified and made ready for signature. Occasionally, of course, one also meets them in bars and night-clubs, where they are welcomed as guests of honour.

In other ages such personages would have been recognised as evil and even dreadful; in a world where evil has become generalised, however, they make an authoritative impact. One immediately senses that they embody the dominant principles, that they are leaders. But they show no interest in honours; they find their reward in their work. In their cells they construct thoughts sharper than any sword, or invent little powders that can render whole nations defenceless. In appearance they are modest but sure of themselves: they know their rank. One feels that they have mastered the problems which occupy their contemporaries. This knowledge endows them with a faint, unobtrusive irony.

The stranger's gaze rested on me with critical benevolence. It exhibited the careful attentiveness of a doctor who lifts the bandage from an abcess. Then he repeated.

"You must fortify yourself, my friend."

I lifted the glass and drained it. I felt the drink pouring through my veins, fiery, revivifying, and looked around me with a clearer head. The fog inside me disappeared, my senses became keener. The encounter, however, now seemed all the more strange. Nothing was further from me, by nature, than to believe in human kindness, and I decided above all to be on my guard. On the other hand I was in a situation where I had nothing to lose. The stranger smiled.

"Perhaps you think that I can read your thoughts? And if it were so, why should that surprise you? Thought-reading is no magic. It is entirely a deductive art. It can be acquired and it's displayed at fair-grounds. Don't let it worry you. What could be simpler than to guess that a man sitting in front of an empty glass expects it to be filled? There are no thoughts without impulses behind them—in this case thirst. That is a simple example; one's insight grows to the extent to which one knows all the possible combinations. Then one can unlock all heads with one master key. In that situation, there are games which one always wins."

"Ah, a cardsharper. No doubt he's looking for an accomplice. The fellow couldn't have come at a more opportune moment. Now I've got to keep my wits about me."

Off-handedly I replied:

"Games which one always wins? For that one would have to do a bit more than thought-reading."

"A bit more? Not at all. Just watch," and as I had thought, he produced a pack of cards, which he shuffled and spread out with a practised hand.

"Name three cards, just as they come into your head."

I called out the seven of spades, the jack of diamonds and the ace of clubs.

"Now draw."

And indeed, I held the three cards, in the correct order, in my hand. The chap was worth his weight in gold; my spirits rose by several degrees.

"Splendid. Except that I don't know what it has to do with thought-reading. One might even claim that I had guessed *your* thoughts when I drew those cards."

The stranger looked at me with amusement and laughed softly.

"Excellent, I saw straightaway that you have a good head on your shoulders. Your objection is quite in order. The experiment was too simple. We'll have to start off differently."

He shuffled again and placed the pack in front of me.

"You will now think of three cards, but without telling me. There, draw."

Again I drew and, with an expression of surprise I was unable to control, turned up the three cards I had thought of. The stranger enjoyed my astonishment, which was obvious enough.

"Who's been reading thoughts now—you or I? You won't be able to answer that question, since you do not know what thoughts are. Thoughts are nothing but matter in action. That matter forms the substance of the brain no less than of a roulette ball or a pack of cards. Only it is infinitely easier to guess what lies hidden on the other side of a playing card than to do the same thing for a human forehead. But if you like, I shall teach you the art."

It became more and more clear to me that I had been hooked by an extremely clever swindler. At the same time I still could not imagine what he was after. Anyone with eyes in his head must have realised that I had nothing worth the taking. No rag collector would have looked at me twice. The simplest explanation was probably that he had some practical joke in mind, and I decided that I had better fall in with his plans. I laughed and replied :

"If you had mastered the art of seeing through cards, you would hardly walk through waiting rooms at four o'clock in the morning, looking for company like mine."

The stranger's good humour seemed to increase still further; he started to whistle softly to himself.

"Yes, quite right, very clever. You've touched on another sore point. That is the argument the alchemists are afraid of : what makes you peddle your arts in the streets, instead of sitting comfortably at home coining sovereigns to your hearts' content?"

He fell silent for a little while and smiled at me. Then he added :

"You are too intelligent—you don't know the power of sympathy. How if, coming upon you here, I had simply felt that something had to be done for you? But quite apart from that, there are other possibilities which you cannot fathom. There could exist operations at which your assistance was absolutely necessary. What made the Mauretanian turn to Aladdin, of all people, when the lamp had to be hidden? I repeat that I want to teach you a knowledge which will enable you to win always. But this is hardly the proper place."

He looked round and added, sarcastically :

"I'm not keeping you from anything important, am I?"

The scoundrel ! He must have known that my only worry was where to lay my hands on a piece of rope. So I hastened to reply :

"I am unworthy of your interest. But since it seems to please you, I am entirely at your disposal.

"I think you will not regret it. Follow me."

He called the waiter to pay my bill, and we left.

*

The station square was already illuminated by the first rays of daylight. The stranger walked unhurriedly through the empty streets, whistling snatches of melodies. I kept at his side, his miserable client. Dark, uncanny forebodings filled my mind; I sensed that I had fallen into evil clutches. What did he want from me, what was he planning to do to me? For the first time, like a subtle pain, a longing for my childhood took hold of me. But what did I have to lose, in this dawn preceding the void?

Soon we had arrived. The stranger stopped in front of one of those tall office blocks that are wrapped in a crazy quilt of business name-plates and publicity hoardings. We entered and went up in a lift. The stranger opened a door. Above the bell I read:

DR. FANCY
Oculist
Consultations by Appointment only

We entered through a bare antechamber into his consulting room, which looked like the workshop of a highly intelligent craftsman. A table was heaped with spectacles and optical instruments and the walls were hung with charts, covered with numbers and letters. The room was dominated by right angles and straight lines; to me it seemed to be filled with a hard, pitiless radiation. I particularly noticed a showcase of glass eyes. They lay on a cushion of red velvet and glowed with colours surpassing those of life. They were almost reminiscent of opals, and indicated an optical craftsman of the first order.

Dr. Fancy motioned me into a chair covered with oil cloth, and sat down opposite on a stool. He now wore a little smock. He looked keenly into my eyes, and it seemed to me that from his almost point-like pupils two subtle rays passed into mine. I became sleepy, but clearly heard the words which, slowly and with an irresistibly mild voice, he was addressing to me:

"I shall not keep you longer than is necessary. Your secret wishes have been known to me for a long time. Though you did not realise it clearly, you were on the right path; you shall be rewarded. You guessed that there exists two sorts of men: fools and initiates. The former are the slaves, the latter the masters of this world. What is the reason for the difference? Quite simply that two great laws rule the universe: chance and necessity. Remember it well: there is nothing else. The slaves are governed by chance; the masters control it. Among the nameless legions of the blind, there are a few who can see."

The voice was sending me to sleep. My intoxication returned more strongly than before. I heard the doctor handling instruments. At the same time, he continued his lecture in a measured but extremely penetrating tone, so that I did not miss a single word :

"The world is constructed after the archetype of the *chambre double*. As all living beings are basically formed of two leaves, it is constructed in two layers, related as inside to outside, of which one has a higher, the other a lower reality. The lower reality, however, is determined by the higher, down to its minutest details.

"Now imagine the following : you are standing in a room in the midst of a large company. People gamble, debate, do business, in short, do all the things people usually do. To the uninitiated, everything, all the various groupings and happenings in the room, will be more or less a matter of chance. Hence none of them are able to predict with any degree of certainty what even the next moment will bring. Everything is ruled by the unforeseen, by a blind force.

"Now go further. The room is covered by a second layer, which is invisible, like an aura. It is almost without extension, but significative. Imagine this layer as a kind of wall-paper, covered with a script of images and numbers. I shall remove the scales from your eyes, and you will discover to your surprise that these characters furnish the key to everything that is happening in the room. Until now you were like a man who follows the course of the stars every night, but without a knowledge of astronomy. Now you are one of the initiates, and your power is like that of the ancient priesthoods, who foretold the eclipses of the sun and moon. You have undergone the initiation into a magic nobility. This is the world where the secret lies hidden; there is no other. You will be eternally grateful to me."

With these words, Dr. Fancy bent down over my face. I saw that he wore a strap on his forehead, carrying a round mirror with a hole in the middle. A movement of his hand placed my chair in a horizontal position, and he approached closer, holding a pointed glass tube.

"A maniac—he wants to burn out your eyes !"

An icy shock of terror passed through me and left me petri-
fied. I saw him turn down the mirror; he looked at me as though
through a huge, empty eye. I heard him murmur :

"The brandy has taken effect."

The hair rose on my head. I opened my mouth, but no sound
came. He placed the tube over my eyes, letting fall two drops
that burned like acid. The pain was unbearable; everything went
black and I felt myself fainting.

When I came to again, Dr. Fancy had already levered the
chair upright again. He was dabbing my eyes with a wad of
cotton wool.

"Did it hurt a little? Well, nothing is gained without some
suffering. It's all over now and I repeat, you will be grateful to
me."

I could hardly believe that I had managed to get off so lightly.
Discreetly I looked round for some blunt object with which to
knock him down, if necessary. Then I said politely :

"You've had your little joke, Doctor. Please let me go now—
I feel very weak."

So as to disarm any suspicion he might feel, I added :

"If you had a few pennies to spare, I would be most grateful . . ."

The doctor laughed :

"Croesus begging alms! Ah well, they say that millionaires
often carry no small change."

He stepped up to his writing desk and handed me a bundle
of notes, without counting them.

"Use the small denominations first, as long as you look like
this, or you'll get yourself arrested."

He looked me over once more, like someone who is satisfied
with his handiwork.

"Of course you'll soon realise that locks and keys are not
made for people like you. You now stand above the law."

With that he dismissed me.

*

The streets were already crowded. I plunged into their tur-
moil. The fright I had received had not yet worn off, and I
would not have repeated the adventure for all the money in the
world. I hastened to a public park and sat down on a bench,

utterly exhausted. Only when I put my hand in my pocket did I remember the bundle of banknotes. I took them out and counted them carefully. They were undoubtedly genuine. It was a large sum—this made the whole thing a complete mystery to me. But I did not think about it long. I felt like a shipwrecked traveller who feels firm ground under his feet once more.

It was a beautiful, warm morning. Gradually, while warming myself in the sun, I managed to get my thoughts into some kind of order. That Doctor Fancy undoubtedly had a screw loose somewhere, only no one else had noticed it as yet. I had profited by his lunacy. The adventure could have ended badly: I had been lucky. From time to time I discreetly leafed through the bundle of notes.

I began to think about the new start I would be able to make. Now I had to emerge gradually from the state into which I had fallen. First I would look for an old clothes dealer and get myself some cheap clothes. Then I would rent once more the little room I had occupied before I became homeless. Once there, I could order a suit from a tailor, and then move again. Thus I would gradually raise myself from the dregs as though through a series of locks.

Filled with new-born courage, I walked to the Metropolitan Railway, to take a train to the old city. The yellow train entered the station, the doors opened. The crowd pressed forward into the compartments, but I was held back by a strange vision. It seemed to me that I was on the point of stepping into a hearse. The conductor, the passengers, stared at me with dreadful eyes. This was no doubt an after-effect of the shock I had received. All the same it made me feel uncomfortable, and I decided to walk rather than go by train. I followed the route of the Metropolitan, whose rails rested on high pillars, in the direction of the city centre. At a crossing near Gleisdreieck Station I was stopped by a crowd. There had been a terrible disaster: the Metropolitan train had crashed down. I saw the conductor being carried off on a stretcher, with a crushed skull. Quickly I made off, as though I had not only foreseen the catastrophe but had somehow been responsible for it too.

That evening I was sitting in my room, drinking tea. Above all, I was going to give strong drink a wide berth from now on. I wore a pair of sailor's trousers and a woollen sweater; I was

freshly shaven and bathed. Next to me stood a small suitcase
with shirts and underwear. I filled my pipe with Virginia
tobacco. My landlady had been somewhat suspicious, but when
I paid off my old debts to her, she had let me have the room
with pleasure. She was not so very particular. The tenant before
me had been arrested a year ago for embezzlement, and yet she
still visited him in prison. He had lived in her house for a long
time : a small employee living in unobtrusive style, until large
sums had been found missing at his place of work.

As all this passed through my mind, I suddenly had a strange
idea. It had never been discovered what he had done with the
money. Probably he had hidden it away. What if he had hidden
it quite nearby, perhaps in this very room? His continuing
attachment to his landlady was rather strange. I felt a ravening
cleverness awaken within me. I looked at the familiar room with
new eyes, intent on putting myself into the frame of mind of
someone who wants to spy out a hiding-place. Immediately I
realised that everywhere except the fireplace was out of the
question. Of course the police had already conducted a thorough
search, but then policemen are notoriously lacking in imagination.

Carefully I locked the door and set to work. I removed two
candlesticks and a clock that stood on the mantelpiece, and then
tried to raise the marble slab. It did not come off, but could be
lifted up a little, like the lid of a locked trunk. It seemed to be
held in by some kind of catch, and there was, indeed, a bit of
decorative metal which, when pressed, removed the obstruction.
The slab could be lifted up, uncovering a hollow space beneath.
It was filled with bundles of banknotes and gold coins. I had
discovered the secret hoard.

Thus, for a long time I had passed my days in abject poverty,
in the immediate vicinity of a treasure hoard, like someone dying
of thirst above a subterranean stream. How many times had I
walked up and down the room, brooding over my fate, and had
put my glass of grog down on the mantelpiece? Countless times
I had knocked out my pipe on it. And it seemed to me con-
temptible to pass one's life with one's senses as dulled as mine
had been. Carefully, and with a growing pride in my newly
discovered intelligence, I counted the notes and gold coins. With

such means at one's disposal, one does not let oneself be arrested. The fellow deserved his punishment.

There was no doubt that my encounter with Dr. Fancy had changed me. He was right: I should be grateful to him. From now on I experienced my new power ever more clearly, like a child that day by day learns to see things more exactly. In just the same way, I learned day by day to employ my second sight to ever greater advantage. At first, as in the case of the train disaster and the hidden money, it had forced itself upon me in an almost somnambulistic fashion; I obeyed it as though in a dream. Then it became conscious. I learned to control it at will, coldly, at the behest of my reason. Above all I used it only in situations I considered suitable. It was as if I could raise my power of vision to an abnormal pitch, as soon as I made the effort. I was like the owner of a microscope in the midst of a population that does not even guess at the existence of such an instrument. But I made use of it only when it suited me. Then, I saw the elements, the atoms, that determine events, the seeds in which fortune and misfortune lie hidden. But I proceeded cautiously, as though under a cloak of invisibility.

Of course I immediately sought out my familiar gambling dens. I knew now how the cards fell, where the ball came to rest. The change of colours and numbers had lost its threatening aspect; it took place within me, behind my eyes. Different problems occupied me now. I had to learn to control the new power with which I had been endowed; I had to become used to it and at the same time keep it secret. Thus, at first, I remained seated at the green table hesitating for a long time, like someone who has brought but a single gold coin and hesitates anxiously before risking it. I wanted to test my power. Soon I found that it was infallible.

Then I began to stake money carefully, so as to lose. I made a reputation for myself as a bad player. Dr. Fancy had picked himself no fool. Later I began to win in a modest way—thirty pounds here, fifty pounds there. I saw to it that it was my losses that were noticed, not my winnings. The most important thing was to cover up my art. Of course no one would have the slightest inkling of it, but it would be unwise for people to see me winning in long series. I *knew* now, by the way, what I had always suspected: that all habitual gamblers cheat.

Very soon I lost the taste for gambling. The wild excitement that had formerly gripped me and had made the night pass in the twinkling of an eye gave way, after the first surprise, to boredom, when I realised that I was unbeatable. I sat at the gambling table like a civil servant at his desk, waiting for the clock to strike. The one amusing thing was the passion of the others—the spectacle of greenhorns being caught, and of cheats being cheated by me in turn.

Soon I turned my attention to subtler transactions. I moved to the West End and rented a house complete with servants. The first transaction I engaged in from there had to do with an inheritance case. I knew of a big inheritance, and knew, too, the poor heirs of the vanished relative : two data which, through a dummy middleman, I turned into ready cash. Thereby I acquired a number of ships listed as overdue and made some risky insurance deals. I also made pleasure trips to places traditionally linked with legends of hidden treasure, and found the treasure without much difficulty. I did not go to the trouble of having it dug up, but left it where it was, safer than in any bank. I made a record and deposited the maps and sketches with my securities. In the course of these explorations, I learned that legends of this kind, that have remained current among the population, are usually well founded, and that the number of hidden treasures is far greater than is usually supposed.

Speculation in minerals was easier still. I knew the places where they could be found. This knowledge I kept to myself and added it to my capital. On the other hand, it amused me to derive profits from plots of land where I knew there was nothing to be found. I entered into contracts with the owners and set up co-operatives. The shares sold like hot cakes. I pocketed the money and left the buyers to their dreams of rich strikes and the need for further investment.

After enjoying a series of sizeable successes, this method of pursuing single objectives began to seem rather laborious. It kept me from my distractions. I was necessarily attracted towards the field of large-scale finance, where the movement of money is determined almost entirely by the pure intellect. I penetrated into the secrets of the stock exchange and soon mastered its techniques. I learned to judge values and the opinions that determine prices. Like all the powers of this world, money is both a completely real and a completely imaginary entity. Big financial coups are achieved by those who have mastered its dual character. Hence that extra quantum of imagination which none of the princes of money lack, and which makes them capable of compositions similar to those in music. An ear for music, after all, is supposed to be due to the perception of fine differences in the realm of numbers.

"Sell rising shares and buy falling ones." This maxim contains the essence of stock exchange strategy, indicating that one must interrupt a series at the right moment. Our instinct, our inborn gambling passion, pushes us in the opposite direction; it always assumes the series to be infinite. But I knew the laws that govern prosperity.

I now entered that circle of select beings to whom human wealth, human labour, has become tributary. Business is other people's work, other people's money. The Negro searching for diamonds in the blue clay, the engineer who, with legions of feverish diggers, joins two oceans by a canal, the farmer worrying over his harvest, the ruler weighing up war and peace with his cabinet—they all are almost unconscious of the fact that their efforts are caught up and reflected in the mirror of speculation, in cells where the world's values are seen as monetary ones. Money is life's real force, its most meaningful symbol and abbreviation; hence the tremendous, universal urge to get hold of it.

Mysterious, too, is the ebb and flow of big money, by which fortunes are made and lost. In the highest echelons, the knowledge of these changes is completely divorced from the current prices. Rather, it influences them by means of powerful fictions. And there are occasions when losses can be no less profitable than gains. Here business assumes an entirely abstract character.

I had soon arranged things so that I made a maximum of profit with a minimum of effort. Partly through agents, partly over the telephone, I gave orders to banks to buy up securities that were moving towards their lowest point, and to sell others shortly before they reached their peak. The real problem was not the choice of securities—here I was infallible—but that I had to work within certain limits, in order not to create a disequilibrium between supply and demand through my own purchases. I was in the position of a punter who knows the winner in a race, but

would shorten the odds if he went on betting without a limit.
This situation fascinated me from a philosophical point of view,
too, since it provided exquisite insights into the interwoven pattern of free will and determinism. From time to time I used to
interrupt the series and simulate losses, so that my strategy should
remain obscure and I did not acquire any fellow-travellers. This
brought ruin to many; my fortune, however, soon grew
enormous.

In all the capital cities and wherever there were stock ex-
changes I opened up small villas: *pieds-a-terre* furnished and
decorated with the utmost elegance. My buyers scoured the
market for pictures and *objets d'art*. It had always given me
pleasure to dress well and to collect exquisite objects. Now I was
able to satisfy my every whim. I became a dandy, who attached
importance to unimportant things and smiled at important matters. I avoided even minor chores. Thus I grew tired of fittings at
my tailors': dummies, made to my measurements, were used for
that purpose. I saw to it that my horses and carriages were of the
best quality and, though I was but a moderate drinker, my wine
cellar housed the choicest vintages. A major domo with the manners and the salary of a Venetian ambassador relieved me of all
bother with the servants.

I was seen at Longchamps in the company of Princess Pigna-
telli, at Epsom with Sarah Butler, whose stage career had then
reached its summit. I was able to see clearly what women hide
all the more carefully the stronger they are affected by it: the
attraction exerted by an unknown stranger who enters their
sphere. I was always conscious of the effect I created. Hence I
was free from that timidity which beauty tends to induce in us.
I was always absolutely sure of myself, and it made me
irresistible.

I was having breakfast at my villa by Lake Wannsee when a
Mr. Katzenstein was announced. I knew him by name as one of
our ablest financiers, and had him admitted. After a few generali-
ties he came to the point. It was this:

He had, for a long time, observed the orders I placed, and
those of the brokers I employed. He knew my "dummies". It
seemed to him that, apart from an occasional error of judgement,
these transactions were controlled by an exceptional intelligence.
He went into details and spoke of strokes of genius. His imme-

diate reason for coming here, he claimed, was a pure feeling of admiration, similar to the irresistible desire for a personal meeting with the author, which the perusal of a book can induce in the reader. He looked at me craftily and made clucking noises, like someone tasting an exceptional vintage.

Listening to him, I experienced a lively feeling of anger. It seemed that I had recently become careless. The best thing now was to assume an authoritative manner and to accept his admiration. With a gracious smile I offered him a glass of port. What was more natural, after all, than that financial success should be based on a specialised knowledge of money and its circulation? What was necessary, in the first place, was insight into world politics and its effects on markets and heavy industry. From here, numerous links led to various other industries. Then there was the problem of free money and the places where it collected. Trade cycles had many, often invisible, causes, but they were not incalculable. If one saw a stone drop into a pond, one could calculate the ripples that would appear. It was possible to work out when this or that spot of the pond would begin to move.

Katzenstein listened attentively while I produced these commonplaces for his benefit. He replied with great politeness :

"Very true, so it says in the textbooks of economics. That is how an experienced meterologist is able to predict the weather with a fair degree of accuracy. Of course, not without meteorological stations, instruments, ships, and a world-wide staff."

He spread out his hands and inspected the palms.

"What are you implying?"

He gazed at me with delight, as though admiring a Raphael :

"A first-rate brain, I always thought so, absolutely first-rate. And what a port—you must be one of old Sandeman's personal customers. What I mean is that, in practice, a scientific knowledge of money is not enough. Capital is required, too. Money's power of attraction increases in proportion to its quantity. The advantage of the banks lies in the fact that they can pursue a series for longer, and over a wider field, than the small gambler, so that they have probability on their side. There is only one way of playing that can stand up to them—the way that corrects the series, that can make its own weather."

My anger increased. Without a doubt, this well-nourished fellow with the liverish eyes had made careful enquiries about me; he knew that not very long ago I had been a beggar. Of course, he was far from the truth. He regarded me as an agent of those powers that stand, invisibly, in the background of the market. Only he was not intelligent enough to realise that this background was an irrational one. He did not and could not suspect that I received my tips from the world's greatest stage manager and carried his *plein pouvoir*. He did not know with whom he was having breakfast.

With the necessary discretion, I let it appear that his guess was not entirely improbable. But if I had, indeed, the connections he suspected, they could only be effective so long as they remained unknown. Of course my reaction only increased his interest. It increased to the precise extent that I appeared to withdraw from his enquiries. In every deal the advantage lies with the partner who shows less concern. He practically thrust himself upon me, and swallowed my bait with shark-like avidity.

From now on Katzenstein sought me out repeatedly to ask for my advice. Without realising it, he thereby took a considerable amount of work off my shoulders, particularly the contact with agents, which is always a troublesome business. I became his partner. In this capacity, I installed an insurance company in his group of firms, which gave mortgages on harvests and generally engaged in financial business that carried a high risk. This company I reserved to myself as my share in the partnership.

Shortly before the end of the Moroccan crisis, I allowed the shares to drop by cancelling the war clause. This coup was directed against Katzenstein. Although he did not see through it, he became suspicious. Cleverly, I advised him to undertake large-scale liquidations, but he would not listen to me. The slump seemed unnatural and promised twofold gains. At such moments, everything becomes ambiguous. They cannot be described in words but require a special flair. Here money rises to fictitious heights, into the realm of the pure imagination. My advice was correct, why did he not follow it? He knew only arithmetical probability.

Then came the treaty of Tangier, which was followed by Black Friday. The bank collapsed; the insurance company made tremendous profits. Constantly, in such crises, the old game of "War or Peace" is being played, as one plays heads or tails with a coin. There followed a conversation between Katzenstein and

2—GNP

myself. He recognised his error. When his butler entered his room the next morning, he found him dead in bed. The reports spoke of a heart attack. The grief of his creditors was immense.

I was now the owner of the firm of Katzenstein & Co. No-one could now be surprised to see me immersed in worldwide financial operations. I turned to government loans, the highest, royal sphere of finance. I was made a baron in Germany, and received the ribbon of the Legion of Honour. I was ranked among the great philanthropists. The Princess now openly parked her carriage in front of my house; people crowded around me at the Jockey Club. It was known that I lost large sums at the gambling tables there.

*

So much for my outward circumstances. They could not have been more prosperous. Yet I felt more and more unhappy, the more I gained in power and prestige. I began to suffer, ever more tormentingly, from boredom. I noticed that the tension was lacking, the uncertainty, the pro and contra, the red and black, that give life its real charm. I played the part of a duellist who cannot be defeated. All chances were calculable for me. They lacked the mystery, the indeterminacy, that make the heart beat faster.

I have already said that gambling quickly lost its attraction for me. The same soon happened with everything else. It became onerous for me to pocket the money of the fools who pressed it upon me. Often I felt tempted to pocket the stake before game had begun. Who wants to work out the solution of a puzzle when he knows the answer? The only thing that still attracted me was to contemplate the excitement and despair of others. But in time I lost the taste even for that. I had lost my own destiny, to become the destiny of those I encountered. As I grew more jaded, my cruelty increased. That, no doubt, is the reason why men who gain unlimited power, like the Roman emperors, necessarily turn to murder. The world becomes a spectacle, a circus.

The same applied to my relations with women: the main thing I felt was my own power. They came to me like moths to the light. While I caressed them, I was constantly conscious of my claws. I played with them as a partner who cannot lose. And like Shylock I saw to it that they paid to the full, with their flesh and blood. I heard the softest falsetti in their melodies.

A strange thing was my fear of being cheated. I knew the exact price of things, and saw to it that I was not overcharged. As my fortune increased, I became more and more strict in this respect. The wealthier one is, the more cheaply one can buy. When wealth becomes absolute, one buys for nothing.

A picture, a house, a piece of furniture were particularly precious to me if they were linked with the memory of a good bargain. It was the logic of money which occupied me more and more, which was taking control of me. At the same time, my spleen increased; I felt that my enjoyments satisfied me less and less. To the extent that my fortune grew, it lost its value for me. After years of excesses, I was forced to lead a life such as is lived in expensive sanatoriums. I loved the colour of grey, noiseless service, days spent in curtained rooms, unspiced dishes, impersonal conversations, women who combined great elegance with absolute nullity.

But it was something else that disquietened me far more than the exhaustion of my *joie de vivre*, something that made itself felt soon after my first triumphal successes. It became ever more clear to me that I carried a dreadful, incommunicable secret inside me. And equally clearly I knew that this secret was a criminal one. My plot against humanity was monstrous, was devised by the arch-fiend. It was so powerful that it was beyond the reach of the law. The thief on the look-out for a favourable occasion, the cardsharper preparing his cards, the man planning evil in his room—they all still took their chance and fell under an all-embracing law. They acted as human beings, while I possessed automatic powers. Hence they could have accomplices, while my knowledge presupposed the profoundest loneliness. I realised this through the fact that I would immeasurably have preferred to be regarded as a forger, than to have my secret even suspected. The delicate hand, the faultless success for which I was admired would have aroused disgust, horror and a frightful hatred if their sources had become known. A usurer who knows the laws of money better than the poor whose blood he sucks; a Don Juan who coldbloodedly repeats the technique of seduction like a clockwork melody: they all did not approach my infallibility. I had parted company with the human race and entered into a new sphere. The man who gains magic power, such as is symbolised by the cloak of invisibility or the magic ring, loses his balance, the tension that keeps us part of the world's course. He controls levers whose powers are infinite. Soon these powers strike back at him.

I first became sensible of this through a vague feeling of malaise, as I more and more clearly recognised the situation I found myself in. The world became empty—a desert where spectres moved according to mechanical laws. I felt that I had lost my way and was gripped by a longing to retrace my steps. The void was growing—how enviable even the most unhappy of men became! They felt hunger, thirst and hope, they had their destiny. All this I lacked.

At that point I realised that side by side with and beyond mechanical laws, a higher law governed the world and made it fruitful. I guessed that it could only be found in those who give lovingly. The void within me drew me to that which was fulfilled, cold was attracted to warmth. I felt that I had to link myself with a human heart, that here alone salvation could be found. But such was my blindness that I employed magical means to aid me in my search.

*

One evening, when my disquiet had become almost unbearable, I let myself drift and felt that I was being drawn to a railway station, the Schlesische Bahnhof. I entered its huge hall, lit by arc lamps, which was swarming with travellers. As frequently in such situations, I experienced a kind of knowing tension—a feeling of curiosity as to why I had come here. I was like a huntsman, who never doubts that he will encounter the game he is after.

I found it when I came upon Helen. She was sitting in a niche formed by a bricked-in window, on a basketwork trunk, such as is carried by girls who are going into domestic service. I saw, from behind, the cheap coat and bent shoulders of a lonely, weeping woman. At a glance, I had grasped her situation: lost, without money or acquaintances, in a strange city. These are the victims for whom procurers, exploiters and mediators of murky deals lie in wait.

I walked up and spoke to her. She was grateful to me, for she was in a situation where one grasps at every straw. Also there was no suspicion in her nature. She saw in me the good neighbour, for whom one longs in times of trouble, and trusted me entirely. I offered her my help and a roof over her head. We carried her trunk to a cab and I took her to Treptow; I had there one of my *pieds à terre*, where I lived occasionally under an assumed name and followed my spleen. It was a modest little place—a small garden house by the river Spree. Helen moved into one of the rooms.

She had dinner with me; we drank tea and talked. I found her unspoiled and unself-conscious. She showed hardly any surprise at our strange meeting. To her I was a kind, chivalrous, gentleman; she could not suspect, of course, that ours was a meeting between complete naïvety and complete self-consciousness. Soon I escorted her to her room and handed her the key, even though I knew that she would not lock her door. She was like a bird in my hand.

After I had left her, I walked up and down in the garden for a long time. The night was dark. From time to time a string of barges, festooned with coloured lights, floated down the river. I knew that innocence yields soonest to seduction. But this was not what concerned me. I wanted to find once again the tension, the inner meaning of life. That was only possible if I set up prohibitions in my realm of limitless freedom. I knew this could be done only through the medium of a human being. I would devote myself to this person, would lavish care upon her as upon a precious being on which my recovery, my salvation depended. Helen should be for me a virginal mirror, into which I directed the rays of my knowledge and received them back, concentrically focused and radiating warmth. I did not see that in this way I made my crime even worse, in that I conjured up love by magical means.

At first everything went as I had intended. Helen took over the running of the little household, while I occupied myself with books and studies. In the morning I drove off to Wannsee or the City, from where I supervised my business operations. They went even better than before. Helen thought of me as a bank official with a good income. I allowed her to think that while I did not have to count the pennies, I had to keep track of my expenditure. My actual wealth would have frightened her. I tried to educate her by developing her own individuality. Soon I realised that she was acquiring a taste for my favourite colours, shapes and odours. Occasionally we visited shops and bought materials, china, or a piece of furniture. I made her presents of books which I had selected. On Saturdays we went to the theatre, and had lunch out on Sundays—in the country, if the weather allowed it. With all this, I kept luxury at a distance or disguised it as simplicity. I fulfilled her wishes before she had even formulated them.

It was not surprising that my plan was successful. I could have possessed Helen the very first evening; we would then have gone on living together in an animalic intimacy. Instead we entered into a spiritual relationship. I became aware of how she attached herself to me, like a sensitive plant, with all her roots. I became her lover in the sense in which one becomes a lover of rare plants, of choice works of art. The soil was virginal; it brought forth crystals and blossoms in beautiful profusion. Before me was the spectacle of a soul unfolding and, as it grew, miraculously gaining in power.

In the course of a year, our relationship had become reversed. It was I who was now the debtor. The fruits that were ripening were too heavy for me. Helen became the source of a higher life for me; I saw the world through her eyes. To the degree that I became dependent upon her, my fear returned, more strongly than before. I realised ever more clearly that by being able to control chance, I had turned into a success machine, an automaton, a worthless void. Inside me I carried a dreadful knowledge, worse than that of the man who had lost his shadow, and with the help of this knowledge I had tied another human being to myself. The moment she saw through me and realised my secret, her love would give way to horror or even disgust. Already it seemed to me that Helen was glancing at me thoughtfully from time to time. I thought it possible that her intuition might be capable of penetrating the web of deception I had spun around her.

It was at that time that my breakdown occurred. I came to one of those turning-points that either annihilate a man or confront him with new decisions; everyone knows them from his own experience. Such a breakdown can be physical: for a long time we feel from small symptoms that some change is taking place in the depths of our physical nature. We should take a rest, but choose to overlook the danger signals. Then, suddenly, comes the stroke that fells us. Similarly before a mental breakdown we turn a deaf ear to the soft voices within us, until there comes the blow that unhinges the entire system. Frequently such a break-down may even be preceded by a period of particularly strong self-confidence. And finally there are moral breakdowns, whose horrors surpass even those of apoplexy and madness. Here the very foundations of one's existence begin to totter.

Yes, the encounter with the void is dreadful. It became clear to me that I had sterilised, annihilated myself from within, and that my wealth gave me a false glow, like the thin laquer with which mummies are varnished. I was gripped by a tremendous disgust for myself.

Helen thought me seriously ill and consulted doctors. I knew, of course, that no physician would be able to help me—especially not those psychologists who regard the soul as a mechanism that can be analysed and treated on technological lines. Our world is full of such charlatans; their influence leads only towards demoniac realms.

I tried to pray, but found that my lips were sealed. Disgusting phrases came into my head. Opposite our house, at the Stralauer Ufer, stood a little church, so I paid a visit to the parson. He knew me, since I lived in his parish and had occasionally sent him some charitable donations, and received me with great res-pect. I tried to make my situation clear to him, but realised immediately that he did not understand me. My words distressed and confused him; undoubtedly he thought that I was mentally disturbed. He talked to me politely, as one talks to a madman whom one wants to get rid of without unpleasant incidents, and urged me to see a doctor.

I then sought refuge with a cleric of the old church, where the knowledge of demonology, of evil's subtler stratagems, has not yet altogether died out. He listened attentively and then turned me away with horror.

I often visited the central district in order to find Dr. Fancy's house again, but in vain. From time to time I thought that it was all imagination, nothing but weird dreams, but this did not diminish the pain I felt. I knew that I was lost.

*

At this time I began to drink again; the hours of drunkenness were the only bearable ones. They seemed like a colourful tent I erected above my head in the desert. Helen brought me wine like a nurse bringing a patient his medicine. It saddened her, but she knew that I had to drink. What is the use of prescribing empty sobriety to a man in pain? Intoxication to him is his last remaining stronghold, the last coloured hem of the garment of darkness.

Then, after midnight, I made for those quarters where life goes on round the clock. I felt the urge to join the crowds that, under the glare of coloured lights, exhibit such a disquieting activity. Every big city has its dark centre, where evil resides. I was attracted to it and even knew its location: a corner of the Grenadierstrasse. Here, at this hour, everyone except the policemen was under the influence of drink or drugs. One saw nothing but women who were selling themselves and men belonging to the criminal underworld. I circled restlessly as part of this crowd that collected in the redly illuminated basin of the Alexanderplatz, then spread out once more as far as the quiet bridges of the Spree. From time to time I fell in with one of the groups that formed around a drunken tart who was being arrested, or some obscure quarrel. Then again I entered one of the big cafés, whose walls were radiant with mirrors, and, like the other guests, sat staring in front of me to the sound of a mechanical orchestra. The sight of this architecture aroused dark thoughts in me.

As before, these peregrinations ended, in complete exhaustion, at one of the railway stations. There are ways of life which, beyond wealth or poverty, are ours and have been cut to our measure. And again there came a morning when I saw myself inescapably confronted by the idea of suicide. I did not realise that I was sitting in the same place as before. As always around this hour, I was very drunk. From time to time I patted my breast pocket; I felt there the vial filled with a powerful poison that I carried on me. The news of the sudden death of an unknown man would still be in time for the morning papers. I shook the powder into a glass.

At this moment a traveller in a blue suit entered hurriedly and approached my table. I saw with vague surprise that it was Dr. Fancy. He sat down opposite me and gave me a searching glance.

"Ah, an old patient, if I'm not mistaken. And how, if I may ask, are your eyes?"

I looked back at him morosely, filled with hatred :

"You should know that better than I. But this time I'll arrange my affairs myself."

Dr. Fancy smiled and whistled his old melody.

"We know, of course, that there are patients who are discontented when their eyes have been sharpened. They complain that their sight is too keen. People seem to prefer an average state of vision—a *clair obscur.*"

He lifted my glass and breathed in its odour with relish. I watched him malevolently and expectantly. The doctor smiled again and repeated his melody in a higher key :

"I see you've made some progress. An excellent smell—bitter almonds."

He poured the contents on the floor and went on :

"Let us talk seriously. It seems that you regard the operation as deleterious, although it was entirely successful. I had even intended to write it up in the professional journals. But you could be given back your old sight without a great deal of trouble."

I hardly dared to believe my ears, and cried out :

"If you'd do that, Doctor, I would give you my entire fortune. You know how vast it is."

"I know. But I am one of those artists who do not work for pay. Since you have, as it were, arrived once more at the same intersection point of the double loop, matters would now have to proceed in the opposite direction. To start off with, you would have to invite me to a blackberry brandy. Then we would be quits in essentials."

He called the waiter, and I gave the order. We emptied our glasses and set out as before. He led me to the house and the consulting room I had searched for so often. After putting on his overall, Fancy made me sit in the oil cloth chair and inspected my eyes with a large magnifying glass. In the manner of some doctors, while getting his instruments ready, he began a monologue that was half addressed to me as well.

"The eye," he said, "is imperfect, like all the demiurge's instruments. A little moisture, a little colour in a dark chamber, looking out on a middle range of light, full of vague impressions. As an organ of insight it is limited by the unforeseen. If we sharpen it, so that it sees the play of chance a little more clearly, the patients complain of pains caused by an excess of illumination. They ask for their illusions back. They prefer their images veiled. The eye was created for a realm of shadows, not for the unbroken light. Light, the great power of the universe, would incinerate you if it approached you without its veil of rainbow colours. Beauty, truth, knowledge are unbearable to the murky eye: mere shadows of them suffice. Why do you press beyond your limits?

"But of course," he added, "how could it be otherwise? The universe is a work of art—hence its imperfections. They are intentional."

He turned to me:

"I sharpened your eyes with an acid. They can be dulled again with a base. But you would have to accept a diminution in your power of sight."

"Get to work—whatever the risk."

The doctor shrugged his shoulders and turned back to his instruments. Then he moved me into the proper position and squirted two drops into my eyes. Again a blinding pain passed through me, followed by loss of consciousness. When I came to, I saw that Dr. Fancy had his jacket on again. He looked at me searchingly and said:

"You can go now."

"I thought you would give me some instructions."

"Oh, I see—you mean that your bank balance should now be divided among the poor? Don't worry about that."

He opened the door and let me out. I felt very ill and groped my way along the walls. Everything seemed to be veiled, but more colourful than before. At a street crossing a car grazed me, knocking me down. With my last strength I got home.

Helen had expected me. With one glance she grasped my condition. She caught me up in her embrace and pressed me to her. . . . "At last," I heard her murmur, close to my ear.

*

My health was shattered; my eyes hurt and my power of vision was greatly weakened. A brain fever nearly carried me off. For weeks I darkly felt Helen fighting for my life, recognising her at rare, luminous intervals. Then I was able to sit in the garden, to attempt my first steps.

Frequently and urgently my managers had sent for me. At last came the day when I drove into town to look after my business. I found it in utter confusion. Insurance losses through catastrophes, drops in the value of shares and defraudations had swallowed in weeks what had been accumulated in years. Above all, I had lost my affinity to money, the keen nose which is indispensable in finance. Gone was the hollow, ever unsatisfied condition which is needed to make the abstract sums flow in one's direction. My taste for speculation had disappeared; its symbols lost their meaning, their reality, for me.

I had an inventory of my securities, real estate and goods and chattels drawn up. All in all, gains and losses probably cancelled each other out. A liquidator was found, prepared to take over my assets and liabilities at his own risk. All that remained to me was the house near Stralau and the presents I had given Helen. They furnished the basis for a little second-hand bookshop I acquired. My taste for old and beautiful things was of help to me here. We married and lived like everyone else.

In our modest round and its daily cares, the past soon appeared to me as a tissue of wild imaginings, the work of illness and dreams. The wave had broken on the shore and rolled back into itself, but without any merit of mine. I had renounced evil and its splendour, but less from detestation than because I had not measured up to it. Evil had taken me into its service and later dismissed me, as though on behalf of a very distant, invisible master. If I had not lost myself altogether, the reason must be that I had still retained a contact with goodness somewhere. I had then adapted my life to a weaker version of evil, and had returned from its acute to its chronic state.

I also returned to the church, into which I had once been baptised. I am one of those whom this age of anxiety has driven to the altars. I obey the commandments, I follow the law. And yet I feel, deep in my heart, that the mysteries have lost their power and the prayers do not penetrate. There is no merit in my righteousness. I feel no answering echo in my breast.

That is the reason why I said, at the beginning, that my name was unworthy of being recorded. I live, like my contemporaries, in a no-man's-land, and like them shall pass away. We have invoked tremendous powers, whose answers transcend our measure. Horror consumes us. We have to choose between entering into demoniac realms or retiring into the weakened domain of the human. Here we may still make a living, for as long as the soil provides an after-crop. Like countless others, I chose the second way.

BIOGRAPHICAL NOTE

Ernst Jünger. Born 1895 in Heidelberg. Officer on the Western Front during the First World War. *Reichswehr*, 1919–23. Studied science and philosophy in Leipzig and Naples. Freelance writer since 1925. Captain in the German Occupation Army in France during the Second World War. Has lived in Wilfingen (Wurttemberg) since 1950.

Select Bibliography

Afrikanische Spiele, 1936 (*African Diversion*, London, 1954)
Auf den Marmorklippen, 1939 (*On the Marble Cliffs*, Norfolk/ USA, 1948)
Gärten und Strassen, 1942
Heliopolis, 1949
Strahlungen, 1949
Gläserne Bienen, 1957 (*Glass Bees*, New York, 1961)
Werke in 10 Bänden, 1963–67

Uwe Johnson

Translated
by
John Cumming

UWE JOHNSON

TRIP INTO THE BLUE, 1960

KARSCH was nearly forty and didn't feel too good. Not that he could say exactly what was wrong: he found it difficult to get to sleep; his joints ached when he woke up; at breakfast it was some time before he came round. As the day went by his mind would sometimes begin to drift: he wasn't really looking at anything; all he wanted to do was close his eyes. He seemed to have been shut up in himself like this for some time. He arrived at a simple diagnosis: a number of minor defects had mounted up in past years; he was just getting older.

And so, whenever he could, he kept to himself. To help isolate himself the more he did something a little unconventional—he took a tidy sum from his savings and bought a loft from a smallholder in the northern district of Hamburg. The fellow had heard of the vogue for selling parts of houses—making something on the side with them—but he couldn't bring himself to do the same with his own bricks and mortar. This chap from the newspaper who came every weekend asking him to make up his mind —he usually told him it was a crazy idea; but at last he found something in it and charged extra for an option on the place itself. He was content to go on living in the same building with the added satisfaction of having made a good deal. His co-owner proceeded to empty out the loft and brighten it up with a large north light.

Karsch left nothing out. Quietly, he bought up all the pieces of furniture that had caught his eye in other people's places and installed them there, under the vast skylight of his new home over the smallholder's head. One day he sold his old place, and with it all the things he had brought with him from West Berlin or kept from his student days. The only familiar thing under his new roof was the telephone. The machines and filing cabinets he needed for his work seemed so right against the sloping walls; he felt he had lived there for so long already, and used up so much of his savings that he wouldn't be able to move for a long time; anyway, he had decided to grow old there.

47

Outwardly, little more than his address had changed. For the
best part of the year, anyway, he was moving round West Germany and the neighbouring countries, collecting material for the
type of feature that had made his name in the newspaper world.
When he was in Hamburg you'd run across him in the city
centre in the afternoon, as before. He didn't change his ways :
inquisitive but slow to say anything, absolutely reliable, a good
bloke; sometimes you might take him for a local man. And for
the present no one seemed to want to know why they had to ask
at the post-office for his address and not just look it up in the
telephone directory. Night or day, when he came back from an
assignment or just from the city, and encased himself in the
quiet, grey-toned room, it seemed as natural as his own skin : he
didn't want it to mean any more to him. For the first few days
after he got back, the long table held his attention at every meal;
the short trips between typewriter, darkroom and kitchen were
enough to occupy him otherwise. But soon he was sitting at the
keyboard again, hands on knees, dissatisfied with what he had
written, full of doubts about his work and whether they paid
him for the right reasons—really for the sake of democracy, as a
custodian and critic of public morals, to find out where the taxes
went : in short, for accurate reporting. But he felt that he had
spent too long now writing as Karsch; that perhaps he wasn't
Karsch any longer. In the evening, when he lifted the receiver
and asked the answering service for the day's calls, he was reluc-
tant to follow up more than seemed absolutely necessary. He'd
rather have waited for something else—something too imprecise
to put into words.

At night, he would often go round this home he had put
everything into, switching off the gramophone or the television,
and lie there in bed listening to the pains in his head, his eyes
still open. In conversations with friends he would avoid talking
about himself, and only drank a lot in order to keep up a cheerful appearance; but he didn't want to ask anyone back. He was
puzzled to know why he so seldom saw the child he had left with
his wife when they were divorced, although six years ago he had
fought quite absurdly for the right to see him. He tried to win
back the boy with excessive gifts and then forgot appointments
with him. Now he was alone as he had wanted. That was the
way he felt. But if he spent a couple of evenings within his own

six walls, tied-up and confused, he would often get away out of Hamburg in the middle of the night, on a job far from the house.

A trying condition to be in; so, happening to be at home when a phone call came from East Germany, he didn't hesitate but accepted the invitation to pay a visit there—all the more readily since he wanted to hear more about Karin F. than she cared to write on the margins of photo-prints. In general, he supposed he would spend the time comparing notes on the years they'd lost. He went because of the balcony outside the leafy-green room where they had lived together in West Berlin, years ago. He left early in the morning; after all, he was awake.

He left a note only for the cleaner, and didn't warn his friends; so his disappearance seemed suspicious—almost menacing to the people in Hamburg. He hadn't thought of it that way.

And he wasn't prepared for the guards on the other side of the border: they picked him out of the line of traffic after West Berlin and had him pull up in the inner check-point enclosure with its beds of stunted flowers—an apologetic display between barrack-huts. The journey came to seem less commonplace, less a matter of everyday choice—so much so that he was already thinking out the first paragraph of an article: he should have prepared carefully for this trip. He was even more disconcerted when he saw the slogans on sign-boards and cotton streamers which the rulers of this country used to measure almost all their achievements against those of West Germany. He knew the emphasis from hearsay—it had made him laugh at home; but the police were in earnest, so he kept up a casual, almost pally tone—the sort of thing common during the war—and got through like that. But he hadn't understood what they said: the constructions seemed cumbersome, and he was rather downcast when he went into a restaurant; he had on his pullover with all the holes in and his oldest pair of trousers, and was immediately recognised as a West German. He got self-conscious and didn't really taste what he ate. He hadn't dared to take his camera in with him.

The visit started with a private welcome: people embrace when they've been apart for some time. And a handshake afterwards—that seems right as well. A "Well, how are you?" could bring out the reason for the invitation: no, he didn't want a drink for the moment. But she didn't talk about times past, moved briskly about him, made as if to hit him on the belly with the back of her hand: "Tennis?" she said. And he replied: "Oh no!" and so on, and so on—the quick, choppy way they used to talk; they fell into it quite easily. No, there was no particular reason at all, that she could single out. No, the thought just came into her head, like that; it was more for the sake of the exercise that she'd tried to get the residence permit from the registration office to the border. She knew people there. She had contacts there. She was well thought of here. She did well. Eventually he relaxed, accepted a drink, watched her movements in the large, comfortable armchair—she had it here, too—in which she lay back, tired, her perm already coming undone about her head, drinking slowly, talking; after a while, sitting there, they seemed as unconcerned as when they were together before—before they separated, against his will. He decided to stay a week at the most.

He felt uneasy before he met the racing cyclist Achim T., for he couldn't imagine that Karin and he were anything else but lovers; he was afraid that the other man would be embarrassed to encounter her former lover—all the more apprehensive since he didn't think the conversation would be disinterested, in view of the chap's profession. And in fact Achim looked ill at ease when the door opened; he was long-limbed, bony, shuffled nervously when they were introduced; sat there trying to appear unconcerned, rolling his lapels back. At first Karsch suspected that the fellow might be ashamed of his Party badge, but over and again his face broke out in so unforced a smile that Karsch became more puzzled than certain. He pretended to be less loquacious than usual, the better to find out the fellow's opinions; he was vexed to discover that Achim thought a lot of him, actually admired him for the weekly articles he wrote—out of resistance to the Federal Government, Achim thought, for the sake of the march of reason and despite strong opposition. Karsch restrained himself. He glanced at Karin from the corner of his eye. Clearly, all she found inept was the way her friend expressed himself. Karsch insisted volubly that as far as he was concerned his profession was only a moderately decent means of earning money. He didn't explain any further, as he had to look down at the floor, for this fellow Achim said not a word, but blushed from ear to ear—the way blond types do easily.

Karsch took for granted that he wasn't exactly welcome, that he ought to keep away when they were together. Lunch, visits to the theatre and to sports halls, walks, sightseeing and similar entertainments for visitors wouldn't suffice for seven whole days here. He tried the town. The sandstone of the public buildings was just like the sandstone familiar to him in Hesse; the sky above the suburban allotments seemed just like the sky he knew over Franconia; and he couldn't pick out anything particularly East German in the Saxon speech. The sparse traffic, the cracks caused by frost on the asphalt of the town centre, the specks of white though yellow-streaked foam on the water in the park : none of these would help him to say what he should have said. Buying things in the shops didn't help him to get to grips with the place. There was nothing to suit his friends among the things on sale : the toy for a ten year old easily came to bits. The picture postcard views of architectural monuments announced where he was; but he wasn't there. Not with his foot on the shoe-shiner's block, with sausage in his hand, or the tinny change in his pocket; he felt at home with none of these. He'd just stopped off on his way through.

He was comforted to think that the leaves above his window would have grown more closely together by the time he was home; he hesitated to sit down in the hotel lobby, for you take a seat if you intend to stay. He would lower himself slowly into the chair, his hands groping gingerly. After all, when your waist thickens so, you begin to look out : you can easily come a cropper.

Then he decided to carry out a survey that would give him some material for a report on hotel accommodation—a project of his in West Germany. He measured his hotel room, noted down the furniture, remarked the porcelain doorknobs in the bathroom with the old-fashioned lettering and the hook for a razor-strop of the kind his grandfather would have used. A glass-covered notice admonished the guest : he was not permitted to introduce visitors into his room. The carpeting on the creaking staircase had been worn threadbare. He ordered breakfast in bed—orange juice, bacon and egg, salami; he would be called down only against precise explanations and have nothing but butter with his roll; their cooking wasn't very hot in the morning. He professed to be thinking of changing his room, and asked for the tariff. He asked to be woken up in the morning, and checked the knock on the thin door against the time he had ordered. Unwittingly, he handed in shirts to be laundered and learned they took two weeks over them. He found that the older members of staff soon warmed to him; the head waiter in particular attended to his wishes with an understanding though bitter nod, and slipped conspiratorially across the street so that the fastidious guest should at least have the sausage he wanted. The younger ones—room-maids, manager, apprentices—resented this West German for his nonchalant references to inadequacies of service and equipment: politeness turned to ill-disguised hostility. Only eventually did he discover that the hotel had rated as a good middle-class establishment before the war, and that since the bombing it had unavoidably aged like any animate being amidst standards that should have provided it with shining floors and functional stretches of glass and light-coloured wood. And this was only one hotel out of many, so that he no longer compared its charges with those of one of the same class in Kassel: the currencies of East and West had a common nominal value only for governmental reasons, and he did not want explicitly to assess the cover and actual value of the East German mark. His purpose here was not so clear-cut.

Once again he tried to get to know the town. The German language and the many national similarities of fire-alarms, phone-boxes, traffic-signs were familiar. He drove to the pawn-broker's and tried to lodge his electric razor as security. The official behind the steel wire of the counter fence glanced up from the West German product to survey the shirt collar and suiting of a citizen after credit. "Is it working?" he asked at last. "How d'you want me to prove it?" said Karsch, quickly. The fellow rubbed his chin and turned the shaver round in his hand. Karsch snatched it back, switched it on and sheared the hair from his wrist until there was an island of clear flesh: then he wiped the stubble away. Smooth, like a baby's, works. He got enough money for a pair of shoes imported from West Germany. He didn't stop in front of the three-cornered sandstone tower, for passers-by gathered round the foreign convertible; instead he pulled up two blocks farther on and made a note of the conversation, the three people in the queue in front of him, and the girl—a student with a typewriter whom he'd made way for on the landing. It was morning—halfway through the week.

Next morning he went to the barber's in the station, and he was caught up again into the past in the midst of this palatially large, opulently furnished basement, in this splendid chair, under the hot towel—just the thing to soften the beard. As the cut-throat blade moved over his face he tried to judge how the East German state managed to get along in the estimation of its rulers. Pawnbroking didn't get it anywhere. How often did a pensioner pop his wireless set? The debtors' prison wouldn't say on the phone; but they understood the question—it was recognised as a question there—and Karsch introduced himself as a West German newspaper correspondent. As soon as he got there he found himself forced back into his chair with maxims about the social function of a pawnshop in the capitalist system; he asked about the place of interest in the socialist system. The man sat there with his arms set firmly on the desk, then looked Karsch straight in the eyes, jumped up suddenly, relaxed against the desk edge, then returned—his hands stretched out as before—to stare again at Karsch; he affected an unworried tone, spoke slowly as if he really had something to say, but stood when the visitor's questioning became obstructive. He mentioned the name of Karsch's paper again, doubted the possibility of a straightforward and other than inimical West German interest in figures, claimed to have none in the files at present: "I'll give you an example here, pure guesswork, say we put it at ten thousand, well, I'd be equally justified in saying a million, it's all out of date! And now, you really must excuse me." Karsch had just begun to speak to the receptionist in the ante-room when the director interrupted them. His mind in a whirl, he went to the pawn office and redeemed his razor; he passed it thoughtfully over his reddened chin—the net profit to date of his initiative.

The incident had involved him. Not so much the refusal of information as the mode of speech drew him on. Karsch felt that in the monstrous sentences of this official he had begun to discern the nature of East Germany for the first time—and found the basis for a report on his visit. He was fairly certain now that he had contacted the ruling power. In fact, after a few inquiries of this kind, he was able to mark off the committed with their peculiar loan-words and constructions, their formulas and hesitations, the direct though vacant stare of a parrot-child reciting or a second-rate bureacrat in front of a West German television camera. This form didn't apply only for foreigners : it was self-sufficient and paraded against the natives too. He began to learn the novel meanings of foreign loan-words no longer or never used in his own country : he noted down the variants of structure and perspective with increasing familiarity, but never learned the language so well as to be able to use it intelligibly. Even in casual conversation with ordinary people he found his way of speaking noticeably ill-adjusted to theirs, for he had missed ten years of their history : it didn't take them long to tell where he was from. They spoke of distribution, and of production bottlenecks where he could speak only of the wholesale trade and hold-ups in delivery; they called his hire-purchase the economy payment system. He soon noted exactly the relation of the people's speech to the idiom of the officials; he would sometimes sit there mentally preparing his next statement, like someone about to speak a foreign tongue, trying not to muff his phrasing. Until he left he remained astonished at the impoverished scraps of workaday language with which the inhabitants rehearsed their allegiance to the regime and, in each case, subsequently dropped into silence or morose agreement. After that June he forgot this latter aspect most easily, since it was the nearest to his own practice.

For he stayed until June. At first, just a week more, then another. At first, for the sake of his notebooks, and finally out of curiosity—and also self-interest. He managed to get his residence permit extended because of a political consideration—it was thought that the East German performance in sport might be employed in neutral countries and also in West Germany to effect a change in world opinion on East Germany. When the task of writing the biography of the racing cyclist Joachim T. was put to Herr Karsch, a West German journalist, he took the job on with only moderate seriousness : he was more interested in the chance of making trips outside the city, and generally in being able to stay longer in the East. He felt like an explorer on the brink of some discovery. Sometimes anyway. At other times headaches, lack of sleep, exhaustion and aching muscles took all resolution away from him. His brain seemed to spin round, knocking against the walls of his skull. Medical men have their own terms for such syndromes, but even when he was thinking about it afterwards his mind would cloud over, and thirty minutes later he would find himself lying there as before; he hadn't been asleep: he hadn't been anything. He would rather have been sick like this at home; but, from inertia, he didn't go back.

One day he visited some relatives who had been turned out of West Prussia after the war and who had ended up in Thuringia; they had reproduced the bedroom left behind in the East—even the cooking had the same reek of tallow soap about it. The relationship was not close enough to justify the long silences between gulps of coffee. After a day he was back in the hotel, but the day had been spent. Or it might have been the waitress in the beergarden just outside the town-limits who didn't want to start anything with the West German, since the certainty that he would be going back and his country of origin would naturally ruin any affair. He spent long mornings in the gravelled yard of the beer-garden, before the customers arrived for lunch, chatting evasively with the girl who leaned on the table there by him: sometimes she would laugh as she rested on her swarthy arms, or bent down to this foreigner who yet again hadn't cottoned on to something. Perhaps it was the dental technician who had fixed on his East German car a superannuated radiator from some hefty West German model. Or the bricklayer who had stayed on the sick-list for years in order to wangle a higher income by illegal private housebuilding—who said he preferred work to sitting around doing nothing. Or the man in the leathertrimmed oilskin jacket who had got three years in a labour camp for some witty innuendo about the local M.P. in a public bar— he'd been back there to find the informer. Or a four year old creeping about on the ground shouting out military commands, distinguishing hostile from fraternal tank attacks. Or the three police mechanics who couldn't pass Karsch's car as roadworthy after a lengthy inspection, rear lights check and brakes test, but had first to scorch three times round the square like mischievous kids. Or the stout though solid youth who ejected Karsch from a dance-hall because of the American way he held his partner. Or the photographer who had his professional licence withdrawn because his flashbulb had upset the composure of a member of the government: now he re-applied every month for restoration of his licence with an assurance that the bulb had been bought in East Germany. Or Frau Liebenreuth, to whose house Karsch had moved; a landlady for the first time in her long life, she would stand behind the breakfast tray, diminutive, clad in black, gossiping about the neighbours. Or a wide avenue suddenly asparkle with tiny, glittering leaves. Or the semblance of recognition when he rounded a street-corner. After a time he felt himself so close to knowing the country that he saw no danger in discarding the projected travelogue.

On his way about he heard talk now and then of the racing cyclist whom the authorities took to be his host. The young people had an absurd admiration for him. It wasn't just the terrific speed he could get up to—but more his provincial dialect, his embarrassed smile during the presentation ceremonies; the fact that he had remained approachable despite his rise to fame, and that he slept with an actress. Some found Achim's hair so blond that they were moved when they saw the contrast with his grey face beneath at the end of the race. He was said to be rich; if he sold everything up he'd be a millionaire. He had a reputation for influence and integrity—as though he could intervene on behalf of the unjustly imprisoned—and above all for impartiality. There was no need for evidence: many people in need had written to him for his money, his advice, his intercession. His association with the Government, to whose Chamber of Deputies he had been appointed, was proof of his indispensability; and in his company the rulers seemed for once conceivable human beings round a table, with their arms on Achim's, chatting; one might even go so far as to say they looked friendly.

Gradually Karsch came to realise how much respect and love a man could win in this country by being no more than a racing cyclist; that the subjects met their rulers only in places where ski-jumpers and actors exhibited their success and lived their public lives like any others. Karsch remembered the talk of a biography and began to take advance payments; he hired a typewriter. This was the first and only time that Karin warned him. Otherwise she didn't criticise his behaviour. He was introduced about the city as the guest of Karin F., the actress, who brought him along, left with him, presented him as a West German (not as a superseded fiancé): so that the commissionaire at the theatre greeted him as an old acquaintance, the management sent him tickets, and—because of her—officials were less ready to refuse him an interview. At the start, she had warned him about his more infuriating West German characteristics; since then, when carefully preparing the data for a television interview, he didn't expatiate any longer on the West German traffic system, drew his comparisons without emphasising them, parked his car more unobtrusively, dressed like the locals, sent hardly any dishes back to the chef, and didn't ask to see the kitchens. At one go, she let him know the right way to behave; you just don't do that—it isn't practicable—it's not possible here : she was showing a foreigner the ropes.

He didn't really fathom it. He understood at best that she wanted to protect a friend of hers from publicity. But anyway, as far as Karsch was concerned, biographies were worthwhile and entertaining work. He usually found it instructive to analyse a man's formation and discover the life behind the persona. It was enjoyable to pick out the hard facts of someone's past, to lead a person's memory back into the labyrinth and see him arrested in self-recognition. He was pleased to know that up to now everyone he'd taken on had finally come to the same opinion of himself as Karsch. It wasn't just the detective work— the questioning, research and revision—that had gripped him : he was also surprised to realise how much an individual retains of social conditions, military procedure, class mannerisms, and remembers about his or her contemporaries. Karsch was indebted to such assignments for his knowledge of the world sugar market, Stock Exchange law, married life *circa* 1925, legal sentences, and specialised technical fields. Two such biographies had appeared in the bookshops, and in each case he had kept a proof copy in which the subject had not yet blue-pencilled his indiscreet disclosures : one was the life story of a trade union official, the other the history of a firm's struggle for existence.

Nevertheless, Karsch had foreseen Achim's initial resistance. Achim, who up to now had emerged in his popular rôle only with dates, photographs and clippings from his victor's laurels, was unwilling to back it all up with his real biography, and certainly not to confide any details of it during the tape-recorded interviews with a certain Herr Karsch, the West German with whom Karin had once almost departed for the West Germans, a house of one's own and the bourgeois way of life; he would always rely on Karin's presence at these interviews, once Party officials had familiarised him with the plan—after all, he was a member too. He grew to trust in Karsch's work—he found the printed examples from the past readable and lucid. Still, Karsch's ready supply of words and his way with them sometimes made him peevish.

Karsch tried to suit himself to this man he'd been inclined to disregard. For Achim, an affable tone was a prerequisite of personal friendship; he allowed Karsch to question him about other areas of his life. In a number of places in the city and outside— mainly in one of the larger industrial estates in southern Saxony and a market-town in Thuringia—Karsch discovered, in his usual meticulous way, Achim at six, Achim at ten, and Achim at sixteen. He recorded these years of Achim's life as contributions to the history of the German curriculum : the demoralisation of a nation in a bombing war, the social position of children in the black market, the reassessment of rural relationships in times of urban destitution, the dislocation of adolescence as a result of pedagogical, fortuitous and inevitable circumstances. Karsch learned from Achim's grandmother, from official registers, from retained and discarded friends, teachers, foremen, fellow-bricklayers, room-mates and, finally, from Achim's father; he discovered that Achim's sensational cycling career grew from the time he was sixteen and used to ride off from this place at weekends to visit a girl a hundred kilometres away in the south —until he learned to replace the girl with sporting organisations and finishing tapes. Karsch had his moment when Achim T. read through the years 1936 to 1947 of his life, at one sitting : read with many gestures of agreement, nods with lips pursed, startled laughter, and embarrassed rubbing of his neck; read for about two hours, and finally handed the sheaf of paper back to him, looking up and giving that jerky hand salute which— among the more illustrious racing cyclists—passed as a recognition of equality, or praise for a good performance. Karsch wasn't taken aback when Achim didn't give him permission to print what he had just read.

Until now no one had written so thorough a study of such early years : indeed, some might not find the chapter of childhood long enough, and the chapter of the subsequent years too slow in passing—the years when one's behaviour is, if anything, more liable to be unwary; when one can be forced to do things that one can afford to be ashamed of only in more generous circumstances. At first Karsch thought it was just the usual lack of correspondence between the actual occurrence of an event and time as the individual memory measures it; but here guess-work was too painful for Achim, and there he was willing to allow a forgotten year to be reconstructed for him—with the classrooms, evenings spent dancing, charges for meals and weather conditions which his biographer had brought back. Similar aberrations made Karsch aware that this time he wasn't up against the usual difficulties involved in writing a biography. Indeed, Achim's acknowledging hand had served only to confirm how closely Karsch's typescript echoed the life of the famous racing cyclist; but his face had shown he was anxious to turn this information to a different account. Again and again Karsch was sure that Achim was not merely concerned that his adherents and supporters should have an account of his life, but saw it rather as a direct means of influencing the nature of their support and adherence; that was why he censured—or, more precisely, praised and yet found erroneous—things that had actually happened to him and ought therefore, with all the witnesses and circumstantial details, to remain as such in Karsch's typescript; but Achim wished to forget the rain when it had actually rained. Karsch was learning what value to put on the process of re-appraisal Achim went through when, as now for example, he attributed the onset of his age of reason to the sight of the same Soviet troops to whom the fifteen year old Achim had reacted by leaving the pavement with his fists clenched in his trouser pockets. Karsch's account didn't accord with Achim's hindsight, which wouldn't allow him to accept the "incorrect" incident; and in this way he lost twenty pages, and also a girl from East Prussia. Karsch got used to a certain look which appeared during these conversations—the faraway look of a man simulating deafness when he hears truth. He questioned the official expressions which Achim used for these interviews; more evasive and awkwardly phrased than in anecdotes of his past, the synthesis he arrived at in his dialectical progress was as valueless to Karsch as the prevailing theme of Party-consciousness. He resisted Achim's optimistic exhortations—he'd got along well enough with his

own opinion until now and intended to stay the same way. And
Achim was displeased at the disputatious, bored rejoinder with
which Karsch yet again explained that he did not understand, if
Achim happened to recall things from his trips to racing tracks
in West Germany—things which weren't even as much as con-
ceived of over there. Fortunate that Achim found his biographer
amusing on the quiet, was willing anyway to give him due credit
for his knowledge of the cycling world; fortunate too that Karsch
didn't lapse too readily into irritable replies and hasty contra-
dictions, which was what he'd really expected after that enervat-
ing heaviness in his limbs, the slight dizziness and pains behind
the eyes, which would lie low for days on end and then return
all at once.

    And all this time the days grew longer, the evenings lighter;
but the Saxon dialect he heard through the open windows of the
tramcars scarcely brought him joy. One day the girl from the
inn came dancing with him—he'd been able to promise her an
introduction to Karin. In the meantime he had so many ex-
posures in a shoebox on top of Frau Liebenreuth's wardrobe,
that he checked his car for hiding-places for the trip over the
border. He understood why the citizens of this State thought the
mail was censored; he didn't want to suffer the imposition himself. A young doctor, whom Karsch had only met three evenings
in a row, had already offered him the use of a darkroom in the
pathological section of his clinic; Karsch would have liked to
have seen the lab, but he didn't want to leave his negatives
hanging up there to dry. Recently he had taken to going to the
post-office in the evening, zig-zagging from one counter to the
other for a long-distance call to Hamburg. Headaches, no headaches; he didn't want to get treatment here: anyway, he
thought, it'll take two years. He no longer spent every day on
the road; in the afternoons he would read for a long time with
his feet up on Frau Liebenreuth's window-ledge, glancing now
and again at the milk-white cloud above the dusty green of the
park. He didn't confine his reading to works of cycle-racing
history, but also tackled the post-war volumes of liberal newspapers, the fiction and poetry of this country, textbooks of economics; and gradually he found several pointers to where it had
begun and had proceeded until now, when a Herr Karsch from
Hamburg wished to stay here only for the holidays and no

longer. Sometimes, when he happened to try to talk those war-mongering barons of industry in the Ruhr out of Achim's head, he was embarrassed to think that perhaps all the close knowledge of the Ruhr district he possessed himself was the night express once between Dortmund and Cologne, on its way to Italy, near the road—and Karsch and a girl: she sat there in their car, sleepless, smoking, set against the glow of the firebox that the windowscreen reflected through the November darkness outside. Karsch felt like looking the place up; he missed the West German papers, wouldn't go so far as to say he was homesick; still, every day here seemed to him a day long gone by. Later he would recall that last week in the East as he would any other ordinary snippet of time.

He had been allowed to visit whatever came into his head (except for the prohibited military zones, so he had to exercise his imagination and suppress the pine forests and the tanks garlanded with foliage that the newsreel releases showed him as they did the other citizens—he was warned about prison sentences). For most of his last week there he was round and about. In order to visit a camp for West German refugees, he had his papers stamped, obtained recommendations; it was reported too, and so he had to talk to the newcomers in front of the television camera as the distinguished visitor from the West under discussion: but he asked questions in the West German way, inquired after precise reasons, used colloquial expressions, described his experiences in this country: it was ridiculous, they didn't broadcast it. (His partly objective, partly subjective mediation fell short of the desired political orientation of the news-report: he wanted it all in black and white.) Most of the immigrants had already been here at one time: they hadn't got along over there with a State that took no notice of them, didn't find them work, didn't set them in a harmless groove with regulations, decrees and civilities; which didn't want to know anything about them other than that they were working as hardily and efficiently as possible, acquired and consumed, lived for themselves and blow the rest—lived better than the rest. And so they came here, sent back by instalments that couldn't be met, by inadequate housing, by piece-wages, by sickness: their hopes had been groundless, they said. They let Karsch write away. All the younger ones really wanted was just to keep out of his way and see him go;

they were new to this place and came for reasons they didn't trust anyone who was going back there to understand. Karsch soon gave up; at any rate none of them would confess to being one of the deserters from the Foreign Legion he'd been promised. They'd come to escape West German national service: they wouldn't accept what Karsch told them about the same obligation in East Germany. Some had been pursued by a police-warrant, denunciations, the criminal investigation squad; it was true of a good number of them that if they'd gone to any country in the West, they would still have been too near the parents, girl-friends, private or civil offences they left behind them; here they were entirely out of reach, cut off, safely away from it all; and if the place itself was one big house of correction, well, after all, it was *voluntary* hard labour, wasn't it! What struck Karsch most was the way they talked—how cold these West Germans were with him, as though they shared neither country nor way of life—hardly even the same idioms. They told this fat bloke he should scram, make himself scarce, shove off out of it to Hamburg—they knew it all already, thanks very much. But they would only let the East German reporters take profile shots of them. One of them had come on private grounds and wanted to make that clear. The house was still full of orphanage furniture, had the odour of damp unaired washing about it: the upper floors were silent and empty.

Karsch got some things together and drove straight to Mecklenburg to look up the Niebuhrs, with whom he had stayed for a month in 1945—waiting. Just before, when he was discharged from the army hospital in Poznan, he wasn't sent back to his tank unit but ordered to set out for Danzig and to proceed west from there with a lorry-load of heavy wooden crates. There were four men—two in the driver's cab, and two on the loading platform—armed only with a couple of carbines. At the end of March they headed along the Baltic coast towards Greifswald, and then—on account of a rumour—turned off to the south by way of Demmin and Malchin. They had petrol with them—on top of the crates; they weren't to stop in any town. In April they came across a procession of refugees in the half-light, blocking an intersection with a cross-country road: they took three unaccompanied children with them, and an old woman with a hand-cart she didn't want to leave behind: it jolted behind the truck now, taking the bends on two wheels. Karsch gave the children some of his bread and generally saddled himself with them—one ragged little creature tried to go to sleep in his lap. During the night he'd opened one of the crates and didn't want to go on to the west with what he'd found. Since dawn they were once more driving between apple trees in blossom and woods in their new April clothes, along poorly surfaced second-class roads, on bumpy winding tracks above stretches of grey water; just before six, when they came to a cluster of mixed forest, he jumped into the ditch, and could still see the disappointed children's faces when the hand-cart had already passed on its unsteady way round the low thicket. Bent down, he ran across the grit surface to the ditch on the other side. The engine stopped, then started again. He found a narrow footpath behind newly planted birch-trees: damp and winding, it led him to a lock-basin. The low-built, tile-roofed house stood glistening with dew against the reddening sky. Sheets flapped as the wind drove half-heartedly against them. Just round the corner of the house he'd seen old Niebuhr standing at the bench for the milk-urns, erect, arms at his side as if on guard, with his back to Karsch; he had slowly turned his head and motioned the stranger to approach with just the same sober nod that now met Karsch on his return, as fifteen years were milled to so many grains in the second it took Niebuhr to turn his head to one side in his bee-keeper's veil, and beckon Karsch over—carefully, so that the swarm did not creep in a flurry over his veil and neck. He did not speak until the swarm had formed into a mass and could be turned warily into the bee-skep. Then he pushed up the veil and held it there on his forehead with one hand: "I'd always said you'd be back." But those weren't Niebuhr's eyes that looked from that vague tired face with its stubbled chin past Karsch, in such a way that he turned his own head to stare. And then the figure in the blue mechanic's overalls raised his hand to his hip—in the same warning gesture he used that past April when a military police patrol or a stranger had come to the house, and Karsch had to creep from his attic into the cupboard beneath the roof-tiles, nine times before the armistice, once in the middle of the night. At that time there was a lad of ten working on the lock, who later threw stones on the roof for him when the Russians had finished raking around for watches and German soldiers : Karsch would lift a tile until there was just enough room to see through, and there was the boy, standing with his brother in the yard and signalling to him with a crooked finger— the kid tried to imitate him—and in the house he coud hear the voices of the old Niebuhrs through the ceiling, calling him down. Now the house was silent : no steam misted over the kitchen window, and no clogs clattered on the stone paving of the lock yard. Karsch asked a question. The old man held the skep in both hands before his chest and moved his head as he followed the convolutions of the swarm. Karsch asked again. Niebuhr carried the skep to the bee-shed, stepping between the apple-trees. Karsch called out to him. The faded blue overalled back tottered steadily on, away from him. The back door of the house was ajar. Karsch put his hand on the latch, then stepped back. This time it was midday in June; there was a calmness compounded of the scraping of chickens, the water moving between the moles, and the wind puffing through the garden-shed. On the other side of the lock-basin stood the unexpected figure of a man in the uniform of the border guards : straddle-legged, he rubbed his damp hands in the back pockets of his breeches, returned the greeting, spat in the half overshadowed water between them. Karsch tried to think what he should do. The boy, who had brought the doctor for him before, was no longer there : nor his little brother, who had always wanted to help look after the concealed soldier for his father. Karsch and the other fellow stood so alone in that wide expanse, it was hard to find anything to look at. A pause. The guard spat in the water. Karsch asked about Niebuhr's wife (that time before she had cut him a jacket from a loden overcoat and used his black uniform to make a confirmation suit for her elder son)—was she dead? All of a sudden the soldier spoke louder, didn't answer the question, warned him off. The lock was a prohibited area, he couldn't give permission, you can't stay here. He turned round and went towards the black-tarred shed. The wood with its mixture of bright green trees had been called the Little Oakwood. Karsch went along the side of the house and looked through the window behind which the Niebuhrs' bedroom used to be. On the table by the window were out-of-date service regulations, a pack of cigarette papers, an opened envelope; an iron bedstead had a coarse cover over it; in an open locker there hung askew a raincoat with shoulder-straps on; there was an officer's cap on the roughly plastered wall. The lock-keeper's desk on the other side of the room looked just the same as fifteen years before: papers were piled on the up-turned desk-lid; the wall clock had stopped. Karsch turned round quickly, but no one was watching him. He went on the mole and sat there for two hours, smoking and looking at the town which squatted there on the other side of the flat curved inlet, with low-lying lines of houses at the water's edge, then higher roof-tops, and then the rust-coloured mass of the cathedral tower. The wind took the foam from the mole-end and blew a fine spray over him. He'd never been inside the town; even after the capitulation they let him out of the house only at night time. He'd never seen the river— always the town above the water, from the attic window. Niebuhr had spoken then. He had sat up all one night and tried to talk to the sappers who wanted to open the lock into the lake: Karsch heard them through the floorboards. He managed to get an unincriminating identity card for the deserter. He taught Karsch his first words of the local dialect. He was forty-six then; could drag a heavy rowing boat without any help over the basin wall; could run at a trot into the town and come back breathing easily. One night afterwards he'd seen Karsch on his way through the English lines to Grevesmühlen. The fifteen years since then were missing. When Karsch saw a woman coming over the lock-gate with a basket, he stood up. He bent down once again to look at a spade which lay there in the reed-grass, rusted and grown over with damp lichen. He stood a little longer on the edge of the basin, near Niebuhr, as a barge went through the lock to the upper reach. Niebuhr let the bargee open the gates and range them up himself, took the money without a word, said nothing as he held out the ticket, put two hesitant fingers to his cap, picked up his lunch basket, wanted to get along. "Good-bye," said Karsch, and swallowed. The old man didn't see his raised hand. He turned back for a moment, kept his head down —it tremored inadvertently—and said, slowly, dejectedly: "I'd always said you'd be back ... ," went in at the door and closed it behind him. Karsch left the place by the pathway that had taken him there once before. The path had been trodden hard and went round the two birches at the opening: but they were decayed, and stood there half dried up, both dead.

Next morning Karsch turned into a small town to the south of East Berlin and stood for a while in front of the municipal hotel; then it occurred to him that he shouldn't leave a car with West German number plates at the kerb all night. He couldn't find any public garages; uneasily, he left the car in a road planted with firs, with single—family houses. Still feeling ill at ease, he went to the station for the city line. When the officials had made out his residence permit, they had spoken of the sacredness of the boundaries of their State—borders which no one might pass over lightly, not even a guest, just as he wished, and certainly not to visit West Berlin, the open wound in the democratic State, the void, the scar, the barbarian islet, the filter, the fissure through which already nearly three million had fled from the embraces of the supreme power. But Karsch wanted to visit a refugee camp. He was standing at the station kiosk, sipping a soft drink, when an old-fashioned passenger train emptied its occupants on to the next platform : they packed the stairway to the city-line, many of them past their working days, and carrying cases; he noticed particularly the old women dressed in black on this fine weekday, who, with heads bent, blinking, stepped well out of the way of any uniformed figure, as if a suspicious odour had caught their nostrils. Karsch had his East German papers in one jacket pocket, and the West German ones in the other—an adequate disguise, he thought. At the first checkpoint he almost went wrong, but eventually showed his East German identification, and through the hum in his ears heard himself give false information—as if in a dream, watched the sham Karsch, seemingly conspicuous in comparison with the other passengers, who gave their East German destinations with studied casualness and presented themselves as innocent citizens, instead of the people they really were with their actual life that until now and their place had been submerged by the ingeniously immoderate demands of the State : they wanted a change. Karsch not only thought he had noticed something specifically East German; he was also bewildered at the similarity of his own behaviour, so that he didn't observe the details of the journey over the zig-zagging river, open boat-houses and barges; and to a question from the refugees ventured "the Spree" as an answer. He showed his West German papers at the checkpoint before West Berlin—puzzled again by the slow beating of his heart behind the superior front he put on: the West German mask his face automatically became. He didn't stir when some passengers were taken out. He followed the others and entered the camp without having to ask the way there: his mouth was dry, he was inexplicably weary, footsore. He looked blankly at the crowd passing over the courtyard, didn't stop to think but went along with them, and near by the city police moved the East German television cameras on to the street. Nothing occurred to him except that everything seemed inevitable and that he was watching it. Without taking a word down, he kept near a reporter from the West Berlin radio, was knocked into, pushed forward, shoved to one side, and—craning his neck— observed them, intimidated, lowering their eyes in front of the slick, solicitous microphone that was ready to hear and retain their reasons for being there, all together.

And now the East German tongue came to grief. It had no currency here, conveyed only what they had left behind; its linguistic signs were powerless to transmit what their users wished them to signify. All that the new arrivals had brought with them was a language which was incapable of helping them to come to terms with their new environment: they couldn't rely on even this common cultural basis, hardly even on hearsay. Earlier on Karsch too would have interpreted the following only as a pouring out of the general stupidities that were East German policies—thought at most of the imposition of the farm- ing co-operatives: "I'd have stood it longer but my wife had had enough of it; we haven't had anything for ourselves except for the home, next to nothing; they came with their loudspeakers and the police; we thought they were going to seal the border; we've waited so long for things to improve; I wasn't going to be allowed to study; so many have gone from our road—I didn't want to be the only one to stay; I was made redundant yester- day; they were going to force us to join the army; my grand- children are over here; I wanted something more out of life." So they declared, self-consciously, as if they deserved mistrust. But in the meantime Karsch had seen the things they spoke of, and thought of himself as an eye-witness, someone who'd actually been there. Listening to these people gave one only a very narrow conception of what the other Germany was actually like, al- though from here it seemed as if a fine, hard-fibred mesh had been placed over it, to change its appearance. Instinctively, his ear decoded what they said, analysed the suasions behind a certain phrase as one of them made a hurried and yet timid attempt to speak West German. Not all of them were entirely to be respected: in fact, he couldn't wish more than a few of them anything more than just good luck; but all and every one of them spoke like the place they had left and which still clung to them. This was a foreign country, but still it helped them to retain what was past: in a foreign country one has to speak precisely, simply and unoptimistically—perhaps someone will understand. They had come because the country they left was different, but scarcely because the country they had sought out was as it was. They still didn't belong here; just as they no longer belonged over there. And in this moment of indecision Karsch was closer to them than a West German, was set apart from the West Germans; for he felt he had something special in common with these foreigners—knowledge and allusions, expressed in the pursing of lips or in silence—something retained from the ninety days he had spent as their guest; and he regretted the amount of reality and neighbourliness that would fade from them—fade into oblivion with their move to West Germany. A few days here and they were no longer the same, the bond between them already long broken: and each of them would have to go before the reception committee by himself, to exchange the finished stretch of his life for foreign values: various refugee's documents, a residence permit, coupons to buy clothing, a job, a loan, and a ticket for the plane that would carry him over the country that in the meantime he had lost. Karsch left the interview hall where he had allowed the crowd to take him; he made his way across the hot, dusty, crammed yard of the camp, and returned to the station. On the platform, he recognised new arrivals from outside: they had already forgotten their customary wariness, and innocently left the train as people who had surrendered their homes and owned no more than their luggage. Once or twice Karsch went too far, and changed trains without thinking, until he got to the housing estate where he had lived at one time. Many of the shopkeepers he'd known then were no longer in business, others didn't recognise him; and when he bought two hundred cigarettes, carrier-bags full of things in the chemist's, in the stationer's, in the fish-market, almost all the dealers took him for an East German who'd found his nice old gran in the West an easy touch. With packets under both arms he walked for a long time in the shade. The façades of buildings seemed to quiver as he gazed half-consciously before him. The back of his head felt numb. He had to lean against the wall of the telephone booth when he rang an acquaintance he'd known as a student, who was now practising as a doctor, and asked him to prescribe something. He didn't want to make his diagnosis over the phone and invited Karsch over. But Karsch pleaded a pressing engagement : he didn't want to pour out his three months in a single afternoon's conversation. He would have liked to have resolved his confusion, but would have done it injudiciously. He had to forgo the pleasure of spending the evening here. At the border with East Berlin, his purchases were noticed, and he gave a ludicrously implausible address in Köpenick as his destination; but the customs official had also been standing in the heat, and didn't feel like picking on this West German who spoke so slowly, and whose forehead was beaded with sweat. At the outer border of East Berlin he remembered the East German papers in his jacket pocket.

That afternoon had pressed him hard with the feeling of facing both ways : so uneasy a sensation that he settled his East German affairs—in an attempt to settle himself. With regard to Achim T., he abandoned the dispute he would otherwise have entered on, and left him the manuscript of the biography—unpublished, it seemed a fair exchange for the advances he had taken; he was in such a hurry that he forgot to make a copy. As he said his goodbyes, he surprised them with a kind of wit which passes for something other than banter in these parts; he invited Frau Liebenreuth to spend a week in Hamburg—he didn't advise anyone to go there for good. He was thoughtless enough to give a lift to a hitch-hiker on the autobahn without asking the youth why he hadn't got anything on under his mechanic's overalls. He very firmly refused to assist any prisoner to escape : the chap was turned out—that suited Karsch (in this way he thought he would assure himself an entry permit for next year). For the first time he was impolite enough to offend against his hosts' traffic regulations : on the four-hour drive to the border they stopped him once and then again because he had exceeded the speed limit—he wanted to get rid of his East German currency somehow. He hadn't been able to close his eyes all night. He felt really knocked up and just managed to keep his car on the road. On the other side of the barrier he didn't resist the attraction of the more modern roads, still whistled softly when his dusty crate got caught in the shining columns of excursion traffic, came home through the small towns that afternoon as if suddenly released from privation, wouldn't have liked to have defined exactly what pleased him in comparison about the faces and clothing of the passers-by, felt naturally back where he belonged, noted (not without the pleasure of anticipation) the shop-window displays of all the objects and devices that ensure an easier life, still breathed in the higher-quality petrol in the air as the welcome fragrance by which the returning traveller knows his homeland; and then, as he pulled up at the corner-kiosk for papers, answered the headlines with a mental "Just a minute!" —for he had two months until September to produce a series out of the sensational report he decided he now had in him. He already saw it set up—and the banner announcing it at the top of his paper—"here, hold on!" As dusk came down, he found the crush of traffic taking him as usual over the Hamburg Elbe bridge, towards home, for this was where he'd lived for a couple of years.

He couldn't start straightaway. The empty flat had used up his bank balance and he had enough in hand for only eight weeks: that was too unsettling, he had to do something. Since his student days, he hadn't let himself borrow money—in obedience to the small shopkeeper's principles that had caused his parents to sacrifice their own grocer's business. He began to telephone. Since he didn't want to travel, and would write only if he had to, he got—only with some trouble—an Italian documentary film-script to translate, forced himself to sell some East German photos (he only took photographs for his own enjoyment), and accepted an advance on the series on hotels he'd planned, until once again he could ply his typewriter with an easy mind. But you have to see people too, have to talk to them; then, when you're drinking, talking, what's been happening slips out: "Been away, have you? But why East Germany?" Karsch used the term "residence permit". An East German residence permit for a journalist was unusual to start with: "Why were you there

so long? After all, one's seen it all at the first glance." Karsch
didn't expand about his first impressions; but gave the book
about the racing-cyclist as his business there. "About a racing-
cyclist—you're not serious?" Karsch tried to let his explanation
rest there, but he had to answer with East German bread prices,
living conditions, educational and cultural policies. Fortunately,
these conversations soon turned into tepid discussions about the
prospects of reunification, and finally into gossip. But East German idioms came so readily to his lips that he found himself
advising them that you just had to see everything in its context,
if you found the other man's opinions too muddled. They looked
at him in such astonishment that he didn't manage just the right
emphasis when explaining that this official precept of the East
German party was understood ironically by the people over there
—taking into consideration the pressure of different circumstances. . . . They let him have his say—he decided to give it more
thought. (It wasn't as insignificant as someone back from a trip
to England with a few foreign expressions on the tip of his
tongue.) Even the taxi-driver for whom Karsch sometimes did
the night-shift sounded his horn outside the house, and said—
between friends—surely Karsch could tell him what it had *really*
been like. Again and again, he retold Achim's entire life—
attempting to be purely impartial only in order not to anticipate
the report he planned to write. And still in the night his telephone
would ring and someone would ask: "Are you quite sure you
haven't made a mistake?" He collected his son and drove him
to Travemünde, but spoiled his fun at lunch when the boy tried
to tell him that in East Germany the police turned their machine-
guns at random on the passersby. He repeated his lecturette on
comic-strips—but the kid would rather have stayed on the
beach, and the inflatable rubber-toy he bought now came too
late—he should have brought something back from his trip. He
dropped the boy in the city, didn't show him his new home, saw
him get on the tram, couldn't overcome his inclination not to
call him back. In the meantime the headaches had become
so insignificant that he put them down to that exceptional summer in which the heat hung without a breath of wind over the
town, and the same went for the attacks of sweating at night. He
promised himself a check-up in the autumn, but first of all he

wanted to get everything settled. When you're fagged out, feeling a bit under, you let them walk you into the editorial conference—he didn't think about the wave of muck and printed matter which every morning flooded the space behind his door at home, and left in its wake an atmosphere of vociferous denial. He took his old place between Third Page and Sport; the white sunlight bore down insidiously on the dormer-window—out there the glittering arms of the gantries in the harbour were on his side. The cold schnaps felt like a sharp-edged mass in his belly. He'd known everyone at the table for ages, he counted on that, said what he thought as the mechanism in his head dictated; he didn't go cautiously, probe, avoid insinuations; he spoke out; not many of them would have expected that.

They commissioned—to begin immediately and finish at the end of August—a series on East Germany: to be forwarded to subscribers in the holidays. Karsch hadn't thought of doing it as a piece of reportage. They prescribed the sort of easy, palatable style everyone knew and liked to read. Karsch hadn't thought of that. If a regular staff man takes an unexpected holiday and leaves Third Page high and dry for twelve weeks, at least you expect an excuse, if not reasonable behaviour and conformity to usual practice. Karsch—yes, of course, I'm sorry—had thought of an analysis of the administration, an economic report with reference to reunification, a presentation of East German consequences of West German politics—if necessary, tricked out with anecdotes to satisfy the readers' imagination, but that came last. That wasn't suitable for August; politics were on holiday then. Yes, but Karsch had really had September in mind. And the paper should doubtless go so far as to propose the recognition of East Germany? Yes, in my opinion, the answer's yes. Must be clean off your rocker. All right then. Are you out of your senses? What do you think we're letting ourselves in for; what do you expect; I'm telling you; let him have his say; just listen; this has always been an independent weekly. That's why I'm suggesting.... An independent paper aimed at a middle-class readership can't suddenly in the middle of July without any directive from the board abandon the guiding principles of official West German policy, according to which there can't be any discussion of reunification with East Germany, since their State just doesn't exist and they rig their elections anyway. Quite right. But look here, I've seen it myself: how do you think it was I let five policemen inspect my car to see if it was roadworthy, if I didn't think a government had put them there? This is an editorial conference, not a readers' opinion poll. You should print it straight. Well, I think we'll take the report on the market gardening show —new feature in September—copy for information of directors —get a line to Ibiza. "Well then," said Karsch, "that's it."

And then he thought he'd just managed it rather clumsily, presented it poorly, got out on the wrong side that morning. He tried to work out then how he was breaking so many rules of the game, all at once. A good salesman doesn't put his goods over by sticking them in the window bare and plain—just as they are. He sees to the packaging—gives them an image that sets them apart from the routine lines. The good salesman sees to it that there's no debate about his wares. Too much persuasion makes them suspect you're on your uppers. And he'd used East German expressions again: when the market gardening assignment came up, he'd asked what the slant was, just like any politically trained East German—but you didn't get that kind of education over here. He hadn't thought it would come out like that; he had let himself be caught out; had given in and acknowledged himself the victim of some sort of logic. He didn't go out alone after the conference, Your Guide to the Week's Trumpery Affairs said let's have lunch, and talked of the hazards of ideological journalism. Karsch sensed curiosity again. Finance and Sport explained the paper's refusal to go along with him as the paper's recognition of his close relationship with the paper. He sensed an attempt to console him; and if he happened to glance over their heads as they spoke, he saw others there giving him that kind of sizing-up look—he couldn't make it out at first —ah yes, sympathetic; and at last he realised he'd been overruled just like eight years ago as a greenhorn. Quickly, he excused himself and walked slowly along the concrete corridor to Page Three's room. Page Three had his feet on the desk but used his arms quite vigorously to explain how first-class, how effective a writer Karsch had been in the past—our eye-witness, he said— and Karsch couldn't help thinking of the East German news programme with the same name: only the fellow's silence brought his mind out of its vague drift. He hadn't been listening —"you didn't seem to have got through, in the end", said Page

Three. Karsch's own estimate of his performance was so low that he cautiously refused a second schnaps, although he needed it—but without ice. The lunchtime traffic rolled along between the red houses as it did every day. Someone jerked across the road in front of him so clumsily that he narrowly missed two cars at the intersection : neither of them had thought he would slow down so suddenly—or so he fancied anyway.

He didn't worry particularly; didn't apply to another paper, as he'd been used for years to this one, its more substantial sheets, the bold column lines and head rules, the dignified make-up—hardly affected by the incursion of small-ads; was prepared for the copy-dates and vagaries of its sub-editors, whose emendations he anticipated with his own cuts; it was this sort of allegiance that made him turn out his copy as usual. In case of extremity, he thought of putting out his report as a book, with full page photo-illustrations, wide margins, and bound in the flexible, functional boards that held the West German market at the time; although it was still just an idea he had to make a start. Anyway he found the work pleasant at first. In the morning he drove to the library, left the reading room only once every hour to smoke, was soon cooking his own lunch, wrote his notes on record cards in the afternoon—in time these became a case book for the history of political ideas. In the evening he was fairly tired, spent just another hour in his darkroom, occasionally went round the corner for a beer, or out to a film which featured girls in low-cut dresses in incredible predicaments that just numbed his mind into sleep. But he slept poorly—sometimes a sudden pain would startle him in the small hours, but had disappeared as soon as he was conscious of it and was walking the empty, early-morning streets, awake. He became more and more perplexed. The more he learned of political theory, the more obvious it was—however he worked things out—that East Germany as much as West possessed the traditional characteristics of a State—the features requisite to a State in classic political theory : its own territory, its own administration, and a population under it with a particular nationality—even culture. He was almost completely baffled by the impudence with which current official policy duped the experts; all of a sudden he was nonplussed at the ingenuousness with which a country so attuned to the variations of foreign politics—whose economy was integrated on a supra-national basis—presumed to deny another country existence, despite all these characteristics. In the process, he revised his previous patient impartiality. He understood the East German economy better, although its statistics were made more adroitly cryptic; he had attended economics lectures for a few terms, and despite all the dogmas of political economy he kept coming back to the undeniable total of the four thousand million marks by which Soviet war reparations had denuded the East German economy—far more than those paid to the Western Allies had hit the West German one before the currency reform. And then there was the lack of natural resources, the construction of a heavy industry, and so on : all this both explained the East German standard of living and showed it to be worse than he had feared : his pride in the West German disappeared. And, with a clarity that was almost alarming, archives, newspapers and documentation confirmed his impression—which had had little more than memory to back it up. He wasn't far from dismay when he assembled the proposals made by the East German to the inflexible West German side; until recently there was no longer any German unity to be had on the question of neutrality, of disarmament, of loans, even though no attempt was made to sue for recognition and negotiations at governmental level. He didn't touch the typewriter for days, when he should have been using it to interpret the details of thirteen years of West German politics recorded on his cards—to summarise them under the heading of reunification, the doctrine which the West German government upheld so immovably. It was already the end of August and he felt the matter was urgent : only half the manuscript was ready for the press, from then on it was patchy. At last he decided to reduce it to the size of the less formal travel article that he had originally thought of. Moreover he kicked himself for starting so haphazardly on a project which could have been done at any time—but before his trip a certain Herr Karsch would hardly have considered reunification to be the most pressing problem of West German politics, and would probably now be writing about market gardening exhibitions if the East German Rent Restriction Act hadn't been made so plain for him in Frau Liebenreuth's corridor, if the locality hadn't become so real on that threadbare staircase : and to think all that was accidental.

He would have liked to have taken his thoughts somewhere other than the local television studio in which five people sat at an unsteady table with two tele-cameras on them, boring one another with doubts about the civic boundaries of Hamburg. He felt a bit of a charlatan as—with less concern for the price of a square acre of land in Garstedt than for the cheap tumbler of water in front of him—he was just about to set his forehead on the hands he'd kept together before him all the time, when the sprightly discussion happened, here too, to turn to the possibility of a future reunification. Karsch—though omitting the simple politeness of raised shoulders and a stare straight into the camera —muttered away in the carping tone of an aggrieved spectator : he couldn't stand the word any longer, his own opinion didn't count for much, but as far as he was concerned . . . and with similar civilities he began to speak, waxed harsh about reunification always coming in the future, was sick with all the pandering with decorous reports on all the Third Pages, and all the trying to use a vexed question to use up all the expense accounts of all the popular pundits, or otherwise turn his life into a procession of received political ideas; thirdly he wouldn't be persuaded that he was master of his own soul one moment and a fellow-traveller the next. As he babbled on, his mind filled with the clear memory of outer suburbs and the rattle of early-morning workers' trains, a street with some gable-ends picked out in colour against the mass of grey ones, the whole East German land that he had seen : thrown out of their order of time and intercourse, forgotten but living. Over and again he used the words "actuality", "reality", "just look"; too quickly he rattled off his statistics in thousands, and tens of millions. Strange to say, he omitted to mention a characteristic smell on the East German autobahn, and that later odour of carbolic mixed with the vapours that came from kitchens, stairways, open pub doors and tramcars. He used the word "recognition" in the precise epistemological sense but left those present and the viewers (who were feeling rather limp on a hot afternoon) free to take the expression as understood in diplomatic usage, and finally tied things up neatly by returning to the subject of Garstedt, so that the volume faded only with his closing look to one side; for the staff at the control desk hadn't been picked out for such contingencies and helplessly allowed the ensuing row to appear on the screen for

another minute, until—probably by mistake—someone's finger
happened on the fade-in button for the so-called technical inter-
ference effect, behind this the unusual scene disappeared from
the viewers' sight, just as a certain Herr Karsch was moving
away from the cameras and slipping into the wings: but with
no bounce in him, no head held high, no defiant stare—just
rather stiffly, stooping a little, looking half worn-out, half-asleep,
and giving only that automatic nod back at them over his right
shoulder. He took note of the pains in his back: they seemed
serious, not just troublesome; they affected his neck muscles. An
empty feeling under his skull, in front, made him afraid that he
wouldn't be able to keep going through the usual sort of September without cracking up. In fact he didn't give himself enough
time to ask for a check-up before December.

That very evening the girls who saw to the answering service
at the exchange spent three-quarters of an hour redirecting calls
to him: some of them they would rather have sent by post to
avoid having to repeat them; they hadn't thought a caller who
spoke so nicely could have said such things. In the next few
weeks he was on his way to youth groups of the officially permitted parties, to student gatherings, to individuals: who invited
him to give a paper, take part in a discussion, give his opinion in
strict confidence. And so he got to see a good number of hotel
rooms without beginning the series on hotels, for at night he
would sit at the apologies for desks, getting down a few sentences
of his report and trying to find other words that would make it
as highly nuanced and evocative as his own memories—but he
couldn't escape the feeling that it was ineffectual, inaccurate, a
waste of time. For why still try to let the two German provinces
know more about one another: why take notice of the cheap
sordid tricks they used to assess one another, as if the year nineteen sixty finished at the border for each of them; why write,
answer letters, give information, if the meetings terminated in
applause or in a beer-hall, as after any ordinary discussion or
foreign travel lecture; why, when the postman brings the supposed Jewish swine the compliments of the Wandsbek watch-
dogs, if one by one the columnists of the smaller newspapers
deny this obscure journalist anything like a representative opinion
and moral justice; why, if on account of that, almost every
evening, he must repudiate political ambitions, bring down on

himself the contempt of nineteen-year-olds for this cowardly citizen; why, just because he wouldn't answer for anything but his report, wouldn't pass judgement. Soon he was engaged in conflict when he spoke from a public platform; for recently he'd taken to opening his talk with the questions, why, on what grounds, for what just cause, and for what purpose, these ladies and gentlemen wanted to unite with the strangers, brothers and sisters they'd been able to do without ever since the war? Under the quiet firmament in his home, under the blue slates of the roof, he so longed for that now darker sky, that towards the end of October he would certainly have chucked it in of his own free will, if the police hadn't forestalled him by searching his place on suspicion of high treason.

He wasn't at home and a search hadn't revealed his name in the Bremerhaven hotel register, so that in the night, when he stopped on the squeaking boards of the entrance hall, he heard loud voices down below waxing indignant with righteous citizen's oaths against this fellow without any sense of national responsibility, whom the rotten trick of buying the upper floor wouldn't help when he was up against those solicitors in Hamburg who knew all about terminating contracts. Karsch put his case down and went down the steps to the door, which gave when he pounded at it; but no one answered. His own door hung open; the lock was undamaged. The chairs stood neatly about the table, equidistant, one placed at each side—just like any furniture shop window. They'd left the official notification next to his typewriter, and nearby another note told him his cleaner had given notice. The things in his drawers were arranged with the precision of a batman; the mattress had been turned and the bed remade as precisely as any housemaid could manage it. His in-tray, all his card-indexes and negatives were missing from the top of the steel filing cabinets, which had all been locked again; the ink had gone from his desk. The list of confiscated objects didn't go into details, gave no total, but had a sort of waiter's receipt stuck on at the end with a note in a childish hand. Karsch stayed for half an hour without sitting down, left the house with two suitcases, drove over the city limits, made an appointment with L. The next morning he took the tram into town and waited in the canteen at the dubbing-studio.

Herr L. (about whom we need say no more) had the money

with him, and took the letter of attorney; but also tried to dissuade Karsch, for he just couldn't see how someone without relatives in East Germany could go on for weeks on end with all this wish-wash about reunification. He thought the way Karsch had found his flat was a misunderstanding—"on whose part?" asked Karsch, and didn't require an answer, but stayed huddled up instead of venturing out into the early morning air. He clutched his arms against his chest as if he was freezing, occasionally rubbed his stubbly chin against one shoulder, couldn't keep his eyes open. He didn't want to talk. He just remarked that when the card-indexes were taken away he had lost eight years' work—he couldn't go on working without the card-indexes. He stayed at the table only out of politeness; they parted after fifteen minutes. In the meantime, although the authorities neither profited from their raid nor made any retraction (though this was for lack of an address), Karsch hunted for some explanation through all the peculiar letters he had received since his return from East Germany—letters or post-cards from people there he'd happened to meet on the platform at Jüterborg, in the Erfurt civic restaurant, or who had otherwise got into conversation with a visitor from West Germany; people to whom he'd given his name and address in case of some eventuality—pleasure or assistance—scribbled them on railway tickets or matchboxes. Now they had had to write to him, notes in which he might perhaps catch the allusion, although the East German censor certainly would not. Karsch had often sent back these post-cards with their mysterious greetings, in case he would open the door and see someone standing there with his bags and the somewhat trying information : "But you know me!" In the meantime the bell had been disconnected, no one moved behind the door, there were no more letters with this secret society stuff—no more answers sent.

Herr L. (who, I promise you, doesn't go around telling everyone about Karsch's affairs) tries to make something of an incident which happened before he met Karsch in the studio. The people there had to get a tape-recording done in a hurry, and since the speaker—alone with the flickering lights and microphones in the recording-booth—didn't think his performance was up to his usual best, they asked a chap who had obviously had a sleepless night and was waiting in the corridor, leaning there against the wall, if he would play the audience for twenty minutes so that they could get their money's worth of ability out of this sensitive actor bloke; and the stranger didn't say a word but let them take him through the two sets of doors, and sat down to watch the sensitive actor's lips moving. While he was there he must have seen his wife behind the glass in the control room, sitting at the cutting table she had gone back to after the divorce : she was six years older now, still had the same taste for full skirts and multi-coloured jumpers, wore her hair shorter than she used to, was nibbling at some sort of sponge-cake, arched one hand below the other, turned towards a part of the room he couldn't see, and hardly moved her lips as she said something in a facetiously guilty way to the sound engineer, something that Karsch can't have heard through the two layers of plate-glass, although per-haps he wanted to hear it as much as the faint sound of the laugh she gave, putting her hand to her throat as if to arrest the noise. He certainly didn't want to disturb her—L. supposes that's why Karsch turned his chair round to sit with his back to the control room—and so the recording had to be repeated; and later on they recognised Karsch's face, although the photo in the paper didn't come out very well. He spent December in a nurs-ing-home in Milan, then he tried to find work in Rome. Finally he went back to Milan : for some time the right people had found his Italian invaluable. He's got two rooms outside town, you only get him back to West Germany if it's absolutely neces-sary—and the necessity is never so absolute. He's got more eccen-tric since then : never answers private letters—if they're on business he only sends a few lines back—doesn't give a phone number, posts his manuscripts without a covering note, pays his taxes in Italy, on which subject he holds certain opinions which we take to be justifiable prejudices if occasionally we happen to talk about him, citing his case as one where an ill-advised action on the part of the police led a man to consider himself for ever excluded from his fellow-citizens; or holding him up as an ex-ample of one who interprets the symptoms of ageing as special insights. His articles read as they used to, and an increasing number of readers probably buy the paper for its third page, where he writes with a nice choice of detail : the sun and wind play about his words as he reports on individual problems of Italian politics and industry, or simply hits off a misty sun-drenched morning in the western Alps, so well that some people would give anything to be there rather than here, day after day and in the anguish of the divided Germany which is often on our lips and which we must live with.

BIOGRAPHICAL NOTE

Uwe Johnson. Born in 1934 in Cammin (Pomerania). Studied German philology in Rostock and Leipzig. Since settling in Berlin in 1959 he has won two awards—the *Theodor Fontane-Preis* in 1960 and the *Prix Formentor*—the international publishers' prize —in 1962.

Select Bibliography

Mutmassungen über Jakob, 1959 (*Speculations About Jacob,* London, 1963)

Das dritte Buch über Achim, 1962 (*Third Book About Achim,* New York, 1967)

Karsch und andere Prosa, 1964

Zwei Ansichten, 1965 (*Two Views,* London, 1967)

Siegfried Lenz

Translated
by
R. P. Heller

SIEGFRIED LENZ

LUCAS, GENTLE SERVANT

To the south the grass was burning. It was burning fast and almost without smoke. The flames moved towards the Kenya mountains. The fire was on its way through the elephant grass. It made itself a wind, and the wind tasted of smoke and ash. Once a year they set the grass alight. The fire followed its old path towards the mountains. At the foot of the mountains it lay down, and with the fires the wind lay down. Then the antelopes and jackals returned—but the grass had gone. Once a year the grass burned, and when it was burnt out, they ploughed. They dug and furrowed the earth, added new ashes to the old, and upon this land of ash and stone they cast their maize. And the maize grew and bore good cobs.

I got out of the path of the fire and drove in a wide arc down to the bamboo forest by the river. Driving slowly between thorn and elephant grass around the fire, I felt the hot squally wind on my skin and tasted the smoke. I intended to drive home along the river and beside the bamboo. In this way I could overtake the fire, and then I could drive back to the grassland. It was not a big detour. I had only another fifteen miles to cover and I should be home before dark—I had to be home before dark.

It was then that I came upon them—or rather they came upon me. I don't know whether they had been waiting for me. They were lying at the river bank, at the edge of the bamboo forest. There were more than twenty of them, gliding from the bamboo, silent and grave, twenty haggard men. On their foreheads and bodies they bore little scars—red marks of hatred. In their hands they carried pangas—short, heavy chopping-knives with which they killed our womenfolk and children, and their own people and cattle. They surrounded the car, looked at me and waited. Some of them stood in the elephant grass, others in front of the thorn. They did not come any closer although they could see that I was alone. They clutched their pangas to their thighs and kept silent—twenty gaunt Kikuyus looking at me gently and quietly, with condescending pity. I switched off the engine and stayed where I was. My revolver lay on one of the shelves, I could see it but dared not take my hands off the steering wheel. They kept their eyes on my hands; calmly and with apparent indifference they watched my movements. I left the revolver on its shelf. In the distance I could hear the fire crackling through the elephant grass. One of them raised his knife. He lifted it and beckoned me quickly. Leaving the revolver where it was I slowly got out. Then I recognised the one who had beckoned me—it was Lucas, my servant. It was Lucas, an old, haggard Kikuyu wearing a pair of my linen trousers. They were clean but shredded by thorns. Lucas, a quiet, gentle man— Lucas, my servant for the past fourteen years. I moved towards him and called "Lucas". But he was silent, looking past me towards the Kenya mountains, and the burning grass, across the backs of the fleeing antelopes. He did not acknowledge me. I glanced around, looked each of the men in the face, and tried desperately to remember whether I had not previously met one of them who might give me a nod and confirm that this was Lucas—Lucas my gentle servant for fourteen years. But all the faces were strange and all of them rejected my searching eyes. They were strange, distant faces gleaming in the sultry heat of the bamboo.

They opened the circle; two men stepped aside and I walked past them into the bush. The thorns ripped open my shirt, and tore at my tanned, wrinkly skin. They were hard, dry thorns. They grabbed at me, hooked on, broke—and the shirt hung in shreds from my chest. We have a name for thorns—we call them "wait-a-bit". I heard them turn over the car. They left it lying there and followed me. They did not set fire to it—just left it; that was enough. That would do in this land of deep sleep and decay. Nobody would ever raise it to its wheels again. Someone might one day push it into the river . . . perhaps . . . But I should never use it again.

They all followed me: more than twenty men trailed behind me. We walked through the bush as if they and I had a common destination.

Lucas walked behind me. I could hear his panga scraping against the branches, the ones my body had pushed forward and which then snapped back. Occasionally I stopped, giving Lucas a chance to catch up. I still had not abandoned the idea of speaking to him, but he always sensed my intention and slowed his pace; and when I turned round he would look back or past me. I followed them to the river. I followed them although I was walking ahead. And before the river I halted. It was the shallow, sluggish river which I had twice waded through—twice up to my hips in mud; once during the war and the second time when the missionary had had an accident. That was a long time ago but I still remembered how it felt. I stopped at the river. They came up to me, surrounding me, more than twenty men with heavy pangas, strange, rigid faces marked with the little scars of hatred. Black river ducks paddled hastily to the opposite bank, and when they got there they looked across to where I stood within the circle which the river completed; I stood at the centre of their numb hatred. They squatted down, holding the knives in their laps and saying nothing. Their silence was as old as the silence of this country. I knew it, I had withstood it for forty-six years. When he came here from England the country received us in silence; it remained silent when we built our houses and staked out the land. It remained silent when we sowed and when we reaped. And it stayed silent. We ought to have known that one day it would speak.

A snake swam across the river. It had come out of the bamboo, keeping its head rigidly out of the water—a small snake with flattened head. Then it disappeared in the river escarpment—I made a mental note of the place where it had vanished. I turned my head and looked into the men's faces trying to find out whether they, too, had been watching the snake. I wanted to humour them because I dreaded the moment when they would start talking. I had become used to their silence and so I feared their speech. But they kept silent, staring ahead, behaving as if I were their guard, as if they had silently surrendered to me. They were silent as if their lives depended on mine; and they kept me in their midst until darkness fell. I had tried to sit down on the ground, too. My shirt stuck to my back, my knees trembled. I was limp from the sultry heat oozing from the bamboo, but hardly had I sat down when Lucas apathetically made a short gesture with his knife. He just lifted its point a little and I knew it meant that I had to stand. I was sure they were going to kill me. I looked at them at length and searched their faces, one by one—including that of Lucas, my gentle servant for fourteen years. I gazed at them, trying to find my murderer.

After darkness had fallen, some of the men rose and disappeared. But they were back soon, laden with dry, thorny brushwood. They piled it up and lit a small fire in the centre of the circle. One of them remained seated and kept feeding the flames.

I remembered the times I had shared with Lucas: it was only two days since he had vanished. I recalled his silent pride and his tendency to complicate life. As I looked at the men and thought of their ritual killings, I remembered that in bygone days they used to take dry leaves to wrap around thieves and set them on fire. In my forty-six years here I had heard a lot about their imagination, their ritual sacrifices and their guileless cruelty. A Kikuyu has more imagination than all the whites of Kenya put together, but it is a cruel imagination. We have tried to wean them from their natural cruelty but by doing so we impoverished them. We have tried to discredit their secret tribal oaths, orgies and incantations, and all we have done is to make their lives boring and empty. They want back not only their land, they also clamour for the return of their magic, their cults, their natural cruelty. I had only to look into their faces to understand: this craving for the land and yearning for their ancient soul was reflected in all the faces across which flickered the dark glow of the fire. I considered whether I should flee: I had not seen any crocodiles in this part of the river. But perhaps they had merely been lying in the grass on the opposite bank or in the bamboo, or perhaps they had slid into the water during the hours of darkness. I could swim under water, I was a good swimmer, despite my age. I might make it, for crocodiles do not strike all that quickly.

But the men who had flung a circle around me would not sit idly by; they would not squat silently and watch me run away. Frightened, I tried to read their faces; I was afraid they might have guessed my thoughts. But their expressions were inscrutable and unmoved—even that of Lucas, my gentle servant. Perhaps they were hoping that I would flee; perhaps they were merely waiting for me to throw myself into the river—their faces seemed to be waiting for it.

Lucas rose, went over to the fire and squatted down. His arms

rested on his knees as he gazed into the glow—a haggard old
Kikuyu absorbed in memories. I could have hurled myself on
him, he was squatting so close to my feet, engrossed and impassive. But it would have done me no good if I had thrown myself
upon him. His knife with its point in the fire was lying before
him only a few inches below his large skinny hands. Lucas seemed
to be dreaming. Then two men, whom I had not seen before
stepped out of the bush. They were received into the circle. Both
men, though barefoot, wore cotton shirts. They seemed to have
lived in a town, in Nairobi or Nyeri. They squatted on the
ground behind Lucas and all eyes turned towards them. They
had both brought two large rolled-up banana leaves. They
pushed them nearer to Lucas and waited. They were strong,
well-nourished men, with flesh on their bones. They looked
different from Lucas and his kind who were gaunt and narrow
chested, their arms dangling from their shoulders. Their faces,
too, were different. They did not have that strange apathetic
look, that look of unconquerable distance. Their faces were good-
humoured, their glances quick and searching, which revealed
that they had been living in a town. I had noticed that as they
stepped into the circle. But I had also seen how they changed
when they spotted Lucas by the fire: their faces were transformed; they seemed to be reminded of some distant sorrow, and
this gave them a weird remoteness.

Lucas removed the knife from the fire. He could not have
seen the two men arrive, but he must have known that they
were squatting behind. He turned on the balls of his feet to face
them. As he turned I could hear the grass squeak under his feet
—it was the only sound he had made so far. Lucas nodded to
one of the men who then took off his cotton shirt, tossed it behind
him and walked up close to Lucas. Quickly, almost with lust, he
squatted down before him. Lucas raised the knife and pressed it
into the man's shoulder blade. There was a hiss as the hot iron
touched the man's flesh. His body reared up and his head jerked
back. I saw his clenched teeth, his distorted face. His eyes were
closed, his lips dragged down. He did not groan. And Lucas,
gentle servant for fourteen years, set the knife to another place—
seven times he laid it on the man's shoulder, chest and forehead.
Upon receiving the second cut, the Kikuyu trembled. After that
he had mastered his pain. After that second wound he calmly

faced the knife—he even bent his shoulder towards it and ex-
panded his chest. He could not get them fast enough—those
little cuts, those indelible marks of conspiracy and symbols of
hatred. Now he was marked and Lucas motioned him away. He
crawled back to his place and squatted on the ground. Lucas put
the knife back into the fire. After a while he nodded to the
second man. He too removed his cotton shirt. The knife sank
into his shoulder, and hissed. There was a smell of burnt flesh.
He too turned numb and quiet after the second wound; he too
received seven cuts and crawled back. I heard thunder rumbling
far away and glanced over towards the horizon, as if the storm
signified my salvation. But there was no second clap. I only saw
the fire in the grass spreading towards the mountains. The moon
emerged; its image dissolved in the lazy river. The sound of
gurgling water reached us from the other bank. In the bamboo
everything was still.

I saw Lucas pull the banana leaves towards him and carefully
unroll them. I noticed that there was a tin in one of them. He
placed it near the fire. The tin was full of some dark, thick
liquid and Lucas poured off a little of it. He then put his hand
into the other leaf. I realised that in it were the entrails of an
animal—perhaps of a sheep. He picked them up, broke them
into small pieces and threw a few of these into the tin. Then he
poured some grains and flour over it and began singing softly.
And while he was singing, I had never heard him do that in
fourteen years, Lucas started to mix a dough. I watched him
beat and work it to the accompaniment of his muted song. It
was a gritty paste.

Eventually Lucas took it in both hands and moulded it into a
big ball. Then he pinched a little piece out of it and began to
roll it between his palms. He turned it into a little ball. The
dough was moist and I heard it squelching in his hands. Lucas
rolled it into fourteen little balls, twice seven moist balls of dough
—and laid them out in two rows in front of him. When he had
finished Lucas nodded to one of the men squatting before him.
The man went up to him, knelt down, shut his eyes and strained
his neck forward. He opened his mouth, Lucas took one of the
moist dough balls and pushed it between the man's teeth. As he
swallowed I could see the ball glide down his gullet. He gulped
several times, his head moving forward and back, forward and

back . . . his face was shining. Then he kept still, his lips sprang open, reaching out greedily towards the next lump of dough. Lucas pushed another ball into the man's mouth. There was Lucas, sorcerer and gentle servant, feeding him the dough of hate. He fed him seven times and turned him away when he had completed the number. A little later Lucas nodded to the second man and he too came forward, opened his mouth, swallowed down the dough balls with an oath, his face gleaming. He too ate the dough of hate, seven times, and was sent away. He walked back erect, picked up his cotton shirt, put it on and rejoined the circle they had drawn around me. I remember, seven is their number, the holy number of the Kikuyu. I had often heard of it in those forty-six years. And now I had seen it. Why had they let me see it, why did they permit me to stand and watch it all? My number was different. It was I for whom the wounds were meant, those fresh marks on the men's bodies. I was the target of their hatred. Why did they not kill me? Why did they hesitate? What kept Lucas from raising the heavy panga against me? Why did they not let me die the death which they had inflicted on so many others? Had they a special death in store for me? Had the gentle Lucas been thinking up a special death for me in those fourteen years as my servant?

We had talked but little in those fourteen years. Lucas had always worked silently and done his job well. I had even asked him to have a meal with us. Sometimes having watched him at work from a distance I would walk over and invite him, but he never came. He always found some simple excuse and declined my invitation with polite regret. No one had worked better for me than Lucas, my wonderful servant. What kind of death had he planned for me?

Lucas rose and walked past me to the river. Slowly he paced up and down along the bank, observing, listening, lying down flat on the ground and looking out over the water. He took a stone, threw it into the middle of the sluggish river, watched where it hit the surface and waited. Then he came back and walked over to me. He stopped in front of me, but he looked past me. His eyes did not see me although they were trained on me. There he stood, knife in hand. He began to speak. At once I recognised his voice, his soft, mild voice. He asked me to go. He spoke to me as if he was begging me for something. The time

had come for me to go, he pleaded. He pointed across the river
and the bamboo forest in the direction of my farm. I was to go,
he begged me, where Fanny, my wife and my daughter Sheila,
lived.

Lucas begged me to go to them. They would need me tomorrow at sunset, he said. I was not to wait any longer. I was to
prepare Fanny and Sheila. For tomorrow, he said, the farm
would burn, the big fire would come and then I must not be far
away from them. He was about to turn away, he had said
enough. But I would not let him go yet. With outstretched hand
I pointed to the black river. He read my question from the
gesture and gave me to understand that there were no crocodiles
about. He had kept an eye on the water. I could go now, the
way was clear.

I looked around the ring of faces, strange stony faces across
which flickered the feeble glow of the fire. Lucas went back, took
his place in the circle and squatted down. I stood alone in the
centre and gazed across at the bamboo forest. I felt the sultry
heat wafting over from it. I sensed decay and mystery. I put one
foot into the water and started walking slowly. I made my way
to the middle of the river; my feet sank into the soft mud, the
water rose up to my hips, then to my chest. It was black, tepid
water. Dead bamboo stems and twigs drifted along and when a
branch touched me I shuddered and stopped. Not once did I
look back. I kept wondering why they had let me go. There must
be some reason why they had not killed me.

What verdict lay behind their decision to send me home? I
did not know and I could not make it out, although I knew
many of their wiles and their bland, cruel slyness.

Why had they let me go? My foot touched something hard
on the ground. I jerked back. If they had not been on the river
bank I would have screamed. Immediately I threw myself on to
the water. Swimming I got ahead more rapidly than wading—
and I swam towards the middle with desperate strokes. What I
touched must have been a sunken tree trunk. The water remained still. There was no new movement in the river. I waded
on slowly, paddling with both hands and taking long, cautious
steps through the soft mud. It was the third time I was crossing
the river.

What deceit lay behind my acquittal? Why had they let me

go? Why had Lucas sent me home? Lucas had shown me the shortest route which was through the river and the bamboo forest. I knew that the grassland—the fields of toil—began behind the bamboo forest, and I remembered that after that I would have to pass the maize fields and the farm. I thought I would make it and could cover the fifteen miles by next evening. The farm belonged to McCormick; perhaps he would give me a lift over the final stretch.

The bamboo stood thick. I could scarcely move ahead and had to squeeze between the stalks. It was hopeless. The soil, too, was treacherous. It was covered with leaves and twigs, up to the height of the first bamboo shoots, and I could not see where I was treading. Time and again I sank, got bogged down as far as my hips and stumbled forward. I just could not go on. I stopped and glanced back. The men had gone, the fire was out and I was on my own, alone in the sweltering bamboo. The wet clothes clung to my skin and my knees were trembling. I had the feeling I was being watched and that lurking, cold eyes were fixed on me from all sides. I carried no arms. I must not go on.

Everything was still. Only now and then the silence was broken when a bird cried out into the darkness or an animal wailed at having its sleep disturbed. I must not go on. I knew that at night, unarmed I could not get through the bamboo forest. Leopards would stop me, leopards or something else. I had to go back to the river and wait for the morning, or else move closely along the river. The night was dangerous for a man without weapons and fire—I could feel it. It was a little too still, too soft. And so I fought my way through the bamboo and liana back to the river. I wanted to make use of the night and walk up the river. At best I should gain two miles, two wearisome miles by the morning. None the less I decided to go this way. I wanted to get to my farm before Lucas brought the big fire to it. I had to warn my daughter and my wife, Fanny.

Once again I entered the river. The water reached up to my calves. With the least possible noise I waded up the river. I was making unexpectedly good headway. The moon lay on the water. If there had been no moon I should not have gone on. The mud was getting harder, and the farther up river I walked the firmer and safer the ground became. I trod on small stones in the water. The shrubs no longer jutted out so far across the river

and everything seemed to be all right. Sometimes I saw a pair
of eyes in the bush, green, rigid eyes. Involuntarily I made towards the middle of the river. I was scared, but I had to suppress
my fear if I meant to get to the farm in time. Occasionally the
eyes on the river bank followed me—calm and cold they trailed
me up the river. I could discern neither head nor body. The eyes
seemed to be suspended in the bamboo and they floated through
the bamboo and the liana. I knew that this night was lying in
wait for me. It pursued the stranger and tried to lull his suspicion with its silence and fragrance. I saw luminous flowers on
the bank, their beauty burning itself to death. At times I saw
them burn in the darkness, as tall as a man, on a tree or in the
very centre of a shrub—flaming flowers of death beneath which
a leopard was lurking.

What treachery was there behind my acquittal? Why had they
let me go, me for whose sake they had burnt the marks of wrath
into their skins? Were they so sure of their plot?

I was getting on quite well. At this rate, I could perhaps cover
three miles during the night and I should be with Fanny and
the girl sooner than they expected. I thought of Fanny—I could
see her sitting on the wooden veranda, listening into the darkness, the old army pistol on the railing. I ought to have been
with them long ago : perhaps they had sensed across the distance
that something had happened to me. They had a good instinct,
which had grown sharper as each of us had started to go his
own way. This land of sleep and decay had shown us that man
is by nature a lone wolf, a lost, solitary hunter, following the trail
to his own self. We each began to go our own ways soon after
Sheila was born. Sometimes we each believed we could manage
without the other. We worked in silence and separately. We got
out of each other's way whenever life was about to draw us
towards a common enterprise. Although Fanny and I walked in
the same direction and our sorrow and our goal were the same,
we approached it at a great distance from each other. We had
said all there was to be said and had confided everything and so
there came a time when we understood one another without
words. We spent whole days without conversation, yet things
went well. Often I had secretly watched Fanny as she walked
through the maize or clambered down the ravine to the river. I
had watched her and noticed that her movements had changed

from the early days. She moved more softly, more like an animal. Her movements flowed out completely, relaxed and easy. She felt secure.

The river became shallower, a few stones jutted out and wherever possible I leapt from one to another, hardly having to wade through water. The river and the air had both become colder and I began to shiver. I stopped on a stone and massaged my body and legs. My shirt was ripped across my chest, and when I bent down the shreds dangled over my face. They smelt sickly sweet and musty. Carefully I covered my skin with the strips, tried to stretch the shirt a little and shove it under my belt. I was beginning to freeze and longed for the warm mud and the spot on the river where they had let me leave their circle. I drank a little of the bitter water and was about to move on when I saw him: he was standing close to the bank, in a little bay of the river, only a few yards away from me. The bamboo around him had been trampled down so that I was able to see his full size. He, too, had apparently just noticed me. He had rolled up his trunk and stood before me, motionless. I saw the dull lustre of his tusks, the small shiny eyes and his ears slowly fanning. He was a huge elephant. He stood there and looked across at me. I was so confounded by the sight of the beast that I did not think of running away. I made no move and gazed at the big, lonely animal. Suddenly I felt the wonderful presence of the wind. After a little while he turned his head, unfurled his trunk and began to drink. I heard a sucking noise. I could hear him brush aside a few little stones with his trunk. They rattled against each other. Then, unexpectedly, he turned round and disappeared into the bamboo. I heard him crashing through the wood and suddenly, as if he had stopped, all was quiet again.

Slowly I went on my way. I had found a bamboo cane in the water and I used it to lean on as I jumped from stone to stone. The stick had been split with a single diagonal blow and had a sharp point. In case of need I could use it as a weapon.

I thought of Lucas, my gentle servant for fourteen years. I visualised him sitting by another fire, with other men squatting before him and swallowing down the dough of hate, which, rolled into little balls, he was pushing into their mouths. I thought I could see their shoulders stretch out eagerly towards his heavy panga, their faces gleaming in the oppressive heat, craving to receive their marks. I visualised Lucas bestriding the whole country and wherever his foot crushed the grass I saw flames leaping up. And the fire followed him incessantly, changing direction when he did, lying down when he bade it—Lucas, Lord of the Fire.

I remember the first time I saw him : with the rest of his tribe he had fled to the north. The cattle plague had almost wiped out their herds, and with their last few animals they had sought refuge in the north. And while they were away we had come and taken their land. We did not know when, if ever, they would return. We took over the fallow land and started to sow.

But after we had sowed and even gathered in our harvests they came back from the north. I saw their silent procession winding its way up the long valley—the women in front, then the cattle and the men bringing up the rear. We told them that they had forfeited the land through their absence. They said nothing. We offered them money; they took it, tucked it calmly in their clothes, and remained silent. They were silent because they regarded themselves as the owners of this land, for to a Kikuyu a sale of land is legal only if it has been carried out with religious ceremony. It mattered nothing that we had given them money. We had staked out the fields without the proper ritual and so it could never belong to us. I remembered how Lucas had come up the long valley in one of these treks. He walked at the end of the procession and he attracted my attention immediately. I was struck by his gentle old face, a face that seemed never to have been young. It was Lucas' land which I had taken. And his face remained calm when I said that I would not give it up.

He said nothing. And when the marchers moved on to continue their silent search for the lost land Lucas set off with the others. I saw him walk gently across the grassland and could not let him go. I called him back and asked him whether he would like to stay and work the land with me. He nodded silently and went to work so naturally that it seemed as if he had only interrupted it for a while and had now returned to finish it.

He worked patiently and never said a word. I did not have to give him many orders. I tried to instruct him a little and took some trouble to make his work easier for him. He would listen politely, waiting till I dismissed him, and shortly afterwards he had forgotten my advice. What trick was there behind my acquittal? What had been going on in my wonderful, gentle servant's mind during those fourteen years?

I continued my journey up the river till morning. The nights in this country are long and I had got about four miles farther than I had hoped. I examined the oblong segment of sky above the river and there seemed to be a thunderstorm in the air. The sky was covered by a single grey cloud which stood above me and the river. Its edges were dark but right through the grey there ran a vermilion track, a line of fire. I thought this might be Lucas' track. I considered whether there was any point in crossing the bamboo forest in these circumstances. But then I thought of Fanny and my daughter, and of the time limit. And I decided to traverse the bamboo at all cost. For the first time I felt hungry. I drank some bitter water from the river and with the help of the bamboo stick I swung myself over the edge. When I stepped on to the bank I realised just how exhausted I was. The walk across the stones had taken all my strength—it had needed so much concentration and skill that until now I had had no time to acknowledge my exhaustion.

Now that I was able to relax I felt unsure of my legs, I saw my hands tremble and I sensed a veil before my eyes—an infallible symptom of exhaustion. But I must not stop. I must go on. I had to let myself be carried right to the farm, dragged, as it were, in the wake of my first exertion. I knew myself well enough, I knew I should make it.

Bending forward, I climbed up a slope. After each step I held on to the bamboo stands and roots and pulled myself up. This had to be done with care because sometimes I grabbed the roots of a dead tree which had decayed but remained standing because there was no room for it to fall. And when I tried to haul myself up on the rotten stem it gave way, the roots snapped and the bamboo came crashing down towards me. Sometimes a tree would hit other trees as it fell and I could hear the roots tearing. I threw myself to the ground covering my head with my hands. At times I sank into the soft soil up to my knees. But this did not happen as often as it had during the night when I tried to cross the bamboo forest for the first time. Now I was able to make out the deeper holes in the ground and could avoid them.

The cold from which I had suffered in the morning no longer

bothered me. I was sweating from the struggle, my shirt stuck to my back, and when I lay face down on the ground my breath bounced back from the leaves and hit my hot face. I felt sweat running down my cheeks. It tasted thin and sour when I licked my lips with my tongue.

I decided to rest a little in the maize but did not dare to lie down or even sit—the risk would have been too great. I meant to rest standing so as not to be overcome by exhaustion. I just wanted to stop for a moment and break a maize cob. I was quite near to it, I already had the sweet-floury taste of the corn on my tongue—it was good just to think of it.

I pulled myself up to a black cedar and put my hand into a tangle of creepers. They felt smooth and leathery like snakes. I caught hold of them, dragged myself towards the tree and stood on a root. Now I could see a clearing. I saw it through the veil of my exhaustion. As I approached it I could make out a number of big heavy birds. They were gathered around something. They were hopping around without making a sound; lazily and flabbily they winged their circles around the object. Some of them sat on it and pushed newcomers off. The birds were black. They would not let me drive them off. I was able to get close enough to touch them with my bamboo stick; and I tried it, too, but they just hopped ponderously and stayed there. The thing they were crowding round was a tree trunk. Evidently all they wanted was to sit on it. But as there were too many of them they engaged in this silent battle.

I went up to the tree trunk, leant against it and succumbed to the temptation to sit down. I sat myself in the middle and used my stick to shoo away the birds. But I was unable to get rid of them: they jumped down, lazily and reluctantly, skipping clumsily around my legs they looked up at me with tilted heads. After a while one bird tried to fly back on to the tree trunk. I ducked because I thought he was going to attack me, but when I saw that he only wanted to sit next to me I let him come and did not bother about him. I leant far back and observed the sky. I saw that the cloud with the vermilion streak had moved further to the west: there would be no thunderstorm and I felt new hope that I would make my way home. I rose slowly and walked across the clearing, threading my way through the big birds.

They did not stir, remained squatting on the ground, only following me with their eyes.

I thought of Lucas' eyes, full of gentle sadness. I thought of them while struggling through the bamboo and I began to understand him—Lucas and all the others who bore the marks of hatred. I felt that now I understood why they were so eager to be branded; we have robbed them of too much but we have also given them too much.

What ruse had Lucas thought up, why had he let me go—why me? After all, he had lost everything and I was among those to blame. I had to get to the farm before sunset. I thought of Fanny and my girl. I could still see them on the wooden veranda, with the old army pistol to hand. I knew they had not slept all night.

When I had got through the bamboo forest, I was so exhausted that I felt I could not walk another step. My body was craving for rest; everything was pulling me down to earth. I stopped amidst the elephant grass and shut my eyes. I should have dozed off and sunk on to my knees, had I not been leaning on my bamboo stick. I was so feeble that a deep apathy overcame me. Fanny's fate no longer mattered. I calmed my fears by telling myself that she was a good shot and was able to defend the house just as well as I could. But for the hunger I should have lain down. The hunger forced me to open my eyes. I raised the bamboo cane, pushed it into the ground and set off. I walked through the elephant grass which reached up to my hips, my lips were burning and the blood was buzzing in my fingers. Not once did I gaze across the huge plain. I avoided looking at the horizon. I had not the strength to raise my eyes.

Towards noon I stood before the maize field. I threw away the bamboo stick. It had done its duty. I flung it into the grass in a wide arc and ripped off a few cobs of maize. I sat down on the ground, put the cobs in my lap, tore the creamy-white, dry husks off one of them and took a good bite. I did not pause to pick out the grains with my thumb. I simply moved the cob along my teeth. It tasted of sweet flour.

Having eaten, I crept into the rows of maize. I felt coolness and shade. I felt oddly safe here in the maize. I crawled through the entire field, imagining that while I was crawling I was gathering fresh strength. Indeed, I felt I was getting stronger. I lifted my eyes and looked ahead. Through the maize I saw the farm on a hill. There it was—the large house with the veranda and sheds, made of corrugated sheet, standing at right angles to it. The farm looked deserted. McCormick had four dogs. Every time I passed I used to see one of them; the dog would always lie in front of the veranda in the dust. But now I could not see any dogs. I was about to leave the maize field and walk across to the house. I had already stood up when they came out of the farm. There were six of them—haggard Kikuyus with pangas, slowly coming down the steps of the veranda. They did not seem to be in any hurry. For the moment they disappeared behind the corrugated shed. Then they came into view again—six gaunt men crossing the yard past a clump of trees, walking erect over the grass in the direction from which I had come. They were heading for the bamboo and the river. I could not make out whether Lucas was among them. They were too far away. I could only guess whether he was with them—and my senses said yes.

I followed them with my eyes until they vanished behind the grass plain. I knew it was useless now to go to the farm and ask McCormick for the car. I should never again be able to ask him for anything. I was sorry for him, he had only been here six years, having come immediately after the war. He was a friendly man with red hair who loved nothing more than a chat. Once a year he'd go away for a month. They said he went to Nairobi where he would mysteriously disappear.

No one came into view on the farm and I slid back into the maize field, determined to return when I had settled things at home. If I had had my automatic, or even the old army pistol, I should have gone over to McCormick's farm right away. But unarmed and worn out as I was it would have been sheer folly. They might have left a man behind; all of them might come back—there was no point in it.

I crawled towards the narrow path which bordered the maize-field on one side. It led to my farm. I had covered the most difficult part of the way. Having had a rest and eaten, I got over my apathy and thirst. No doubt I should reach my farm in time. The nearer I got, the more fearful I became of their wiles. And I distrusted them even more for setting me free. Why had he let me go, Lucas, gentle servant and sorcerer—what deceit had he planned? Fear made me stand up among the maize. I pushed my hands forward and started to run, as well as I could. I hastened through the field, stopped, listened, felt my heart pulsate and continued to run. I felt my thigh getting cramp, becoming stiff and numb. On my chest I discovered the marks of the thorn—small, blood-clotted scratches. My arms were trembling. My mouth gaped, my trunk bent forward. Thus I ran through the maize. And when I reached the end of the field, I allowed myself no respite. I ran on to the road. I thought I was still running; I heard my feet beat against the earth and I thought I was running—but if I had been I should have arrived at my goal much sooner. I was stumbling forward, beaten by fear and heat. I could hardly control my steps any longer.

Then I came to another maize field—well before sunset—and it was my own maize. Behind it lay the farm. One final spurt and and I should be there. I could even see it there ahead of me, although the maize was obscuring it from my eyes—my farm, Lucas' farm. I turned aside from the path and ran through the maize. The plants seemed stronger and higher, the cobs bigger than those in McCormick's field. I ran as far as a furrow—had Lucas torn it out of the soil or had I? I had underrated myself, under-estimated my strength. Now I felt there was still plenty in me.

The maize plants got thinner. It was the end of the field, and I stepped out of the maize. I pressed my hands against my chest, lifted my head and looked over to the breadfruit trees. The farm was no longer there—and it was many hours till sunset. I went over to the trees and looked at the ashes. I knelt down and plunged both hands into them. The ashes were cold.

BIOGRAPHICAL NOTE

Siegfried Lenz was born in Lyck (Masuren—then East Prussia) in 1926, and served in the army. Later he studied philosophy, history of literature and English at Hamburg. For a time he edited the literary pages of a daily paper; in 1962 he received a prize for literature awarded by the city of Bremen. He now works as a freelance writer in Hamburg.

Select Bibliography

Es waren Habichte in der Luft, 1951

So zärtlich war Suleyken, 1955
Der Mann im Strom, 1957
Jäger des Spotts, 1958
Das Feuerschiff, 1961 (*The Lightship,* London, 1962)
Zeit der Schuldlosen, 1961 (play)
Stadtgespräch, 1963 (*The Survivor,* New York, 1965)
Lehmanns Erzählungen oder So schön war mein Markt, 1964

Ilse Aichinger

Translated
by
Eric Mosbacher

ILSE AICHINGER

ANGELS IN THE NIGHT

THERE are bright days in December so penetrated with their
own brightness that they become brighter still, mild days, nourished by the long nights, both strong enough and weak enough
to take their pallor as a challenge and their shortness as a
promise to surpass themselves in mildness. Their brightness is
both of the dark and only of the dark. There are not many of
them, because if there were, too many strange things would
happen, too many church clocks would simply turn into the eye
of God. Such days are therefore rare: so that unusual things
should remain unusual; so that men returned from the war
should not too often feel pain in their severed limbs and should
not hold too much in hands long since lost by frostbite, and
should not know too much about the night, which soothes. But
sometimes there are such days—birds which have forgotten to
fly south. They stretch their bright wings over the city, make the
air tremulous with warmth, and make our breath once more invisible before it freezes; and, having done that, they quickly die.
They require no long twilight or red clouds, they seldom bleed
to death; they simply fall from the roofs, and it is dark. Perhaps,
were it not for those bright days in December, those stray birds,
no one would be left to go on believing in angels, though everyone else laughed behind their backs; no one would be left to hear
the rush of angels' wings before daybreak, though others heard
only the barking of dogs.

It was my sister's fault. It was she who pulled me out of bed
in the dark morning and dragged me to the window. "There!
There! they're flying over there! Didn't you hear the sound of
their wings? Can't you see their trail? Wake up! You sleep too
long!" And later, when Christmas was close and the Christmas
trees on sale in the squares had lost their needles, she would say:
"There's silver in the air, the Child will soon be here now!"
If I said it was raining, she would laugh contemptuously. "You
sleep too long!" she said. I always slept just a moment too long
to see the angels flying round the house.

I had long since started fearing sleep like death. For what is death other than missing the angels? I would lie awake with staring eyes, waiting for the sound of their wings, for the silver in the air. I would creep to the window and gaze outside, but all I ever heard was the voices of drunks down below, and once I heard one of them call out "Hallelujah!" My sister had long since gone to sleep. I heard one o'clock strike, and then two. I bit my pillow and dropped off to sleep. Then I woke again, and this time it looked almost as if silver was in the air. I jumped up and fetched logs from the box, put them in my bed and lay on them. But before three o'clock struck I fell asleep again in spite of them, and in the morning my sister again woke before I did. This time she had seen the tips of their wings, and she would have seen much more if she hadn't wasted time shaking me to wake me up.

"Did you see the angels?" I asked when I went to school, and they teased me. By now I should have stopped believing in them, I should have allowed the small fat cherubs to be shaken from my shoulders, but I only laughed. "You sleep too long!" I answered. From then onwards my angels started circling over me all the time. Everyone who said they didn't exist slept too long and the world was an enormous encampment of sleepyheads over whom the angels flew unseen.

One day my mother fetched me from school. She did not live with us, but sometimes she fetched me from school and walked part of the way home with me. Sometimes she talked to me as if I were a grown-up. That day she told me that she was suffering from insomnia and used to lie awake all night. I loved my mother, and, if there was one person in the world whom I trusted even more than my sister, it was she. If my mother lay awake at night, she must obviously know about the angels. I remember the scene exactly. I can hear it and see it in front of me now. We were just crossing the square where the Christmas trees were on sale, and the sky overhead was too high for December, and the man who sold the trees was dozing. It was a warm, sad day, a stray bird. My mother had long since started talking about something else when I suddenly asked her whether she had seen the angels. "I've never seen any!" she said. She stopped, and looked at me, and laughed, and said: "I didn't know you still

believed in them! I've never seen any!" Immediately afterwards we said good-bye.

But I was too big to accept it like that, because I had believed in angels too long, and if people had deceived me, they
had deceived me too long. I wanted a sign, I wanted to see a
host of angels over the square and hear the rush of their wings;
I wanted to see the complete collapse of all the mockers. But the
angels did not come. Swarms of pigeons took wing and circled
under the quiet sky. But the sky was no longer heaven, it was
only empty air. They had made me look foolish and ridiculous,
and I had taken bright smoke for white clothing and the echo of
the morning bells for the rush of wings too long. They should
have warned me, and I should have stopped believing in these
things, as everybody else did, but now it was to late. The angels
were no longer child angels, cherubs with chubby cheeks and
short, fair hair; they had grown bigger, more serious and more
violent. Like me, this year they had grown too quickly, and
throwing them off now was no joke. For it is only at the very
beginning that the angels who come into the world with us are
as we; they grow with us, become wilder and stronger, and
their wings grow with them. The older we are, the harder the
struggle becomes.

I did not get home till it was nearly dark. I lingered for hours
in the passages between the houses and along the benches by the
river, all alone in the world, all alone among the senseless doors
and windows, which were meaningless if there were no angels to
caress them with their wing-tips at night. It would be better than
this to have no windows, no doors, and no houses, and to have
no smoke coming out of the chimneys. Better to have no lamp
than a lamp that did not burn, better to have no world than a
world without angels.

My sister was waiting; she was always waiting. She seemed to
be waiting for something invisible, for someone who never came
because he was already there. I had always believed that she was
waiting for the angels. She was waiting on the stairs, with her
plaits dangling over the banisters. Behind her the flat door was
open, and the mist which was seeping through the cracks of the
landing window was bits of angels' clothing which had got
caught. But this time it was I who went for her. This time it
was I who tore the stars out of her hair, and when she again

insisted that she had seen the angels I could not believe her. I
asked her to swear that she had seen them.

At that time I did not yet know that it is we who are the
figments of the angels' imagination : it is not we who dream of
them, but they who dream of us. It is we who are the ghosts in
their bright night, it is we who bang doors which do not exist
and jump over cords that rattle like chains. Perhaps we ought
to behave more gently in their dreams, so as not to frighten them.
When shadows fall on the desert they are thrown by the sky. And
my sister could not swear.

When I shrieked in her face : "They don't exist! They don't
exist! You lied to me!" she did not defend herself as I had expected. She did not get angry, or burst out laughing, she did not
even contradict. She seemed to have been taken by surprise,
and to be as dismayed and horrified as I was. She was fifteen
then, and had left school for a whole year, and yet it was as if I
had told her something that she did not know, as if her belief
in angels had been dependent on mine.

"If you've seen them, swear it by their wings, swear it by the
silver in the sky!" But she remained silent. I had been prepared
for anything but this retreat into silence, this sudden defence-
lessness, this half-admission of a lie. I had expected an enemy,
and had struck with all my weapons, but struck into the void.
She had withdrawn her troops, or perhaps they had fled, I still
don't know to this day. She warmed my supper and laid the
table for me, but she could not swear. I pulled her plaits and
her dress, we hit each other, but she could not swear.

We had our supper, we sat facing each other in the dark, we
listened to the evening noises without moving. We sat in the
room, and the room lay in the house, and the house stood on the
earth, which rolled around, rolled senselessly, like a drunken
man. We both sat still, and my sister sat even stiller than I. The
weak light of a street lamp streamed through the window over
her shoulders and turned her hair into angel's hair, the same
that was on sale cheaply in the shops below. We were alone in
the house, and perhaps we were still waiting for a sign, for a rush
of wings in the air. Now, if ever, was the time for them to come,
to lift the roofs of the shops, tear the false angel's hair from its
cheap packing and let their real angels' hair fly, the long strands
of which would cut into one's cheeks like whipcord. Now, if ever,

they should have come to blow out the lamps and set alight the trees in the market-place before they were sold. But they did not come, they did not break the windows or dig us in the ribs. They did not come to set us free from our bondage. They left us alone, with nothing to look forward to but sugar-icing angels whose wings you could bite off.

If there were no angels to fly in advance of the Child, how absurd to think that all this time father was going round the shops, looking for cheap presents to buy, and that in some churches singing was going on. And the Child? The Child travelling in its little white sleigh through the vast spaces of the world, astonished at the huge distances? The Child was nothing but a cloud, and that was all. My sister could not swear.

Her army had been beaten without even making itself visible, but mine had been visibly beaten; and while my army, stricken with terror at the frozen void of a hostile land, retreated and senselessly took to flight, hers lay wounded in deep woods, a paralysed army which made not the slightest attempt to defend itself, an army bleeding to death, the defeated host of the angels. But between the trampling of the fleeing footsteps and the forgotten forest unsuspecting shepherds started pasturing their flocks.

After it had grown quite dark I went to bed. Outside sleet had started to fall. I lay half-asleep, and saw how the sleet made the tired angels' wings heavier and heavier, while the Child in dreadful solitude travelled through the mountains of the moon, past the open craters. I wanted to warn it, but I had no strength.

Later I heard my father come home, and I heard him exchange a few words with my sister. They never said very much to each other. Still later I heard the key turn in the lock; he must have gone out again. My sister opened the door of our room and stood for a time in the doorway, undecided. She tiptoed towards my bed, while I lay quite still. She bent over me, but I kept my eyes shut. Then she went quietly out of the room again. This time when I went to sleep I did not dream. My sleep had grown empty, like the death of people who look forward to no resurrection.

But, just as I had dropped off to sleep against my will, so did I wake up unexpectedly, timelessly, and in a strange room. The bedclothes on top of me felt as heavy as marble tombstones. It

felt impossible to move or to open my eyes. I didn't want the
marble slab on top of me; snow would be better, because snow
melts! What had they done? They had buried me alive. They
had gone home and left me, and now they were lighting the
candles, there was a smell of fresh pastry and burnt twigs. A
snowstorm had started outside. How lucky of them to have got
home before it started! And I? I wasn't dead! Angels, come
quickly, come and save me before the breath leaves my body,
why don't you come and save me? Are you dead? Oh, yes, now
I know, it was you who died, we buried you yesterday evening.
Or didn't you die? Was it you who were buried alive under the
marble slab? Wait, I'll try and help you, I'll lift the slab! With
all my strength I strove to lift it with the flat of my hand. Good
heavens, how light it was! I felt I was flying, like the angels.
The stone was snow.

Moonlight was flooding into the room, it was so light that the
closed doors might easily have been mistaken for open windows.
The walls had turned round, and the beds and cupboards had
secretly changed places. I felt giddy. What had woken me? Who
had turned the heavy slab into snow? There was a noise in my
ears, but it hadn't been that, no one is awoken by his own
voice. My heart was thumping, but it was not my heart which
was thumping at the window and shaking the window-panes and
had torn them open and slammed them from outside. Had it
been you?

How had I been able to doubt? It was not I, my angel, who
thought for a moment that you were the wind. How white your
dress was, there was snow in your hair, it was snowing so thickly
that I could not see how many more there were behind you. But
there must have been many, a whole host! Could I come
nearer? Was I to pray? How still you stood! Should I open the
slammed window? I wanted to see you better. Move! How big
your wings were! What had you on your feet? I wanted to open
the window for you and ask you in, see you upset everything
with your broad wings, and make you welcome.

But as I approached the window I saw the angel shake its
head, and I remembered that my sister always said that one
must not look angels in the face, and I realised that the angel
did not want me to touch the hem of its dress. Once more I had
a horrible doubt that it might be snow, a piece of rag blown

by the wind, a dream. I wanted to see the angel spread its wings.

A gust of wind came through the window, and snow blew into my eyes and mouth, and from behind a veil of snow I saw the angel move as if it were about to stretch its wings. But the snow was falling so thickly that I could hardly see, a snowstorm must have broken out. More gusts of wind came and slammed the window and obscured my view. By the time I had wiped the snow from my eyes and torn the window open again nothing was to be seen but snow swirling about the tall, narrow courtyard, falling, and then being driven back over the roofs in great scurries, like the angelic host that does not want to be touched.

Stop them! Stop them! Rise high, you roofs, you houses turn into towers, you chimneys blow smoke before them to prevent them from finding their way. You sleepers, turn on the light so that you may see them! Who would catch them, who would make it the last day, the day of judgment? Who would call them back for me? This was the time when my sister woke me, but today I was going to wake her. Wake up!

Six o'clock struck, one stroke came hesitantly after the other. The room, was dark now, and I couldn't find the bed. The snow had dazzled me, I had spent too long gazing after them, I should have woken my sister at once. "Wake up, you sleep too long!"

The bedclothes fell to the floor, my sister was not gripping them as I used to, and she did not groan and defend herself, as I did every morning against the cold floor and the angels, she didn't push me away, she kept as still as do those who are not asleep when one wakes them, as still as ony those are who are not there.

And she remained still when we found her in the courtyard and lifted her out of the snow, which had already covered her.

BIOGRAPHICAL NOTE

Ilse Aichinger. Born 1921 in Vienna. Spent her youth in Linz and Vienna. After the war studied medicine in Vienna. Prizes: *Förderungspreis*, Austria, 1952; *Gruppe 47*, 1952; City of Bremen, 1954; *Immermann*, 1955; Literature, Bavarian Academy, 1961. Now a freelance writer in Lenggries, Upper Bavaria. Married to the writer Günter Eich since 1953.

Select Bibliography

Die grössere Hoffnung, 1948
Der Gefesselte, 1953 (*The Bound Man,* London, 1955; New
   York, 1966)
Zu keiner Stunde, 1957
Besuch im Pfarrhaus, 1961 (radio play)
Eliza, Eliza, 1965

Ingeborg Bachmann

Translated
by
James Alldridge

INGEBORG BACHMANN

A PLACE FOR CHANCE ENCOUNTERS

> He hounded himself through life
> with furious speed, and then he says:
> "consistency, consistency";
> whenever a word was spoken by another
> he said: "inconsistency, inconsistency";
> —this was the gulf of a madness beyond recovery....
>
> George Büchner, Lenz

IT is ten houses to *Sarotti*,[1] some blocks before *Schultheiss*[2] five crossroads away from the *Commerzbank*, it is nowhere near *Berliner Kindl*,[2] there are candles in the windows, it is well away from the tram-lines, and it is the quiet hour, a cross stands before it, it is not so far really, and yet it is not *so* near, it is—you're wrong there—a thing and yet it is not an object, one can see it in the daytime and it is also there at night, it has a use and there are people in it, there are trees around it, it can be carried but it need not be, it should perhaps be but it must not be carried or given away, it emerges on foot, it has a blue light but it has nothing to do, it has occurred before, indeed it has, it has been surrendered, it exists now and has done so for ages, it is a permanent address, one can die in it, it occurs over and over again and emerges just as often, it is something—in Berlin.

In Berlin everybody is wrapped in grease-proof paper. It is Sunday the First of May. Myriads of beer bottles stretch from here down to the Wannsee, scores of bottles are already floating in the water, washed against the banks continuously by the waves from the steamers, so that the men can fish them out again. They open the bottles with their bare hands, they press the stoppers open with the ball of the thumb. Some of them call to their fellows that they can manage. One is sorry for the women wrapped in grease-proof paper, some are even allowed out of it to sit on the grass with the equally greasy children. Then even

[1] Brand of chocolate: Tr.
[2] Names of breweries: Tr.

115

the sick are allowed ashore. We have so many sick here, says the
night nurse and pulls back from the balustrade the patients leaning over it, wet and trembling. The night nurse has seen through
it all, for she is quite well aware of the attraction of the balcony,
grabs hold of them and gives them an injection which goes right
through them, almost, it seems, to the mattress underneath them,
to make sure they do not get up again too soon. The last passenger plane arrives; the last medicine is taken and then—quiet;
the later mail and freight planes are hardly audible any more.

An aeroplane flies now through the room at the rate of one
per minute, passes the face flannel on its hook and lowers its
undercarriage a handsbreadth over the soapbowl. The planes
about to land in the air corridors passing directly through the
room have to fly more silently. The hospitals have complained.
True, the planes muffle their engines, but now it is worse than
ever before, they hum away over one's head, over the perspiring
hair, these muffled planes, which go swishing past just below the
ceiling. There is in the hospitals great agitation about the planes,
which muffle their engines and are then so silent that one can no
longer hear them; in spite of this one listens from the very
moment one begins to perceive a whining sound, as when one
holds a tuning fork to one's ear; then one hears them more
distinctly, now they are here and just as soon gone again, and
afterwards there seems to be still a whirring sound and then
nothing more. Soon there begins again the approach sound and
one is less satisfied at hardly being able to hear them at all, so
that the Medical Superintendent has to go out into the street and
wave the medical diagnosis charts at them, page after page of
hieroglyphics. This helps for a time, but in the next moment free
of aeroplane noise there begin to ring all the church bells in
Berlin, churches seem veritably to rise up out of the ground and
seem to come quite near, nothing but new, bleak, unpainted
churches with belfrys and protestant tape recordings. This bell
ringing causes more and more agitation, it is even suggested that
the Chief Burgomaster himself should come, there are heard calls
on all sides that the churches should be moved away from here,
the patients in the hospitals complain loudly, rush out into the
corridors where blood appears, because some have bitten their
tongue in despair over the churches. The hospital chaplain sits in
the chair for visitors, telling all and sundry that he has been a

naval chaplain and has rounded the Cape of Good Hope. He knows nothing about church bells and takes a biscuit from the plate (no one dares to comment about this or the bells), he does not even ask if the patient needs anything and he just sits there twiddling his green shooting hat in his hands. They have to set the ventilation going, so they ask him to leave.

The burn-scarred walls around the Lützowplatz are lit up by large floodlights, all is black with smoke and the fire must by now have died out. And now they are flashing their torches, searching carefully amongst the tufts of grass, but all that is left is charred bones, scorched earth, not a single whole skeleton, only little scattered bones. The programme is in full swing on huge dumps, lit by increasingly strong light, building sites are continually extended but no one has yet started to build on them. Good humour prevails. Someone is carrying around a huge signboard. Scharnhorst Tours.[1] All are agreed, the programme is continued in KDW,[2] the blue and white KDW flag is hoisted, suddenly everyone wants to surge into KDW, but you can soon see that it will not be possible, but the mood of cheerfulness increases, the crowd can no longer be contained, it surges around the saleswomen, all want their palm read and their horoscope cast, lottery tickets are snatched from hands and people rush to the automatic machines, money is put in so noisily that the balls leap out of their runnels and in room after room customers complain that they want sleeping tablets. But tonight there are no more to be had. At least the people stop yelling and are just merry, the decorations are torn down and thrown out of the windows of the upper floors, the escalators are jammed, the lifts crammed with scarves and dresses and coats, all of which are supposed to be taken along as well, but the fat cashiers are in the middle of it all, nearly suffocating and call out: all this has got to be paid for, you will have to pay for it all one day!

The corridors have got to be cleaned again. Some well-known people have been brought in here secretly, at night when only the blue night-duty lamp is burning, but the majority are distant relatives, and none can give any definite information; it is true they have an address but no next-of-kin. For, after all, next-of-kin is the most important thing of all. They all lie there in

[1] Scharnhorst: imaginary name of travel agency in Germany: Tr.
[2] KDW: name of large department store: Tr.

silence. The night nurse says he is on his way from somewhere or other, another plane will be in soon, it happens often enough, you can be sure. Surely they must mean the next-of-kin. The Medical Superintendent is expecting the plane any minute, all his hopes are set on it. Then he says, just for the sake of peace and quiet, that they can all go home next week. There they all are, coughing and hoping, with a thermometer in their armpit, under their tongue or in their rectum, and ten centimetre long needles stuck into them. The dark balconies are ripe for demolition, no one this evening risks climbing on to the balustrade and to threaten the night nurse, who is again making coffee for the doctor on night duty; so they are all left to make their plans, a tunnel or perhaps one ought to go straight out into the desert, free the camel from the zoo, unstake it, saddle it up and ride on it through Brandenburg. You could rely on the camel. Suddenly, in the middle of the night, comes the news of an increase in charges, a sweating anxiety such as has never before been known. It is absolutely frightful. A room now costs one thousand marks in gold. All reach out and frantically press the buzzer.

The war disabled hobble down the steps of Bellevue Station on the Metropolitan, the light sways to and fro like in a vault, most of them wear yellow armbands with black dots on them, use sticks for support, and have attenuated limbs in splints. They are all disabled, not only by shell splinters but also internally, with bodies in utter confusion, too short above or below, the skin on their face is entirely mutilated and quite expressionless, mouth and eyes all awry, and the uncertain station light intensifies it all. The woman ticket collector at the barrier has to prop up the ceiling and the metro as well, for the roar of the trains is approaching again. It is a good thing that she has such huge hands and muscles; while issuing the tickets she supports the whole Metropolitan simultaneously, because at the same moment the train running in the opposite direction to Friedrichstrasse trundles by overhead. A piece of the ceiling falls down, but she picks it up again and down comes another piece with the Pillar of Victory on it, and again a train, this time the Wannsee train, clatters by overhead. It is catastrophic. The people seek refuge in the adjoining restaurant, they crouch under the tables waiting anxiously for the attack, but the ticket collector comes and says there is no attack. They are carrying on, she says, this sort of thing won't occur again.

The Medical Superintendent must not be disturbed, the result has been recorded for some years but is not being communicated. There must be some "disharmony". The news leaks out all over the town, everyone maintains he has read or heard of some "disharmony" or "discord", and many have been thinking the same. But nothing is said about it publicly. More and more trees are being planted, all in the sand, of course—desert experience. In the end all return to work in silence. All in freshly laundered white shirts, fastened at the back of the neck. No more excitement now. Everything is calming down. Most are dozing, anyhow.

The streets rise up at an angle of forty-five degrees. Cars heading for the horizon of course roll backwards, cyclists lose their balance and come slithering down towards one quicker than anything else, and one cannot prevent the cars from doing damage either, a sports car comes tearing backwards smack into the asylum and flings buckets, spittoons, tea trolleys and stretchers all over the place.

The Medical Superintendent stalks over it all while it is being cleared up, for he is on his way in a hurry to play skat[1] in town. But it is beginning in the radio tower restaurant as well. The whole town is rotating, the restaurant rises and falls, shakes and jolts, and everything begins to slide about more and more. Potsdam with all its houses has collided with the houses in Tegel and the pines hang down with their needles firmly clawing each other. In the restaurant everyone hangs on to the arms of his chair and goes on talking, no one admits it, each now looks at the other as though he were looking his last, all eyes firmly fixed on their neighbour, while the tables with roast duck and almonds on them are like a heavy swell at sea; then the glasses swish the wine about, forks bend their prongs over, the knives cut haphazardly into the ketchup, the red gravy runs all over the tablecloth, which is immediately wrenched off the table and displayed to all, complete collapse is imminent. There is a catch in the throat, the thing is stuck half way, there is no remedy.

All doors and windows in the Academy are glass, there are no curtains, so that everything shall be accessible to the light, it gets

[1] German card game: Tr.

light soon after midnight and only the portraits are hung with little doors before them. The Exhibition is open, a sea of heads, all stood present before their pictures. The organisers of the exhibition are still looking for the picture that is to be cut up. This is preceded by long, dreadful waiting, everyone thinks *he* is going to be beheaded, but it is to be someone else after all. In spite of this no one can help crying. They are saved by the fire breaking out suddenly and emerging from the cellar, they all escape into the open, to the cars parked in the grounds and they jump in. Quite a number have been caught by the flames, and they run into the Tiergarten, throw themselves on the ground where the flames are extinguished—all well-known people. They all meet again at Kempinski's,[1] the whole incident is forgotten, waiters bring wash bowls for their feet, each pulls off his socks and puts his feet into warm soapy water. This makes the feet feel warm and light—what bliss. The dirty water flows over the floor. The waiters come up with serviettes and dry the feet.

In consequence of politics the streets rise up at an angle of forty-five degrees, the cars roll backwards, cyclists and pedestrians whirl backwards on both sides of the street, and it is impossible to stop the cars from doing damage. Pedestrians take firm hold on themselves, grit their teeth and do not try to speak, but look out from behind hands held firmly to the mouth, seeking to find some support. In the eyes of everyone there can be read : this is still the safest place, it is best to stay here, one can stick it best here, it is more endurable here than anywhere else. And the whole thing is repeated in the radio tower, but the sandy heathland of the Marches[2] with the last birches and pines lie there so quietly, while everything else is rotating. It is best to look firmly down into the sand. Dizziness passes, the nurse will shake up your pillows for you. That is better. This is the best place, after all.

Thunderstorm over the lake. Two hundred times the lightning was counted flashing down into it. And all the surroundings ran into the thunderstorm as well and so the white birds have flown away. But there was music at the lakeside, as though flung down hastily, entrusted hastily to the billowing waters, which freeze, thaw out, turn to slime and freeze over again. The fishing rods are stiff, immured in the ice, with sounds and notes on their

[1] Name of famous Berlin cafe : Tr.
[2] Of Brandenburg : Tr.

hooks and the music too is frozen up, while the cars race round over the Avus,[1] Berlin's thunderous noise prays for Berlin's uneasy silence. Sleep is quite out of the question. The patients send back uneaten their evening raspberry blancmange, nobody can get a single spoonful of it down, no one wants to count the lightning flashes any more and gulp down his spoonful besides. Disapprovingly the nurses take all the flowers out of the rooms and put the vases in the corridor.

On the way to the Krummer Lanke,[2] near the pearl of the *Grunewald*, who is mad, lies the huge deciduous tree, felled, snapped off a yard above the ground, fallen right across the pathway. The patients, for whom a walk is prescribed, want nevertheless to go down to the water, but the nurse orders them all to stop, climbs alone over the tree, investigates, lifts up the branches to see if the tree has killed anyone in its fall. She waves to them, it is impossible to tell if she has found blood or not. They become restless, everyone wants to know if he has been killed here, it becomes increasingly unpleasant, no one has brought a coat, it is starting to rain again, there is a loud outcry, none of them wants to go back to the ward, because he does not know if it is the right one. "It must be more than just 'disharmony,'" some call out and begin to strike each other. "It does not look like 'disharmony', it must be something worse!" All are wet through to the skin, their shirts are sopping wet, because of the cold, of the rain beating against one's face and into one's mouth and in one's nose, because of the whole stream of rain before one's eyes, it all happens much more quickly. Painlessly the collapse under the tree is complete.

Berlin has been cleared up. The shops have been laid one on top of another, piled up in heaps, shoes and foot-rules, some of the store of rice and potatoes and cabbages of course, which the Senate has hoarded, lie around on the verges, easily recognisable. Now there is sand everywhere, in one's shoes and even amongst the coal. The large shop windows, more particularly those with the less obvious names like "Neckermann" and "Defaka", are glass roofs over everything else, one can see through them, but one cannot recognise much. Underneath a pub in *Alt-Moabit* is still open, no one understands how this can be possible. Surely

[1] Motor race track: Tr.
[2] Name of popular resort in environs of Berlin: Tr.

everything has been cleared away already. The landlord poured out double measures of Doornkaat[1] and one for himself, his pub had been the best and oldest, always full of people. But the people are no longer in Berlin. He stands another round, which is always drunk up at once, and another, that's how it goes, double gins, a large beer, always doubles. The Spree and the Teltow Canal are already brimming over with gin, the Havel is frothing right up to its banks with beer, no one can speak clearly any more amongst all these piled up glasses; everything that is said runs out at the corners of the mouth, almost incomprehensible, nobody wants to talk any more, but just say something, it just runs out of the corners of one's mouth anyhow, always doubles.

Kreuzberg is a coming district now, the damp cellars and the old sofas are in demand again, the stove pipes, the rats, the view over the backyard. For that one must let one's hair grow long, one must roam around and bawl about all over the place, must rant and get drunk and frighten all the old people between the *Hallesches Tor* and the *Böhmisches Dorf*. One must be always alone and in groups, take several others along with one, from one belief to another. The new religion comes from *Kreuzberg*, the gospel beards and the commands, the revolt against subsidised death agony. They all have to eat out of the same mess-tin, a very thin Berlin broth and with it dark bread, after which the strongest gin is prescribed, more and more gin, for the longest nights. The second hand dealers are no longer so cheap, because it is an up and coming district, the "Kleine Weltlaterne"[2] is no longer paying its way, its preachers and disciples are gaped at of an evening and they spit into the curry of the starers. A century which does not want to prove itself even here is challenged. At a door, at any one, there is a banging, a lamp standard is knocked over, some passers by are hit over the head. Laughing is allowed in Berlin.

All the bars are full after midnight, the Egg Shell, the Bath Tub, the Stable, the Kleist Casino, Volle Pulle, Taboo, Chez Nous, Riverboat and Big Apple and the Eden Saloon. They are all nothing but places shaken by vibrations, by bursts of music which break out at night, but always only for a matter of a few hours at a time. The takings are increased, and there is at once

---

[1] Doornkaat: brand of spirits: Tr.
[2] Name of religious periodical: Tr.

an inflation of wet hands and glassy eyes. The whole of Berlin is
at night a place for turnover and sudden changes. Confusion and
muddle arise, then some withdraw. Espionage is made easy, for
every weakness and decay is obvious. All and sundry are anxious
to impart their information, to pass on the message, to collapse
under interrogation. Everyone has got someone else after him,
and no one in the dim light can really check the fraudulent bill.
Outside it is already daylight again, it is too bright there. Nothing
works out any more then.

Only of the transvestites does one know nothing at all, in
what form or with what device upon their painted lips will they
go home to fall happily asleep into every day that is.

Anyone who jumps off in the town uninvited, who passes to
and fro across the sector boundary, or crosses from one zone to the
other, is detained, X-rayed, measured and undergoes the treatment. He is led blindfold into the camouflaged houses, there the
bandage is removed from his eyes, of course he has no idea where
he is and he is not allowed to ask. The men with masked faces
do the asking. Everything is secret. But they ask nothing very
special, just name and occupation, whom he has seen and why
and when, everlastingly how, where, why. It is so secret that
one has to repeat it all to another lot of men, loudly and clearly.
You can always say the same thing over and over again, nobody
minds, very seldom do the questions the other men ask vary at
all. It lasts for hours and hours, for days and days, until one
begins to tremble a little, when one says one's name for the last
time, clearly and with oneself under control. Then they tell you
to forget everything, they lead you out again blindfold and give
you permission to stay. He hasn't betrayed. He has betrayed. He
hasn't lied. He has lied. But in the houses were only chairs and
tables, no black wall, not even thumbscrews. Only a slight clearing of the throat now and again, a drumming of knuckles on the
table, an indifferent look. But you can't find the houses again.
The Security Police stays secret. Night has fallen and all has
grown so quiet. No one has been in the streets since that time.
The old villas are choked up with sand and overgrown with
weeds, and they sink deeper and deeper into the gardens. At the
bend in the *Königsallee* the shots, now quite muffled, strike
Rathenau. In Plötzensee[1] hangings are in progress. Coins in the

[1] Plötzensee: Berlin prison: Tr.

telephone booth all roll out at the bottom again—all put in in vain. No one can get through. Not a soul to be found from *Halensee* to the Centre.

In Cafe Kranzler, with the lights all off, even though it is night-time, the old women with felt hats on their heads, sit at the tables chewing away at their cake, they often put two pieces in their mouth at once, because no one can see what they are doing. The high-heeled waitress gets stuck in the whipped cream and splashes it in the frills of her hair and all over her stomach. The old women go on eating and eating, and the old men stand in front of Cafe Kranzler, hat stands in hand, some kneel on the pavements and draw their old wives on the asphalt, write dirty jokes with blue and pink chalk, chalking drawings of their wives on the ground, naked, with heavy thighs and rifles between them. In the cafe the wives pull their felt hats down deep over their eyes, chew away and reach out for more, as they have done since that time.

The patients are allowed out for an hour and come back after a few minutes. An American, probably made of lead, with a short white helmet and a lowered machine pistol, stands as though rooted to the spot by the roundabout on the southern by-pass. Manoeuvres have been going on for hours, through the cheap curtains one can just hear the rumbling, the dull angry mutter-ing. The nurse says she can hear nothing, it is only manoeuvres, she says; she is polishing the door handles and the taps at the wash basin, laughing and singing as she does so: all this is not a war. The convoy of lorries with red-nosed young Englishmen in them come to a stop, two Soviet guards walk along the road, people, are talking and counting, and finally one doesn't under-stand the other. The nurse interrupts. Suddenly many kinds of tank arrive, one lot does not want to let the others enter Berlin, and there is a fuss. The nurse cannot help laughing and secretly passes a cigarette. Then the guards march to and fro again and show no sign of noticing anything, no one has witnessed the cigarette incident. In Berlin one is allowed to smoke a cigarette. The tanks finally drive on one after the other into the town.

In the Friedrichstrasse there is another crossing point, an en-trance and exit for Red Cross ambulances and for big black cars with curtained windows. It is dark, there is much whispering, policemen and soldiers wave one away and point to where

Checkpoint Charlie is, straight on till midnight, in the opposite direction. At the correct crossing point they are not exactly indignant because one went to the wrong crossing point, but they are whispering again, one thinks one has made a mistake and holds up one's passport, popular music is switched on, and the nicest passports are stamped. Then one has to remove the varnish from the car, it is quite a quick job, the varnish comes off in strips like cold wax, then one has to bang three times on the exposed metal, kick the tyre once, then a coin has to be tossed, heads or tails. Greetings all round, waving to each other in the driving mirror and driving away back again.

The week begins with Nepal and Ghana. On Tuesday the Congolese, to the accompaniment of complaints and furious commentaries, are cursed to and fro across the Friedrichstrasse, on Wednesday Pakistan has a guided tour by bus, on Thursday delegates from the South Pole visit one side and are ignored by the other. The mixture of visitors on the next evening drive away with the wigs from the Schiller Theatre and at the Schiffbauerdamm Theatre are presented with costumes to go with them, then there is a traffic jam, the visitors from Central America are demolishing the Brandenburg Gate to take away as a souvenir, then the Malayans come and disappear with the Reichstag. Suddenly Berlin has been occupied by gipsies, who erect their tents, the Berliner flee to the outskirts, then the gipsies do all their laundry, which flutters as far away as *Lichterfelde*. It must be Sunday, because fanfares introduce a new item in the concert given by the Philharmonic Orchestra. There is a general call to resurrection, black red and gold, Unter den Linden. The Memorial Church ascends to heaven.

Nobody, least of all the new arrivals, believes that the animals all really live by the Zoo station. Nobody is prepared for the camel. The Pillar of Victory stands on its hump now. Because of the animals the platforms empty again very quickly. The men all go to the aquarium, the women to the monkey house. The men hang about for hours staring at the fishes, and finally at the little lizards, they have their eye on nothing but the softest green and gold lizards, which they would so love to take with them, but the keepers at the exit feel even breast pockets, it is no good. The women, all standing far apart from each other and mistrustful, pay a visit to their favourite monkeys. They have brought with them a silver spoon and a silk bag and feed only their own monkey with sugar. Only at closing time do the men and women meet up again, in the hothouse, on the bridge, over a river already indicated. Down below in the stifling heat the crocodiles doze. Everyone looks down with eyes growing heavier and heavier, but the crocodiles are not going to perform, they just wait. But now the bridge could collapse and bring the crocodiles to life, but it does not collapse. No one can fall down as long as no one is deliberately pushed. The temperature is not supposed to rise, because it is exactly regulated, but it does rise, all the same. They don't want to look at the crocodiles any more, they push their way out and want to return for the evening visit.

They have sent the children out into the street, on to the concrete barricades. The children sit astride the barricades and think up a hundred things they want to be and do. They want to be airmen, soldiers or spies, they want to get married and eat chicken on Sundays, they want barbed wire and pistols and liquorice, and to hear and tell stories in the evenings. The guards, who are too big to get involved with children, are however secretly irritated and chase them off home for dinner.

Everyone is waiting for the circus. The compact, restless ponies, the slow elephants swaying along inside their skin, come up the avenue, escorted by the Allies. The circus manager in an open car talks to the passers-by, who have to wait, he speaks continually into a loud speaker, he extols his lions and monkeys, but not his camels, which come last, silent and with heads held high. The camels lag further and further behind and gradually withdraw, they belong to the same circus, but they have nothing more to do with it. The patients have been waiting just for the camels, go up to them and place themselves under their protection. The camels' hides smell as though longingly of desert, freedom and the world outside, each one goes with his camel and advances without let or hindrance, across country, through the forest, each one swims the rivers and lakes with his camel, and mounts it at last, through all the forests and water. The camel shuns no water, it hears no whistle, no ambulance, no siren, no night bell, no shot. One more forest, then another. The camel goes faster and faster in the sand. One last forest. Outside at last.

The wood pile is erected at the junction of the Kürfurstendamm and Joachimsthalerstrasse. The Press is silent. None of the newspapers with which a fire can be kindled has been published. The Kiosk is empty and not even the paper girl has turned up. The people hesitate at first, then take heart and pick up a billet of wood. Some carry theirs away home at once under their overcoat, others begin on the spot to carve out of the wood whatever occurs to them : solar symbols, life symbols. Some people make mean remarks, complaining that the wood is wet. An aged man waves his billet around and shouts : Sabotage! This is playing into the hands of the others! And sure enough the pieces of wood are passed from hand to hand, each passes one into his neighbour's hand, but no one plays with fire, they are all quite sensible. Soon all the wood has gone and traffic can proceed. All of a sudden the newspapers appear at last, first of all the very small ones, with black adipose letters, with thick transverse bars, superfluous cold fat running down the edges. Then come the large newspapers, the lean, quite decocted ones, swimming in thin broth, and which must be picked up with gloved hands.

The letter looks threatening, green and black or green and blue. One can sense already that it is not the expected letter, but quite a different one. It is short. The competent Berlin Insurance Company declares that it can accept no responsibility, since it is a matter of an illness contracted prior to the signing of the agreement. The pain is dulled, and because none of the doctors is present—since they are present only on more important occasions in the forenoon, only when making their rounds—all say to the nurses how unjust it is, it cannot be true, otherwise everything would be incurable. The nurses give no indication of whose side they are on nor how much they know. They set out the tablets with the fruit juice, permit an occasional bottle of beer, behind the doctors' back, wink to inspire confidence in the belief that all is not incurable. Always these favours! The nurses always seem to miss the point, it is "diplomacy", yes, that's what they call it. Slowly the news leaks out. They all say, fighting down their pain, it is now "diplomacy". No one will be able to do anything. The exhaustion is too great. All drink up their fruit juice and lie there, breathing heavily. The shrouds are smoothed out. For one moment all is in order.

Berlin room, dim item in the bright suite of rooms, the comforting stucco work on the high ceiling, a reminder that it was at that time in Schöneberg. A cell for contemplation amongst a mass of rooms. The guilts, the feathers in them, which have all been worn flat, it is long ago, it is not long ago. There is a party, they have all been invited, there will be drinking and dancing, there must be drinking, so that something can be forgotten, something, it is—you're wrong there!—it is today, it was yesterday, it will be tomorrow, it is something in Berlin. All dance in silence, the young people dance cheek to cheek. And then they all drink a lot.

The last guests are shouting their hearts out, they no longer know what they are saying: I can, I can, I've got it, I've got it, I'll do it, I'll do it! None of the cars will start, all want to spend the night in this room. The Medical Superintendent will be late for his skat game, for once in a way he looked in again and put his finger to his mouth. One does not know if there is any hope, but if there is no hope, then it is at the moment not quite so dreadful, things become calmer, there has not got to be hope, there could be less, there is no need to be anything at all, it is nothing, it is all over with Scharnhorst, Insurance Companies, cigars, chocolate, Leiser,[1] Fire Insurance, Commerz Bank, Bolle,[2] all over, the last plane has flown in, the first will arrive after midnight, everything flies at the right height, as it should, not through the room. It was quite exciting, it was nothing. It will never happen again.

[1] Name of large shoe store: Tr.
[2] Bolle: Name of dairy: Tr.

BIOGRAPHICAL NOTE

Ingeborg Bachman. Born 1926 in Klagenfurt. Studied philosophy in Innsbruck, Graz and Vienna, took her doctorate in 1950. She lives now in Switzerland and Berlin. *Gruppe 47* award, 1953

Select Bibliography

Die gestundete Zeit, 1953 (poems)
Anrufung des Grossen Bären, 1956 (poems)
Der gute Gott von Manhattan, 1958 (radio play)
Das Dreissigste Jahr, 1961 (*The Thirtieth Year*, London, 1964; New York, 1964)
Ein Ort für Zufälle, 1965

Friedrich Dürrenmatt

Translated
by
I. Hilton

FRIEDRICH DÜRRENMATT

THE THEATRE MANAGER

THE person, to whom the town was to succumb, was already living in our midst at a time when we were still paying no heed to him. We took notice of him only when he began to attract attention through a mode of behaviour which struck us as ridiculous (for he had been the object of considerable derision in those days). Yet, when we did come to pay attention to him, he was already running the theatre. We did not laugh at him in the way we are accustomed to do in the case of people who amuse us through their artlessness or sense of humour, but rather in the way that we occasionally take delight in things improper. Yet it is difficult to advance reasons for what it was that induced laughter on his appearance in those first days, all the more so since later on he was treated not only with servile esteem—and which we have taken still to be a sign of fear—but also with open admiration. First and foremost, he was an odd shape. He was of small stature, his body seemed boneless so that there was a kind of slimy insidiousness about him. He was completely hairless, even lacking eyebrows. He moved like a tight-rope walker who is afraid of losing his balance, his steps were noiseless, their pace irregular. His voice was soft and hesitant. Whenever he came into contact with a person, he would direct his gaze constantly at inanimate objects. It is, however, uncertain when we suspected the possibility of evil in him for the first time. Perhaps this happened when certain changes on the stage became noticeable, changes that were ascribable to him. Perhaps, but it is to be borne in mind that aesthetic changes are not yet generally linked with the idea of evil when they attract our attention for the first time. Indeed, we were thinking then more in terms of bad taste, or were making fun of his supposed folly. Certainly those first productions in the theatre under his direction had not yet achieved the importance of the ones which subsequently were to become famous, but there were touches that hinted at his general plan. There was, for example, his characteristic favouring of masquerade which marked his theatre already in those early days; and there was also present that abstract quality in the sets which later had been given such prominence. These signs did not obtrude, but the indications that he was pursuing a particular policy multiplied, a policy of which we had an inkling as to its meaning, but could not appraise. He might have been a spider that sets about spinning an enormous web; but he seemed to proceed with his task without purpose, and perhaps it was this very want of design that misled us into laughing at him. Of course in the end I could not remain unaware of the fact that he was pushing himself to the front almost imperceptibly, and after his election to Parliament this fact struck everyone. During the time he abused the theatre, he set about leading people astray in a place where no one suspected there to be any danger. And I only became aware of the danger when the changes on the stage had reached a point where the secret intent of his action was exposed. As in a game of chess we realised the move that was our undoing only when it had been played, when it was too late. We have often asked ourselves what it was that induced the mass of the people to go to his theatre. We had to admit that this question was scarcely answerable. We thought in terms of an evil driving force which compels people to seek out their murderers in order to deliver themselves into their hands : for these changes revealed that he was endeavouring to undermine Freedom, in that he was pointing out the impossibility of it, so that his art was a bold attack on the meaning of mankind. This intention led him to eliminate every element of chance, and to base everything at the most distressingly painful level, so that the events on the stage were governed by one enormous sense of compulsion. Also noteworthy was how he treated language; here he suppressed those elements which help to distinguish the individual authors, so that in his case the natural rhythm of language was falsified to attain the uniform, unnerving beat of pistons pounding away. The actors moved like puppets, not that the guiding force which determined their actions remained in the background; on the contrary it was that above all which revealed itself as a power gone mad, so that we believed we were looking into a factory where a substance was produced which must destroy the world. At this juncture it is also to be mentioned how he made use of light and shade; these did not serve him to allude to the Infinite, and thereby to establish a connection with the world of Faith, but on the contrary they were for the purpose of exposing the finiteness of the stage, since remarkable cubic shapes limited and checked the light—he had been a master of abstract form then; and by means of secret devices all mezzo-tinto was avoided, so that what took place on stage seemed to be played in confined prison-like space. For colour he employed red and yellow with an intensity that hurt the eye. The most devilish thing, however, was the way that every event portrayed on stage imperceptibly had another meaning and the genres began to get mixed, in that tragedy was transformed into comedy, and vice versa. At that time we were hearing a lot about uprisings of those unfortunates who were eager to better their lot by means of force, yet few there were who would give credence to the rumour that this man was the driving force behind these occurrences. But the truth of the matter was that right from the beginning the theatre only served him as a means of acquiring that power which was later to reveal itself as a brutal and terrible despotism. What prevented us at that time from getting nearer to the bottom of these things was the consideration that the business of the actress was beginning to assume more and more menacing proportions, as the intelligent person could tell. The fate of the actress was strangely tied up with that of the town, and he was trying to destroy her. When, however, his intention with regard to her became clear, his position in our town was so firmly established that this woman's cruel destiny could be effected, a destiny which should be an omen to us all and which even those who had seen through the nature of his corrupting ways did not possess the power to avert. She succumbed to him because she despised the power he embodied. It cannot be argued that she had been famous before he took over the running of the theatre, but she held a position in the theatre, which though not terribly important was undisputed nevertheless; and she owed it to the general esteem in which she was held that she could practise her art without making those concessions which others, who aimed higher and whose position was more important, had to make to publicity. How significant it is then that he knew how to destroy her through this very circumstance, for he understood how to ruin a person by utilising to the full that person's virtues. The actress had not resigned herself to his directions. She paid no attention to the changes which were effected in the theatre, so that she marked herself more and more clearly off from the others. But it was just this observation that filled me with concern, for it was striking that he took no steps to compel her to conform to his directions. That she did stand out was his plan. It is true that he is said once to have passed a comment on her acting shortly after he had taken over the theatre, but I have never been able to find out anything positive about that argument. However he left her in peace from that time and took no steps to dismiss her from the theatre. Indeed he placed her more and more clearly in the foreground, so that she gradually assumed the leading role in the theatre, even though she was not equal to this task. It was this business then that made us suspicious, for it was such that her art and his views were so opposed, that an argument seemed unavoidable, a confrontation which would inevitably be the more dangerous the later it came about. There were signs, too, that her position was starting definitely to change. If in the beginning people were in raptures over her acting and praised it with an unanimity that was thoughtless (she was regarded as his big "Discovery"), voices now began to be raised with the object of censuring and reproaching her for not being equal to his directing, and saying further that his allowing her to continue in the leading role was a testimony to his unusual patience (and humanity). But since it was her persistence in following the rules of classic dramatic art that in particular came under fire, it was those very people who had perceived the real deficiencies in her art that took her side; it was an unequal contest, which unfortunately strengthened her resolve not to leave the theatre of her own free will—she might, perhaps, still have been able to save herself, even though our town was scarcely able to escape his clutches any longer. But the crisis only occurred when the fact began to stand out that her art produced a strange effect upon the audience, which must have been distressing for her, and consisted of people starting to laugh at her in private, and then during the actual performance, an effect which naturally he calculated finely and tried to build up more and more. We stood aghast and helpless. We had not reckoned on the cruel weapon of the involuntarily comic element. Though she went on acting, it was certain that she noticed it, as I also suspect that she, more than we, knew of the unavoidability of her downfall.

About this time work was completed on a building which had long been the topic of conversation in our town and which we had awaited in a state of great suspense. It is indeed the case that already many have been put out by this structure, but I must mention here, before I take my own stand over it, that I still would not understand today how he could have obtained the means for this new theatre, had a suspicion not been raised which I cannot reject. However, we were still not able at that time to give credence to the rumour which linked this building with those unscrupulous circles in our town, that at all times aimed solely at unbridled increase in their wealth, and in pursuance of which the commotions of those, whom he was likewise influencing, were directed. Be that as it may, this edifice, which is said to be destroyed today, was like blasphemy. Yet it is difficult to talk about this edifice, which externally looked to be a monstrous mixture of every style and form, without one being able to gainsay that there was something magnificent about it. It was not a building which revealed the living quality that can gain expression in solid materials when transformed by the skill of the artist, but one which consciously aimed at calling special attention to its very lifelessness, where there is no time sense, only inert, immobile mass. Everything there exposed itself to us in all its brazen and shameless immoderation, devoid of beauty; it had doors of iron that were gigantic and seemingly out of all proportion, but which were soon reduced to the level of prison gates. The structure seemed to have been heaped up by clumsy cyclopean hands, in meaningless slabs of marble, with heavy columns put there without any definite purpose : but this was only seemingly the case, for everything in this structure was calculated to achieve definite effects, the object being to render the individual helpless and make him the victim of pure caprice. Possibly in contrast to these crude masses and brutal proportions there were individual objects that had been fashioned by craftsmen to an accuracy, it was boasted, of one ten-thousandth of a millimetre. Still more alarming was the interior of the theatre with its auditorium. It was based on the Greek theatre, but its form was without meaning because a strangely shaped ceiling spanned the hall, so that we did not seem to be proceeding to a play when we entered this auditorium, but rather to a festive occasion in the bowels of the earth. Now we come to the catastrophe. We were waiting for the play to start on that occasion, tense and silent. We sat crowded together in ever widening arcs, pale and expectant, and stared at the curtain covering the stage, on which a crucifixion was displayed as a mocking farce. Even that was not seen as outrageous, but rather accepted in the name of art. Then the play commenced. There was talk later of undisciplined street-mobs being responsible for the uproar that resulted, but on that occasion there sat in the theatre those citizens of our town, who most of all boasted of their illustriousness and cultural up-bringing, and extolled in the director the great artist and revolu-tioniser of the stage; who saw genius in his cynicism, and were unsuspecting of how soon the young fellow was setting about breaking out of the realms of aestheticism (this aestheticism they admired in him!) into spheres which were no longer aesthetic, even indeed as he was receiving the Shakespeare Prize from the hand of the President of the State amid thunderous applause of the social gathering at the opening of the new theatre, before the play commenced. I don't remember any more which of the Classics was performed for the dedication, whether it was *Faust* or *Hamlet*, but the production was such that as the curtain with the crucifixion on it rose, this question became immaterial even before it was possible to pose it. Whether it was a piece from the Classics or the work of another writer was no longer of any relevance to what was taking place now before our eyes, punctu-ated as it was frequently by the rapturous applause of members of the Government, Society and the University elite. A frightful violence took control of the actors like a whirlwind, which tosses houses and trees one upon another, then to leave them. Their voices did not sound like those of human beings, but rather as shadows might speak, but then suddenly and without transition they assumed a cadence which resembled the delirious drumming of savage tribes. We didn't sit as mortals in his theatre, but as gods. We took delight in a tragedy which in reality was our own. But then she made her appearance, and I never saw her so clumsy as in those moments preceding her death, yet at the same time never so pure. If the audience only broke out into laughter when she stepped on to the stage—so exactly calculated was her entry that it had to tell like a pointed and obscene comment —this laughter was soon transformed into rage. She appeared as a transgressor who presumed to oppose an authority which has the power to crush everything, yet also the ability to pardon every sin and absolve all responsibility, and I realised that this was the real reason whereby the crowd was led astray into renouncing freedom and surrendering to evil, for guilt and atonement exist only in freedom. She began to speak and her voice was for them blasphemy against those cruel laws in which men then believe when they want to raise themselves to the position of a god and suspend both Good and Evil. I perceived his intention and knew now that he had set out to bring about her downfall in front of everyone and with the consent of all. His plan was perfect. He had opened an abyss into which the audience plunged headlong in its eagerness for blood, to demand again and again murder anew, because only in this way was to be found the senseless frenzy which alone qualifies for not becoming torpid in endless despair. She stood as a criminal there in the midst of human beings who were transformed into beasts. I saw that there are terrible moments when a deadly transformation is effected, where the innocent person must appear guilty to his fellow men. And our town was thus ready to be present at that deed which was equivalent to a savage triumph of evil. A contraption sank down from the flies. It was like a system of light metal rods and wires to which were attached clamps and knives, as well as steel shafts with peculiar joints, which were linked to each other in an odd manner, so that the contraption seemed to resemble a monstrous and supernatural insect. Indeed, we only became aware of it when it had seized the woman and lifted her aloft. Scarcely had this happened when the audience broke into immeasurable shouts of applause and cries of "Bravo!" And when still more new clamps fastened on to the actress and held her horizontally, the audience was convulsed with laughter. When the knives started to rip her dress, so that she was hanging there naked, there arose from the mass of people wedged in there together a cry which must have originated somewhere or other, and which then was transmitted on and on quicker than the thought could be conveyed; was raised *ad infinitum*, taken up and passed on again and again, until everyone was shrieking "Kill her!" And amid the ravings of the crowd her body was cut up by the knives in such a way that her head fell among the audience, which had risen to its feet; and befouled with the blood from it, they seized the head, and like a ball it flew about from one person to the next. And as the people swept forth from the theatre like a rising tide, stamping on one another, propelling the head before them, through the winding streets in long snaking trains, I left the town, where already the flags that glaringly heralded the Revolution were waving inflammatorily, and the human beings were assaulting each other like animals, encompassed by HIS rabble and, as the new day was dawning, subdued by HIS order.

BIOGRAPHICAL NOTE

Friedrich Dürrenmatt. Born 1921 near Berne (Switzerland). Studied philosophy, literature and science in Zurich and Berne. Drama critic for the *Weltwoche.* Lives in Neuchatel (Switzerland). Prizes : *Tribune de Lausanne,* 1958; Association of Critics, New York, 1959; *Schiller-Preis* of the city of Mannheim, 1959; *Schweizerische Schillerstiftung,* 1960.

Select Bibliography

Es steht geschrieben, 1947 (play)
Romulus der Grosse, 1949 (play) (*Four Plays,* London, 1964)
Der Richter und sein Henker, 1952 (*The Judge and His Hangman,* London, 1961)
Die Ehe des Herrn Mississippi, 1952 (play) (see : *Romulus . . .*)
Die Stadt, 1952
Der Verdacht, 1953 (*The Quarry,* London, 1962)
Ein Engel kommt nach Babylon, 1953 (play) (see : *Romulus . . .*)
Grieche sucht Griechin, 1955 (*Once a Greek,* London, 1966)
Der Besuch der alten Dame, 1956 (play) (*The Visit,* London, 1962)
Die Panne, 1956 (*Dangerous Game,* London, 1960)
Abendstunde im Spätherbst, 1957 (radio play)
Das Versprechen, 1958 (*The Pledge,* London, 1959)
Frank der Fünfte, 1959 (libretto)
Die Physiker, 1962 (play) (see : *Romulus . . .*)
Der Meteor, 1966 (play)

Walter Jens

Translated
by
Lawrence Wilson

WALTER JENS

THE CONQUEST OF TROY

WHEN I left Penelope I was in my prime : life lay before me and I still had much to look forward to. Ten years later, when we had at last captured Troy, I was tired and spent; war had sucked the marrow from my bones, I was burnt out and empty and had no courage left to begin all over again. I trembled at the least excitement, my movements were unsteady and feeble, and when I was alone with no one watching I talked to myself as though to a stranger whose lost happiness I was bewailing. Camp life had exhausted me, hunger had gnawed away my body; rain and snow had torn my uniform to shreds, dew and humidity had stiffened my limbs. How often we had to go without even a piece of bread and how long we had to wait to get a single plate of hot soup! And then the exposure to the cold—those iron winters of Asia when the birds froze to death and the game perished in the snow . . .

Yet everything—the glare of summer and the ice of winter, the vermin and the cries of the wounded—would have been tolerable if the dead had at least left my sleep alone.

But try as I might, I could not forget them. Their faces pursued me, even into my dreams . . . those child-faces with blue eyes and blond hair lying in damp strands on the forehead : dolls' heads of clay and cardboard, grey skulls and masks with grinning mouths.

I know, my Prasidas, that you will accuse me of exaggeration and in my own anguish forgetting the misery of the others. Did they not suffer exactly the same as I? Did hunger and cold strike Odysseus alone and spare the others' tents?

No, child, the others suffered, too : but all of them—Ajax and Menelaus, Agamemnon and Achilles—at least still believed they were fighting for a good cause; they talked of perfidy and betrayal that had to be avenged, and encouraged each other to hold out so that justice might triumph. But to me such consolation was denied. I knew the senselessness of this war, cursed by the common man and long since regretted by the Trojans themselves. But I also knew that no single party was ready to make terms with the enemy and arrange a truce.

So when the tenth year had passed in its turn and an end of the war was still not in sight I resolved to enforce peace on my own initiative. To this end I had a big horse built of wood with room inside for ten men to be concealed.

According to my plan they alone had to stay close to Troy and wait for the enemy to leave the walls and draw the horse into the city. All the other Greeks were meanwhile to feign retreat, withdraw to the nearby island of Tenedos and not return until one of the ten gave the agreed signal with a torch or more than four days had elapsed since the departure.

Admittedly it soon transpired that the Trojans knew how to control their curiosity and to start with they trusted only in their caution; at any rate, they waited until the evening of the fourth day before drawing the horse through the Scaic Gate and standing it in the market-place in the shadow of the city hall. So it came about that I could only emerge three hours before the agreed assault, in the ninth hour of evening on the fourth day.

What happened then, Prasidas, you know from your books: at first it had really been my intention to open the main gate, let in my compatriots and compel the surprised Trojans to a rapid and bloodless surrender. But as I walked through the streets that evening and observed the people in their houses I suddenly felt doubtful: could I guarantee that in the decisive hour the soldiers would preserve order and discipline? After such long privations were not license and excess more probable, plundering and murder more to be feared, so that my plan might all too easily be turned into the opposite?

Silent and thoughtful, in the guise of an old Trojan. I walked through the streets. It was a warm summer evening, soft and mild ... such evenings do not occur in this country. It had been raining and the air was spicy and fresh. The people had opened their windows and were leaning out, chatting with the neighbours. Young couples were strolling along the broad corso, making plans for the future. Now and then a jest was thrown to me, a cheerful word or an inviting: "You there, old man, won't you come up?"

For ten years the people in Troy had borne hardship and privation, but now that the Greeks had gone and peace had returned there was nothing to be seen of either. Old women sat knitting on wicker chairs in front of their homes; old men, arms crossed over their chests, gazed with quiet confidence at the evening sky and drank a glass of wine. At the street corners stood young lads with scarred hands and shattered limbs—they, too, were glad that everything was over and they could make a fresh start.

I saw young girls sewing their summer dresses by candle-light and small children playing indoors with the pearls on the curtains. But while I still looked at them, enjoying their quips, my imagination saw them lying in the gutter, their necks ringed with blood: blood flowed over the girls' dresses, the boys had rejoiced too soon and the contented eyes of the old people opened wide in terror.

In that second I knew that I must act. For the first time in my life I had a chance to save human beings: if I succeeded in warning the Trojans and saving the women and children from the clutches of the soldiers, the years of hardship and privation would not have been in vain.

On me alone it depended, on my courage and determination, whether these children died or not. There was not a minute to be lost: a few hours—and the Greeks would begin their attack. In haste I left the main street, crossed the temple area, plunged into a dark deserted alley and opened the door which led to the house of Laocoon.

When I entered, the priest was busy separating the logs in the hearth with a large rake of blackish copper. He seemed so absorbed in his task that at first I thought he had not noticed me; but after a while he raised his head and pointed to a chair in the corner.

"Sit down, stranger. But do not stay too long; the omens are unpropitious. If you are wise, you will try to escape. The guards at the Scaic Gate can be bribed."

He spoke in short, jerky sentences, panting a little and with great effort. When he had finished I took a step towards him and asked him to listen to me and receive an important message.

I spoke very seriously, Prasidas, and deliberately chose words which sounded weighty and solemn; but to my amazement it was not the sense of my speech which seemed to interest him, but only the tone of voice.

"I know your voice, stranger," he said with slow conviction. "It is long since, but I still remember clearly. Was it in Greece that I heard it? At a festival embassy in Corinth? Or . . . wait a moment . . . did we meet in Athens?"

Suddenly he seemed to remember, his expression brightened, he seized my hands and sat down on the floor by my side.

"How could I ever forget it?" he said gently. "It was your wedding day, wasn't it? You knelt before the shrine of the Virgin Athene; I was standing only a few steps away from you close to a statue of Parian marble which I had dedicated that morning as a gift of the Trojans to Athens. Do you recall how I drew your attention to the features?"

Although he spoke very gently and I had to bend low to hear his voice, not a single word escaped me and the longer he talked the more tangible and solid stood that wedding day before me. A first glimmer of peace, the distant gleam of former happiness touched me softly, and the dark visions faded. A single smile, a delicate chisel-blow in the features of Persephone sufficed to banish the shadows of war.

Captured by his words, caught in the web of his sentences, sunk in the depths of his voice, so, my child, I began to forget time—a sleep-walker between dream and awaking, a dancer touched on the temple by Hermes' golden staff.

On the border between clear consciousness and the veils of sleep I saw once more the smile of Persephone; she had Penelope's eyes and signed to me to follow her. I stood up, went towards her and had only taken a few steps when the scene changed: the shrine and its pillars sank in the mist, the mist became the sea—a silver surface with waves and islands, blue coasts and ships seeking an anchorage. A bay rose up, the harbour of Ithaca, a festively decked roadstead, streets by the shore with flags and lampions, gaily dressed people and a platform wreathed with flowers. Penelope was wearing a dress of bright silk, Telemachus by her side a white cloak. Both were looking at the sea and watching the ship that was slowly gliding into the harbour. As it reached the mole and the sailors threw down the mooring ropes, the crowd broke through the barrier and rushed towards the ship. But when the gangway was lowered and the bearded, sunburnt man appeared at the rail there was a sudden silence; the crowd sank to its knees, mounted stewards forced a passage and laid a carpet leading from the ship to the lowest step of the platform. At the same moment as Penelope, followed by Telemachus, left the podium, the man at the rail went to the gangway and slowly made his way along the black hull of his ship towards the carpet. Penelope came to meet him; she had Persephone's smile and signed to the man to follow her.

I saw him nod and take one more step towards her. Then he suddenly stopped, fell to his knees, bent his head to the ground and kissed the earth.

At that moment, Prasidas, as in dream I saw myself on the shore of Ithaca and my lips touched the stony ground, I believed I knew for the first time that for me, too, the hour of home-coming would arrive. Murder and hunger had made me forget that war was not universal, that in other places men sat in their studies, bent over a book, awaiting the dawn . . .

But now, when Laocoon's words had revived for me the splendour of those wedding weeks in Athens—the hours by Penelope's side, evening talks with Icarius, rides to Eleusis and Cape Sunion—I felt once again the spell of that peaceful happi-ness which had filled me on the evening when Menelaus came to Ithaca.

At that time I had waited passively for the arrival of the black-sailed ship; but now I resolved to act and end the war at a single stroke.

In Laocoon I confided without reserve, told of my battle with Helen, deplored the oath which had compelled me to help Mene-laus, evoked the horrors of war, the hunger and the pitiable slaughter, the lot of the cripples and the suffering of the orphans, and told him frankly of my plan : to put an end to it all with the aid of cunning. I described the doubts and the remorse which had seized me at the sight of the people sitting before their houses and portrayed my experiences as I walked through the city . . . in short, I put myself completely in Laocoon's hands and waited for him, the blind man, the seer familiar with the secrets of darkness, to find a way out.

Yes, Prasidas, I was ready to frustrate the victory of the Greeks; what did a triumph count compared with children's dreams! Impelled by pity, I did not hesitate a second to sacrifice the glory and honour of the conqueror for the lives of those entrusted to me, the hopes of the women, the sleep of the children and the memories of the old people. I might be a traitor in Agamemnon's eyes, ambitious patriots might condemn my action —I knew that I was not loved. I needed no warning from Laocoon: I had long since seen through my enemies and sensed that they were waiting for me to show weakness so that they could attack me together.

No, I had no reason to underestimate the consequences of my deed; I knew the methods of the courts too well not to be aware that I would be stoned to death. The mob is fond of confusing hesitant caution with weakness and fear; why then should it not strike when it caught the Crafty One on the path of treason?

And yet, serious though the situation was: it still lay in my power to avert the catastrophe and not only save the Trojans, but rescue my own head from the noose. If I remained circumspect and did not lose my calm and self-possession everything might still turn out well.

First, Laocoon would have to go at once to Priam and tell him of my arrival in the city. Later, the surprise of the Trojans would have to be exploited and an audience obtained with the Assembly of Princes in exchange for the promise of a free conduct. By taking skilful advantage of the general confusion—the enemy in the heart of the city!—it ought not to be difficult to convince the Trojans of the existence of a secret passage, inspire them with terror and finally bring them to a point where the idea of a great underground system of shafts in which the Greeks were preparing to attack no longer seemed to them fantastic. Once they believed in an imminent assault, then, as I calculated, they would also accept the Greek demands, hand over Helen and pay a suitable fine; and as soon as that had happened I could safely cross over to the Greek camp under cover of darkness, talk of betrayal and discovery, invent a story of bad luck and in particular mention my old friend and guest Laocoon whose sons, I would claim, had recognised me by ill chance on my reconnaissance. The darker I painted the picture, the blacker the fatality, the greater emphasis I could then lay on my own achievement.

There was no doubt, the story about the underground passages would not only arouse laughter at the deception of the Trojans, not only admiration and respectful astonishment, but also quickly stifle any budding doubts. In the end most certainly all would be pleased and shower me with thanks and praise because I had kept cool control in a hopeless situation, enforced the Greek demands and brought about the long-desired peace. With what pleasure I could then return to Troy, secretly release my companions from the belly of the horse—the terrified citizens might take them for Greeks just emerged from underground!—and inform Troy's princes and peoples of our agreement and readiness for peace.

Truly a well concocted plan, my Prasidas, a piece of arithmetic so simple, of such compelling logic that even Laocoon could not conceal his admiration: in this and no other way, he maintained smiling, not only the Greeks and Trojans could be helped, but he himself, my old friend who did not wish to lose me a second time. Indeed, not a moment was to be wasted and as he had to go down to the shore again where his two sons were awaiting him for the sacrifice, he would set off at once, first to the sea and then straight to Priam in the palace. There was no need for me to accompany him: he knew the way and did not wish me to endanger myself.

With these words he rose, embraced me and promised to be back within the hour. "You must be tired, Odysseus . . . rest and enjoy the peace of my house."

He bowed with a smile and nodded to me. The door closed behind him and I heard his steps die away in the street.

What happened then, Prasidas, again you know. When he had reached the shore and was offering a slaughtered bullock to Poseidon by the water's edge, a grey serpent rose out of the sea attracted perhaps by the smell of the blood or by the entrails set aside in a copper bowl. Absorbed in prayer and pious thoughts, Laocoon did not notice the approach of the monster. He was praying, of that I am certain, for the success of our plan and when the serpent touched his body and he tried to defend himself, shouting to his sons for help, it was too late. Throttled by the tentacles, with blue faces, swollen veins and bloated limbs— thus I found all three suffocated on the shore.

My poor friend, I came too late: too late to save you, too late to do my deed. Silently I had to watch as the body of the serpent was cut away with great knives and the dead were freed from its coils, covered with a scarlet cloth and placed on a wooden cart.

Sorrowing I stayed in silent prayer and did not depart until black-clothed women, mourners from Troy, approached the cart and, ranging themselves in a half-circle, began bewailing the dead with shrill cries. Then slowly I returned to the city.

The chant faded; in Troy all was silent, all were asleep and only from an inn came soft, almost tender music. Later, groups of people sauntered through the streets; their voices broke on the walls into lingering echoes, deadened somewhere high up as it seemed by giant cloths.

The night was clear and very cold. The moon had a slim, pink-coloured halo and the stars were shining brightly. It was eleven o'clock: in an hour the Greek attack was due to begin. I felt tired and miserable: my plan had failed and I had no alternative but to wake my companions and give my countrymen the agreed sign.

When I had crossed almost the whole city and was once again near the city hall—the massive shadow of the horse was clearly visible in the moonlight—a group of revellers came towards me: men and women with linked arms who blocked the street in an undulating chain. When they saw me, they surged shouting towards me, surrounded me and laughingly threatened not to release me until I paid a suitable ransom: apparently they had drunk their money and were now trying, half in joke, half in earnest, to extort at least a few coppers.

Slightly annoyed at losing yet more time, I gave them some coins: Greek money, as they noticed to their surprise ... booty from a dead soldier?

Laughing I shook my head and as, somewhat sobered, they decided to take a closer look at me—one of them even held a lantern to my face—I resolved to stake all on a single card and tell them the truth.

"I am Odysseus, friends, the son of Laertes. Ithaca is my home, an island in Western Greece."

What shouts of laughter, Prasidas, when I had ended! What an explosion of merriment! Men embraced me, women caressed my cheeks, calling me tenderly "jester" and "buffoon" ... and finally they all raised me shouder-high, carried me in triumph to an inn and, noisily forcing an entry, toasted me again and again with the words: "He is Odysseus from Ithaca, a rich man. Tonight we'll drink up his money."

Whom the gods wish to destroy, child—they drop pitch in his eyes; they strike his heart with blindness and cloud his mind with the darkness of night. Yet where is the man who notices when the hands of the god are on him? Where the mortal who does not still hope when his feet are already touching the glowing coals?

A curse upon you, unseasonable revellers; not one of you survived that night. And a curse on you, too, guards ill-met at the royal palace. You knew my name as well—I shouted it to you. But when I asked you to help me and waken the King you laughed me to scorn and one of you even spat in my face.

You still had ten minutes, but instead of using them, you seized me and held a spear to my chest. And when, a few minutes before twelve, I revealed everything and told the story of the wooden horse you thought I was drunk, you bound me and with blows led me down to the dungeon. There you threw me into a corner and threatened me with summary trial and sentence next morning.

But when it began to dawn and my countrymen at last freed me, the judge was already hanging from a tree. An old Greek showed him to me; why, said he with a shrug, did he struggle when the soldiers tried to embrace his wife?

It was a scene of terror, Prasidas. The city was still burning. Squads of plunderers were combing the houses—for three days they were allowed to do what they liked. Children lay in the streets with open mouths, still clutching their balls and dolls; the cries of the wounded broke from half-ruined houses; a hoarse voice cried for water; wild-eyed women were running through the city shouting words which no one could understand: the names of their children, perhaps, or curses at the conqueror; old men sat in the gutters begging for a crumb of bread.

But worse, even, than the horrific visions of the burning city was the satisfaction felt in the Greek camp at such an end. Truly, Prasidas, we were miserable victors. Instead of bothering about the wounded, we held pompous feasts; instead of caring for the maimed and distributing a plate of soup at least to the old people and cripples we squandered the booty with flute-players and whores. While the Trojans went hungry we poured wine into the street—banquets and victory celebrations followed in quick succession and the drunkenness at the love-feasts allowed the misery of the conquered to be all too quickly forgotten.

No one thought now of the sufferings of war. The dead were buried and the living demanded their rights. A few more weeks, and all would go back to their native land, settle themselves at home and begin again where they had left off twelve years before.

In everything the past seemed restored. Even Helen had returned and had reconciled herself with Menelaus ... an old woman with hair dyed blonde and a layer of powder on her face which merely accentuated the crows' feet and the wrinkles. But who still remembered that, long ago, it was for this woman that we had gone to war?

Perhaps I was the only one who sometimes still spoke of it. It was not a popular topic, but as I happened to be a hero and triumph and victory were due solely to my cunning I was allowed my say and it was even accepted when I stayed for a while in Troy and on the pretext of supervising the collection of the indemnities prevented at least the worst abuses.

I stayed in the palace of the King, Prasidas. Formerly poets had spoken of "Priam's golden house"; now the only reminder of past glory was a smoke-blackened façade. The roof had half collapsed, the windows were like blinded eyes; weeds were growing in the lobbies and on the steps and the marble basins of the ponds were a tangle of reeds and giant ferns.

Inside the house, cupboards torn open, ransacked drawers and smashed display-cases witnessed plundering by drunken soldiers. Only a small extension, the Prince's Wing, as the Trojans called it, had been partially spared. Here I had a small, not uncomfortable dwelling set up for myself and a royal apartment of pleasant dimensions—both rooms quite close to the modest chamber in which Priam, once King of Troy, was spending the evening of his life.

Not without emotion, Prasidas: with feelings of solemn distress I pronounce the name of the man who once had fourteen sons and now, alone and childless, awaited the hour of his death.

Previously, when the old-fashioned chariot drawn by two emaciated nags had stopped at my camp and, kneeling at a respectful distance, Priam had asked the son of his guest-friend Laertes to his house—he said he was very alone and feared the terrors of the winter—at that time, Prasidas, moved by shame and remorse, I intended to decline his wish with courteous words. But when he pressed me and described the miserable lot of his old age, his loneliness and the darkness of the empty palace, when he wept and raised his arms to me in pleading, I seized his hand and promised to come to him as quickly as I could.

Leaning on a stick, he received me that same evening at the gate; one slave kindled the torch, another opened the door . . . then we were alone and our pilgrimage began.

Priam went ahead, I followed him in silence. Mortar and debris lay underfoot. We crossed innumerable ante-chambers, walked through halls and state-rooms, paused in parlours and secondary apartments, groped through corridors and mouldering passages, climbed stair-cases with broken steps, strode through immense suites, scrambled over rubble, broken cupboards and overthrown tables, stopped in cellars and examined the store-rooms in the attic, had to make repeated detours, lost our way, went in a circle and after many wrong turnings found ourselves back at our starting point . . . It was a tour which lasted until broad daylight, until sunrise, until our return to the Princes' Wing which we finally reached towards four in the morning, confused and exhausted, more asleep than awake.

This walk, my Prasidas, this march through a museum of horror was a pilgrimage of suffering on a gigantic scale.

There was the room in which Hector had taken leave of Andromache; pictures slashed by knives were still hanging on the walls : soldiers had used them as a target.

There was the room where Priam's youngest, the sixteen-year-old Deiphobos, had armed himself with helmet and mail to go into battle with his brothers in defiance of his father's command. His lute still hung in the corner; copy-books lay scattered on the floor.

There was Andromache's chamber : the only reminder that this was a princess's room, an elegant little table with legs cut off and emptied drawers.

There, desecrated and ransacked by feverish hands, was the immense hall, the home of Paris and Helen. Pillows and blankets were in tatters, the head of Aphrodite above the bed had been split by a blow with an axe. The mouth of the goddess gaped with an open wound, the nose was broken in two, a cleft between the eyes had mutilated the charm, the smile had turned into a faun's grimace, the sweetness into the cynical grin of a satyr.

And there, finally, a small, shell-shaped oval, was Helen's boudoir, the only intact room in the whole building. Silver mirrors stood in recesses of reddish wood, stools and chairs were undamaged, the bolster had been spared, pots, bowls and bottles were still neatly ranged. It almost seemed as though the picture of the Queen still rested on the white crystal. Had the soldiers stopped short? Blinded and enraptured, had they held back in fear? Had the shimmer of beauty, its gleaming reflection suddenly sobered their drunkenness and halted their steps? Blinded by the light of youth and humbled, had they respectfully gone their way?

"A miracle," said Priam gently, "it is a miracle, my friend. We will not cross the threshold, either. The goddess might be angry with us." Silently he inclined his staff into the emptiness, described a half-circle and pointed smiling to the three great mirrors which transformed the glowing ball of the raised torch into a heart of red gold. "He who enters this room is bewitched. We were all intoxicated by her beauty: Paris and Andromache, Hecuba and Hector . . . and I, too, my friend."

"I loved her very much," he said calmly, "more than my own children, and I know that the gods are angry with me for it: would they otherwise have taken from me my wife and all my sons? And yet even today I still love her, for it is great good fortune for a mortal to have met perfection itself once, at any rate once in his life.

"Helen, you know—I cannot speak her name often enough—was not only, like many women, very beautiful, neither was she more beautiful than others, admirable and pure. She was Beauty Itself, the mirror, not its reflection; she was the sun, not its light.

"But she was only a human being," he said sadly, "and try as she might to protect herself, craving powders, unguents, narcotics and poisons, the time of ageing was inescapable." He raised his voice: "You see the sun darkened by clouds—soon it will shine again; the stars turn pale, to gleam brightly in the evening; the moon wanes and rounds herself anew; but human beings know neither permanence nor pause, they know nothing about going back, return is denied them: the shadow of the wrinkle destroys beauty for ever, the hesitance of the ageing warrior buries his fame, and the first sign of fear drives the athlete from the arena. It is better to leave the stadium in good time."

He gave a tired shrug. "But what was she to do? For the sake of her beauty the Trojans had taken the field: no one would have fought for an old woman. What alternative had she but to cheat nature afresh every day? At the end, admittedly, neither powder nor rouge could help; she became very lonely, shut herself in her room and even on high feasts only showed herself to the people from a distance, from the balcony. Finally she drove in a curtained carriage to the Greek camp: otherwise the Trojans would have stoned her. Poor Helen, only her mirror still retained the picture of her youth."

Was it on that first night that in solemn speech elevated by imagery and metaphor Priam told me his story? Or was it only later? I cannot remember. At my age, Prasidas, the memory loses power, yesterday and the days before are one and the same, the recent past reaches back into childhood.

For a year and more I went to him almost every day: at first to listen to his stories—and no poet could have invented more colourful ones—later, when his strength was visibly failing and he could no longer leave his bed, to tell him something of myself and my life. Suffering bound us together, knowledge of transience and swift ageing. Thus we concealed nothing from one another and it was not long before Penelope and Telemachus also became Priam's intimate friends.

But much as he enjoyed dwelling in thought in Ithaca, news from Troy interested him most: the talk of the market, gossip from the harbour, sailors' tales and rumours which sped through the city.

Smiling and friendly, not without understanding for the pardonable vice of curiosity still alive in old age, I kept him informed. As I was having the war debt collected with mildness and tolerance, the attitude of the Trojans, at first so hostile, had gradually changed to confidence and respect; I took part in the life of the city and could tell Priam of many a secret matter which otherwise he would never have heard.

When in the following winter he fell seriously ill and the doctors gave him little hope, I stayed at his side, exceeding the year which I had set myself, tended him as well as I could and told him fairy stories and fables—legends which later, through the incomprehension of a slave (or was it the doctor?) were given out as my own adventures and were soon in everyone's mouth: stories of monsters and vampires, one-eyed giants and mis-shapen dwarfs, but also of cliffs which could sing like birds.

Later, when Priam's mind began to wander—he dreamt a great deal and talked confusedly—I read to him from an old book of fairy stories. How happy I was to be able to read again at last! It was only now, my child, that I slowly began to forget the war: for the mind to unfold, you see, the leisure of peace is required and the tranquillity of seclusion.

To the end Priam took pleasure in the old stories—right up to that dark night in March when, peacefully and without a struggle, he passed away. A few days later we buried him beside his sons and when the week of mourning was over and life had resumed its normal course, the hour of parting was at hand for me, too.

A procession of honour acompanied me to the quay, children strewed the gangway with flowers, and when I went on board and the sailors saluted, there were many people weeping for me. But in my heart was peace and I felt happy, almost joyful. The conqueror of Troy was parting as the city's friend.

In the early brilliance of a summer's day the plain of Troy faded in a veil of mist. Before us lay open sea, the ship set a course for Ithaca. Moved with joy I sacrificed a lamb to Apollo, besought the heavenly blessing and asked for protection and escort on the long journey home.

BIOGRAPHICAL NOTE

Walter Jens. Born 1923 in Hamburg. Classical education, 1933–41. Studied classical philology and German literature in Hamburg and Freiburg. Doctorate 1944. Lecturer at Tübingen, 1949; Professor since 1956. Member of *Deutsche Akademie für Sprache und Dichtung* and *Berliner Akademie der Künste.*

Select Bibliography
Nein—die Welt der Angeklagten, 1950
Der Blinde, 1951 (*The Blind Man,* London, 1954)
Vergessene Gesichter, 1952

Hofmannsthal und die Griechen, 1955
Der Mann, der nicht alt werden wollte, 1955
Statt einer Literaturgeschichte, 1957
Des Testament des Odysseus, 1957
Die Götter sind sterblich, 1959
Deutsche Literatur der Gegenwart, 1961
Zueignungen, 1962
Herr Meister, 1963

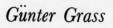

Günter Grass

Translated
by
Aliza Shapiro

GÜNTER GRASS

THE LEFT-HANDERS

ERIC is watching me closely. And I too, cannot take my eyes off him. We are both holding the weapons that we have decided to use to wound one another. Our guns are loaded. Long tried and tested, carefully cleaned after each trial, we cradle them in our hands. Slowly we feel the cool metal warming up.

Seen objectively, a gun really looks very harmless. After all, one can hold a fountain pen or a heavy key in much the same manner and one can even coax a scream from a timid aunt by spreading one's fingers inside a black leather glove.

But I must not permit the thought to enter my mind that Eric's gun might not be loaded or harmless—a mere toy. And I know equally well that, never for a moment, does Eric doubt the seriousness of my weapon. Just to confirm our intentions we took our pistols to pieces only half an hour ago, cleaned, re-assembled and loaded them and, finally, took off the safety catch. We are no dreamers.

As the right setting for our inevitable action we chose Eric's little weekend house. His bungalow is more than an hour away from the nearest railway station and, therefore, sufficiently iso-lated for us to assume that all unwanted ears are, in the most literal sense of the word, far out of our range.

We have cleared out the living room and removed the pictures, which are mainly hunting prints and still-lives of game, from the walls. After all, the shots about to be fired are not meant for the chairs, nor for the warmly polished side-board or the ornately framed pictures. Nor yet, do we plan to hit the mirror or any of the porcelain in the room. It is only ourselves we plan to aim at.

We are both left-handed and have got to know each other through the Club. You know, of course, that the left-handers in this town, as all others who share a common defect, have founded their own club. We meet regularly and persistently try to develop the strength of our clumsy right hand. For a time a good-natured right-hander tried to teach us. Now, unfortunately, he won't come any more. Our honorary officers criticised his teaching

160 GERMAN NARRATIVE PROSE

methods and decided that members of the club should try and
learn on their own initiative.

As a result of this, we now try to combine specially devised
(though non-compulsory) games with various dexterity tests. For
example we try such simple actions as threading a needle, pouring a drink or buttoning and unbuttoning—all with our right
hand. For one of the provisions in our statutes claims that "we
shall not rest until right has become like left".

Apt and strong though this sentence may sound, it is, in fact,
sheer nonsense. Like this we shall never make it. The extreme
wing of our organisation has actually been agitating for some
time that this slogan should be scrapped and that, instead, our
battle-cry should be: "We shall be proud of our left hand and
feel no shame in our inborn ways." Surely, however, even this
slogan is not the right one. Only its pathos and a certain emo-
tional generosity made us choose these words. Eric and I, who
are both counted among the extremists in the Club, know only
too well how deeply rooted our shame is. First the parental
home, then school and later our service in the Army, none of
these helped to teach us bear our defect with equanimity—
minor though it is in comparison with other widely known ab-
normalities.

Realisation that we were "different" came early. As long ago
as the childish command to "shake hands, dear". With aunts,
uncles, mother's girl-friends, father's colleagues; and on the all-
important, terrible family photograph which darkens the horizon
of every child. Everyone's hand had to be shaken. "No dear,
not the naughty little hand, the good hand, the clever, dexterous
one, the only real hand—the right hand."

I was sixteen when I touched a girl for the first time. "Get
away," she said in a disappointed voice. "You're left-handed,"
and drew my hand out from the inside of her blouse.

Such memories remain and if, none the less, Eric and I, the
authors of the new slogan, are prepared to accept it, we are
merely attempting to achieve the definition of an unattainable
ideal.

Now Eric's lips are tightly compressed and his eyes have
narrowed into mere slits. I follow his example. The muscles in
our faces are strained, our foreheads taut and our nostrils drawn.

Eric now reminds me of a film-star whose features have become familiar through many adventure films.

Hopefully I wonder whether I too, now resemble one of the dubious heroes of the canvas screen?

I am sure we look terrifying and I am glad that no one is watching us. Any unwanted witness would undoubtedly assume that two excessively romantic young men were about to fight a duel—over a shared woman; a slanderous rumour; a family feud, harboured for generations; a debt of honour; a bloody game of win or lose. For only enemies can look at each other like this. Note the narrow lips, devoid of all colour, the unrelenting line of the sharply drawn nose. They appear to be choking on their hatred—imbued with a fatal death wish.

Yet we are friends. Although our professions are very different—Eric is head of department in a large department store and I have chosen the remunerative trade of precision mechanics—we have a sufficient number of common interests to make our friendship a lasting one. Eric has belonged to the Club for longer than I. I well remember the day when I walked into the "One-Siders" for the first time—shy, unsure of myself and over-dressed. Eric came towards me then and, giving me a knowing look which was yet devoid of excessive curiosity he said: "I am sure you want to join us. Don't be shy; we are all here to help each other."

You notice that I have just spoken of the "One-Siders Club". This is our official title. But it too, like a large part of our statutes, seems to me a misnomer. It does not really express what binds and should also strengthen us. I am sure we would be better named "The Lefthanders" or even "The Left Brothers". But you can, no doubt, guess why we had to reject the idea of registering the Club under the latter name. Nothing could be further from the truth and therefore more insulting, than to liken us to those pitiful beings from whom nature has withheld the possibility of doing justice to the art of love. Quite to the contrary, we are in fact a very mixed crowd and I can say without hesitation that, as regards beauty, charm or the social graces, our ladies are more than a match for their right-handed sisters.

In fact, if one were carefully to compare the two, a picture of morals and manners would emerge which would cause many a vicar concerned with the salvation and spiritual welfare of his flock, to exclaim from his pulpit: "If only you were all left-handed."

How troublesome this Club-title is! Even our first President, a high official in the Municipal Land Registry Office who is, unfortunately, inclined to think and act somewhat too patriarchally, had to admit that we are not aptly named. The "left" is missing from the title and we are certainly not one-sided, either physically or in our thoughts, emotions or actions.

No doubt, certain political factors also had to be taken into consideration when we rejected some of the better-sounding suggestions for possible names and, instead, chose the one by which we should never have been called. After all, one must consider how Members of Parliament tend to move from the centre towards either one side or the other and how the very benches in the House are placed in such a way that their order gives clear indicataion of the political orientation of our country. It has become an accepted custom to attribute a dangerous radicalism to each article written, to every speech made in which the word "left" appears more than once.

However, on that score no one needs to worry as far as we are concerned. If there is one organisation in our town which is utterly devoid of political ambitions of any kind and which was created for the sole purposes of mutual help and sociability —it is ours. And just to give the lie once and for all to any thoughts of erotic perversion, I merely want to mention briefly that I met my fiancée among the girls in our youth group. We are now planning to get married as soon as a suitable flat becomes vacant.

If the shadow cast over my ego by my first encounter with the female sex should ever disappear, I shall certainly owe my liberation to Monica. Our love had to learn to cope not only with the generally known and often described trials and tribulatitons, but also our physical handicap had to be overcome and even glorified before we could achieve our small share of happiness.

In our first, understandable, confusion, we tried to please one another by using our right hand until we saw how insensitive this, our impotent hand, was. Now we stroke and caress with ardour, using the hand that God meant us to use for this purpose. I am sure I am not giving away any secrets, nor do I mean to be indiscreet when I hint here that, again and again, it is Monica's dear hand which gives me the strength to hold out and keep my promise. Straight after our first visit to the cinema I had to reassure her that I would respect her virginity until we exchanged wedding rings, unfortunately on the right hand, thus giving in to custom and underlining the awkwardness of our natural tendencies.

And yet, in Southern, Catholic countries, the golden symbol of marriage is worn on the left—just as in the same sunny regions it is the heart that rules over the unrelenting brain. It must have been a sign of revolt, attempted in an effort to prove the logic of female thinking under duress, when values are threatened, which drove the younger lady members of our organisation to embroider the words "left side—heart-side" as an inscription on to the green flag of our Club.

Again and again Monica and I have talked about the moment of exchanging rings and we invariably arrive at the same conclusion : alas, we cannot afford to face an unknowing and only too often malicious world as an engaged couple when, in fact, we shall have been long married, sharing both big and small things alike.

Monica often cries about this question of the ring. So, no matter how gladly and anxiously we anticipate this, our day, a slight mist of sadness will veil the beautiful presents, the richly laden tables and the joyful festivities.

Now Eric is facing me once more with his normal, kind face. I also relax, but I can still feel the strain in my jaw muscles, the twitching in my temples. I am sure our grimacing faces do not become us. Now our eyes meet more calmly and therefore with greater courage. We aim, each for that certain hand of the other. I am quite sure that I shall not miss and know that I can also rely on Eric. We have practised too long—spent almost every available free minute in a deserted gravel pit on the outskirts of our town. Surely, we cannot miss today, when so much is at stake.

You may well object and say that this deliberate self-mutilation borders on sadism. Believe me, we are familiar with all these arguments. There is no crime of which we have not accused each other. Nor is it the first time that we are standing in this empty room. Four times we have seen each other armed as we are now, four times we dropped our pistols, frightened and shocked by our plan. Only now, at last, we have found peace in our intention.

Recent events in our personal life as well as in the Club justify our plan. We must go ahead. After prolonged doubts, when we even questioned the aims of the Club and its extreme wing, we are finally taking up our arms. Regrettable though it is, we cannot continue as we are. Our conscience demands that we withdraw from the activities of our fellow members.

A new element seems to be gaining ground there recently, and even among our most stable members there is an encroachment of dreamers and fanatics. The former gush and enthuse on the one side, while the latter curse and swear on the other side. Political slogans are being bantered from table to table—something I would never have thought possible among our group. And a repulsive cult of oath-taking has developed which takes the form of a left-handed hammering-in of nails and is spreading so rapidly that many a meeting of our executive resembles an orgy in which the main aim seems to be to achieve ecstasy through constant and obsessive hammering. And although no one dares to talk about it, and those who have most obviously fallen victim to vice are, so far, being expelled, it is no good denying that the false and, to me, quite incomprehensible love between members of the same sex has found a number of followers among us. To say the worst: even my relationship with Monica has been affected. She spends far too much time with her girl-friend, an unstable and inconsistent creature. Too often she accuses me of excessive weakness and lack of courage with regard to the ring business. I can no longer feel the same trust between us and it is no more the same Monica whom I now hold—alas more and more seldom—in my arms.

Eric and I are now trying to co-ordinate our breathing. The more we harmoniously agree, even in this, the more convinced we become that our action is inspired by sound instinct. Don't think that we are following the Biblical edict to root out evil. It is rather the fervent and constant desire to obtain clarity and ever more clarity, to know where one stands and whether one's fate is irrevocable or whether it can be interfered with and our lives redirected into normal channels.

No more childish restrictions or prohibitions—bandages or similar tricks. Upright and independent, no longer set apart from the norm, by our own choice, we want to begin anew with a happy hand.

Now our breathing is perfectly atuned. Without a sign we both fire simultaneously. Eric has hit his mark, and I too, did not disappoint him. As planned, each one of us hit the vital vein in such a way that our pistols, no longer held with sufficient strength, drop to the floor and any further shot would be superfluous.

We laugh and begin our great experiment by awkwardly fixing emergency bandages, solely dependent on our right hand.

BIOGRAPHICAL NOTE

Günter Grass. Born in 1927 in Danzig. After the war he worked as a stonemason and sculptor and subsequently studied art in Düsseldorf and Berlin, with three years (1956–59) in Paris. He is now a freelance writer in Berlin. Prizes: *Gruppe 47,* 1958; *Kritikerpreis,* 1960; *Le meilleur Livre étranger,* 1962.

Select Bibliography

Die Blechtrommel, 1959 (*Tin Drum,* London, 1962)
Katz und Maus, 1961 (*Cat and Mouse,* London, 1963)
Hundejahre, 1965 (*Dog Years,* London, 1965)

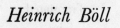

Heinrich Böll

Translated
by
Mervyn Savill

HEINRICH BÖLL

TRAVELLER, IF YOU COME TO SPA ...

WHEN the truck stopped, the engine went on purring for a while.
Somewhere outside a big door was flung open, light fell through
the smashed window into the inside of the truck and I now saw
that the electric bulb on the roof was also smashed. Only its
wires still stuck in the socket, a few glittering wires with fragments of broken glass. Then the engine ceased to purr and a
voice outside shouted : "Bring the dead in here. Have you any
dead?" "Hell," shouted the driver, "don't you black out any
more?"

"No point blacking out when the whole city is blazing like a
torch," shouted the strange voice. "I asked you if you had any
dead."

"Don't know."

"Bring the dead in, do you hear? And take the others up the
stairs to the Art Room. Do you understand?"

"Yes, yes."

But I was still alive. I belonged to the "others", and they
carried me up the steps. We went first along a long, weakly lit
corridor with green-painted walls. Curved, black, old-fashioned
clothes-hangers were screwed into the walls and there were doors
with enamel plaques : VIA and VIB. And between these doors,
gleaming softly under glass in a black frame, hung Feuerbach's
Medea, staring into the distance; then came doors with VA and
VB, and between them hung a picture of *The Boy with the
Thorn*, a wonderful reddish gleaming photo in a brown frame.

The big pillars in the well at the bottom of the staircase were
there too—and behind them, long, slim and beautifully fashioned, a model of the Parthenon frieze, gleaming yellow,
genuine antique, and everything appeared in its right order : the
Greek hoplite, gay yet dangerous, looking like a feathered cock,
and in the well itself—the walls here were painted yellow—the
whole portrait gallery, from the great Kurfürst to Hitler. ...

And there, in that small, narrow corridor where I raised myself for a few yards on my stretcher, was the particularly beauti-

ful, particularly large, particularly gay portrait of the "Old Fritz", in his sky-blue uniform with the flashing eyes and the great, golden, glittering star on his breast.

Once more I lay flat on the stretcher and was carried past the racial faces: there were the Nordic captain with the eagle eye and the stupid mouth; the Moseller from the west, slightly haggard and sharp-featured, and the man from the east with an onion nose and the long Adam's-apple-like winter sports film profile. Then came another corridor, and again for a few steps I raised myself on my stretcher, and before the bearer turned on to the second staircase I could see it: the war memorial with the huge golden iron cross and the stone laurel wreath.

It all went very fast. I am not heavy and the stretcher-bearers hurried. Nevertheless, it could all have been an illusion. I had a high temperature and my body ached all over—my head, arms and legs—and my heart raced like a maniac. What does one not see in a fever?

But when we had passed all the racial faces, the others appeared: the three busts of Caesar, Cicero and Marcus Aurelius, beautiful reproductions, looking yellow, genuinely antique and venerable against the wall. And then came the Hermes pillar as we turned round the corner, and right at the end of the corridor—this corridor was painted rose pink—right at the far end of the corridor hung the great mask of Zeus over the entrance of the Art Room. The Zeus mask was still a long way off. To my right, through the window, I saw the glare of flames; the whole sky was red and black, thick clouds of smoke swept festively across it. . . .

And once more I had to look to the left and once more I saw the plaques over the doors OIA and OIB and between the brown padded doors I could see only Nietzsche's moustache and his pointed nose in a golden frame, for on one half of the picture they had pasted a notice on which I could read: "Light surgery."

"Now if only . . ." I thought swiftly, "if now . . ." But there it was: the picture of Togo—gay and large, flat as an old engraving. A magnificent impression. . . . And in the foreground, in front of the colonial houses, the Negroes and the soldier who stood there aimlessly with his rifle, right in the foreground was the large life-size bunch of bananas. A bunch to the left; a

bunch to the right. . . . And there on the middle banana of the
right bunch, a scribble. I saw it. I myself must have scribbled
it. . . .

But now the door to the Art Room was flung open and I
swayed beneath the bust of Zeus and closed my eyes. I did not
want to see any more. The Art Room stank of iodine, excrement,
mould and tobacco, and it was noisy. They sat me down, and I
said to the bearers : "Shove a cigarette in my mouth. You'll find
one in my left-hand pocket."

I felt the man fumbling in my pocket; then a match spluttered
and I had a lighted cigarette in my mouth. I puffed at it.
"Thanks," I said.

But all this is no proof, I thought. In the last analysis, there
is an Art Room in every college. There are corridors in which
curved, old-fashioned clothes-hangers are screwed into green and
yellow-painted walls. In the last analysis it is no proof that I am
in my school if the *Medea* hangs between VIA and VIB and
Nietzsche's moustache between OIA and OIB. There's obviously
some regulation that insists they should hang there. Household
regulations for humanistic colleges in Prussia : *Medea* between
VIA and VIB; the *Boy with the Thorn* over there; Caesar,
Cicero and Marcus Aurelius in the corridor; and Nietzsche up-
stairs where they learn philosophy. The Parthenon frieze . . . a
gay portrait of Togo . . .*The Boy with the Thorn* and the
Parthenon frieze are, of course, good old school properties which
have been preserved for generations. And obviously I was not
the only one who took it into his head to write on a banana :
"Long live Togo." The jests, too, that they make in school are
always the same. Moreover, it is possible that since I am feverish
I may be dreaming.

My pains had now vanished. They had been bad in the car.
Each time it drove over small potholes I screamed. The big
bomb craters were better, for then the car rose and fell like a
ship in a high sea. But the injection which someone had given
me in the darkness now seemed to be working. I had felt the
needle pierce the skin and my leg below had grown hot.

It can't be true, I thought, the car cannot have driven so
many miles—nearly fifteen. Moreover, I feel nothing. No feeling
tells me. Only the eyes. No feeling tells me that I am in my
school—in the school I left only three months ago. Eight years

are no trifle. Should I be able to remember everything with my eyes alone after eight years?

Behind my closed lids I saw everything again as though in a film : the lower corridor painted green, stairs painted yellow, war memorial, landing, more stairs, Caesar, Cicero, Marcus Aurelius . . . Hermes, Nietzsche's moustache, Togo, the mask of Zeus. . . .

I spat out my cigarette and screamed. It was always a good thing to scream. One had only to scream loud enough. It was marvellous to scream, and I screamed like a madman. I did not open my eyes when someone bent over me. I felt a stranger's warm breath, stinking repulsively of tobacco and onions, and a voice asked quietly : "What's the matter?"

"Something to drink," I said, "and another cigarette. In my upper pocket."

Once more someone rummaged in my pocket. Once more a match hissed and someone stuck a lighted cigarette in my mouth. "Where are we?" I asked.

"In Bendorf."

"Thank you," I said, taking a puff.

So apparently I really was in Bendorf. At home, then. And unless I wasn't really delirious it was also obvious that I was in a humanistic college. It was obviously a school. Had not the voice below shouted : "Take the others to the Art Room"? I was one of the others. I was alive and obviously those who were alive were the others. So this was the Art Room, and if I had heard right why should I not have seen right? And then it was obviously right that I had recognised Caesar, Cicero and Marcus Aurelius, and that could only be in one particular humanistic college. I do not think that these fellows stood on the walls of the corridors in other schools.

At last he brought me water. Once more the smell of tobacco and onions from his face and involuntarily I opened my eyes. I saw an old, tired, unshaven face above a fireman's uniform and an old voice said gently : "Drink, comrade."

I drank. It was water. But water is wonderful. I felt the metal taste of the mess-tin on my lips and I could feel that there was a great deal of water left. But the fireman snatched it away from my lips and walked away. I screamed, but he did not turn round, merely shrugged his tired shoulders and went on. . . . A man lying next to me said calmly : "There's no point in yelling.

They've got no more water. The whole city's on fire, as you can see."

I could see it through the gloom. There was a glow and a rumble behind the black curtain, red behind black as in an oven which had just been stoked up with coal. Yes, I could see that the city was on fire all right.

"What's the name of the city?" I asked the man who lay next to me.

"Bendorf," he replied.

"Thanks."

I stared straight ahead of me at the windows and sometimes at the ceiling. The ceiling was immaculate. White and smooth with a small classic frieze. But in all schools they had classic friezes on the ceilings of all the art rooms; at least, in the good old humanistic colleges. That was quite certain.

Now I had to admit that I lay in the art room of a humanistic college in Bendorf. The city possessed three of these colleges : the Frederick the Great School; the Albertus School; and perhaps I need not mention that the last one, the third one, was the Adolf Hitler School. Did not the particularly beautiful, large and gay picture of the "Old Fritz" hang on the staircase wall of the Frederick the Great School? I had been at this school for eight years. But why should not this picture hang in the other schools in exactly the same place, just as clearly and prominently, so that it was bound to catch the eye when one climbed the first stairs?

Outside I now heard the firing of heavy artillery. Apart from that it was almost peaceful. Only occasionally I heard the roar of the flames, and somewhere in the darkness a roof collapsed. The artillery fired calmly and regularly and I thought : "Good old gunners." I know that this was cheap, but I thought it. My God, how consoling this artillery was and how cosy; dark and raw, a soft, almost well-tuned organ. Almost elegant ... yes, I found that there was something elegant about the artillery, even when it did not fire. It smacked so respectably of war as portrayed in the picture books. Then I thought of how many names would be inscribed on the war memorial if they consecrated it again with an even bigger golden iron cross and an even bigger stone laurel wreath, and suddenly I knew. If I were really in my old school, my name would also stand on it ... carved in stone,

and in the school calendar behind my name would be written:
"Went from school into the Army and died for . . ."

But I did not know what for and I did not know if I were
in my old school. Now I had to find this out at all costs. There
was nothing particular about the war memorial. Nothing outstanding. It was like all the others, a mass-produced war
memorial, and they came from some large factory.

I looked round the Art Room, but they had taken away the
pictures. And who could say that it really was an art room
from the few benches piled up in a corner and the small, close-
set, high windows to let in a great deal of light? My heart told
me nothing. Would it not have said something had I been in
this dump for eight long years drawing vases and copying scripts
—thin, fine, marvellous imitation Roman glass vases which the
art teacher had placed in front of us on a pedestal, and scripts of
all types—copperplate, antiqua, Roman, italics? I had hated
these hours more than anything else in the whole school, and for
hours on end I had been bored. And I had never been able to
draw vases or to copy the scripts. But where were my curses?
Where was my hatred against these sober-coloured, boring walls?
Nothing spoke in me and I shook my head in silence.

I had gone on drawing, sharpening my pencil, drawing . . .
nothing. . . .

I did not exactly know how badly I was wounded. I only
knew that I could not move my arms or my right leg. I could
only move my left leg a little. I thought they must have bound
my arms to my body so securely that I could not move them.

I spat the second cigarette on to the floor between the straw
pallets and tried to move my arms. But it hurt so much that I
had to scream. I went on screaming. It was still wonderful to
scream. I was also in a rage because I could not move my arms.

Then the doctor stood at my side. He had taken off his glasses
and was blinking down at me. He said nothing. Behind him
stood the fireman who had given me the water. He whispered
something in the doctor's ear and the latter put on his glasses
again. I could clearly see his big, grey eyes with the slightly
trembling pupils behind the thick lenses. He looked at me for a
long time, so long that I had to turn my eyes away. "Wait a
minute," he said gently. "You are the next. . . ."

Then they lifted up the man who lay next to me and carried

him behind the blackboard. I stared after them. They had dismantled the blackboard and stood it on its end and hung a sheet in the hole between it and the wall. Behind burned a bright light.

Nothing could be heard until the sheet was drawn aside once more and the man who had laid next to me was carried out. With tired, impassive faces the bearers carried him to the door.

I closed my eyes and thought: I must find out how badly I am wounded and if I am in my old school.

I found everything so cold and bleak that I felt they might have carried me through the museum of a dead city, through a world which to me was as apathetic as it was alien, although my eyes recognised it, but only my eyes. It could not be true that I had been here only three months ago, drawing vases and copying scripts; that in the breaks, carrying my slices of bread and marmalade, I had passed Nietzsche, Hermes, Togo, Caesar, Cicero and Marcus Aurelius. Slowly down to the corridor below where hung the *Medea*. Then to the caretaker, to Birgeler, to drink milk in that dusky little room where one could risk smoking a cigarette although it was forbidden. Obviously they had carried the man who had laid next to me down there among the dead. Perhaps the dead were lying in Birgeler's grey little room which stank of warm milk, dust and Birgeler's cheap tobacco. . . .

At last the bearers came in, lifted me up and carried me behind the blackboard. I swayed once more, now past the door; and as I swayed past I saw that once more it was right. Above the door a crucifix had once hung, when the school was still called St. Thomas's. And then they had taken the crucifix away. But a new, dark yellow patch on the wall, hard and clear in the shape of a crucifix, had still remained; it could be seen even more clearly than the old, unobtrusive little crucifix itself which had hung there. Clean and beautiful, the sign of the cross remained on the new painting on the wall. In those days in their rage they had repainted the whole wall but it had not sufficed. The painter had not found the right tint. The crucifix stood there, brown and clear while the rest of the wall was pink. They had cursed, but that was not enough. The crucifix remained there, brown and clear on the pink wall, and I think that their paint allowance was exhausted and they could do nothing about

it. The cross was still there, and if one looked closely one could
even see a clear trace above the right beam where for years had
hung the boxwood branch which the caretaker, Birgeler, had
stuck there when it was still permissible to hang crucifixes in the
schools. . . .

All this flashed through my mind in a second as I was carried
past the door, behind the blackboard where the harsh light
burned.

I lay on the operating table and saw myself clearly, but very
small and shrivelled, overhead in the clear glass of the electric
bulb. Tiny and white, a small, musty-coloured bundle like an
extraordinarily delicate embryo. That is how I looked up there.

The doctor had his back to me and was standing at a table,
fiddling with his instruments. Broad-shouldered and old, the fireman stood in front of the blackboard and smiled at me. His smile
was tired and sad and his dirty, bearded face was the face of
a sleeping man. Over his shoulder on the smeared back of the
blackboard I saw something which made my heart beat for the
first time since I had been in this necropolis. Somewhere in a
secret chamber of my heart I was deeply shocked and in its fear
it began to beat furiously. My handwriting stood there on the
blackboard. . . . Right on the top, on the top line. I knew my
own handwriting. It was worse than seeing one's face in a
mirror. . . . There was no possibility of being mistaken as to
the identity of my own handwriting. All the rest had been no
proof—neither the *Medea* nor the Nietzsche, nor the dinaric
winter sports film profile, nor Togo's bananas; not even the
mark of the crucifix over the door. All that was the same in every
school. But I did not think that in other schools they wrote on
blackboards in my handwriting. There stood the quotation which
I had had to write in that desperate life which lay a bare three
months behind us: "Traveller, if you come to Spa . . ."

Oh, I know that the blackboard had been too short and the
art teacher had grumbled that I had not spaced the words cor-
rectly; that I had chosen too big a script and that he himself
with a shake of the head had written in script of the same size:
"Traveller, if you come to Spa . . ."

It stood there seven times in my handwriting, in antiqua,
gothic, cursive, roman, italic and copperplate; seven times clearly
and irrevocably: "Traveller, if you come to Spa . . ."

At the request of the doctor the fireman had now stood aside and I could see the whole quotation, which was only slightly marred because I had chosen too big a script and too big a pointing. I shuddered as I felt a stab in my left thigh. I wanted to raise myself but I could not. I looked down and then I saw. . . . They had taken off my bandages and I had no arms left and no right leg, and I suddenly fell backwards because I could not raise myself. I screamed. The doctor and the fireman looked at me in terror. But the doctor merely shrugged his shoulders and pressed on the plunger of his syringe which sank slowly and peacefully. I wanted to look once more at the blackboard, but the fireman was now standing close to me and hid it from sight. He held me fast by the shoulders and I could smell the reek of burning on his dirty, stained uniform. I caught sight of his tired, melancholy face and at last I recognised him. It was Birgeler.

"Milk," I said softly. . . .

BIOGRAPHICAL NOTE

Heinrich Böll was born in Cologne in 1917. He worked in a bookshop, and studied literature and philology for a few months before his army call-up; he served from 1939 to 1945. He was four times wounded, and later became a prisoner-of-war. On his return to civilian life he joined the staff of the *Statistisches Amt*, Cologne. He co-edited *Labyrinth*, and is now a freelance writer in Cologne. Many prizes, among them: *Gruppe 47*, 1951; *Tribune de Paris*, 1954; *Förderpreis*, Federation of German Industry, 1955; *Literaturpreis*, City of Cologne, 1961.

Select Bibliography

Der Zug war pünktlich, 1949 (*The Train was on Time*, New York, 1956)
Wanderer, kommst du nach Spa . . ., 1950
Wo warst du, Adam? 1951 (*Adam, Where Art thou?* London, 1955)
Nicht nur zur Weihnachtszeit, 1952
Und sagte kein einziges Wort, 1953 (*Acquainted with the Night*, London, 1955)
Haus ohne Hüter, 1954 (*Unguarded House*, London, 1957)

Das Brot der frühen Jahre, 1955 (*The Bread of our Early Years,*
   London, 1957)
So ward Abend und Morgen, 1956 (*Tomorrow and Yesterday,*
   New York, 1957)
Unberechenbare Gäste, 1956
Im Tal der donnernden Hufe, 1957
Irisches Tagebuch, 1957
Doktor Murkes gesammeltes Schweigen, 1958
Billard um halbzehn, 1959 (*Billard at Half Past Nine,* London,
   1965)
Der Bahnhof von Zimpren, 1959
Ansichten eines Clowns, 1963 (*The Clown,* London, 1965)
Entfernung von der Truppe, 1964 (*Absent without Leave,* Lon-
   don, 1967)
Ende einer Dienstfahrt, 1966

Herbert Heckmann

Translated
by
James Alldridge

HERBERT HECKMANN

THE PHOTOGRAPH

In March 1933, one afternoon at three, an enterprising young man of twenty-seven, whom however everyone would have taken for much younger, entered a house in the Knesebeck-strasse, went up to the first floor, paused for a few moments outside a large, carved door before ringing the bell, and, full of expectation, took a deep breath. A grey-looking woman in a grey dress, her hair combed firmly into a towering bun, opened the door to him and barked at him that she did not want to give anything and that times were bad enough anyhow. In turn the young man smiled and replied that he was not asking for anything, but that he was only the new tutor. Hardly had he said this when the woman threw up her hands and burst out into a laughter which shook her whole body. Her towering bun wobbled.

"What is there to laugh at?" asked the young man, a little uneasy at this kind of reception. "Haven't I come to the right address?"

"Oh, yes, this is the right address, to be sure," she replied, brushing aside a lock of hair from her forehead. "You know," she continued, stepping a little nearer to the young man, as though about to impart a secret which required only a very short distance from mouth to ear. "You know, I think he's mad." She tapped her forehead with her forefinger to indicate the condition of the pupil he had come to see. Saying this, she conducted the young tutor into the parlour, where he was faced with a bewildering choice of old-fashioned chairs to sit down on. He stood there gazing round the room which looked just like a junk shop; he even detected himself hunting out the price tags, and even the cash desk, which would probably look like a cathedral. Suddenly the folding doors were flung open and an elderly man of seventy or so, not a bad looking seventy, with his hair combed like a boy's, entered the room, arms outstretched, his chin almost submerged in an enormous cravat, such as one can see in the yellowing pages of old picture books.

"Ah, there you are at last," he called. "I am so glad you have replied to my advertisement, and have had in addition the courage to afford an old man like me the pleasure of learning once again as a child, no, no—no flattery, I beg you. You *will* allow me to call you 'tutor', won't you?"

The young tutor had expected to find a lad spoiled and pampered by his parents, and determined not to overdo the learning or the pursuit of knowledge. He was so surprised at the real age of his pupil that he forgot to shake the hand held out to him, and only with an effort did he manage to utter a greeting, staring helplessly at the old man dressed in such an old-fashioned way, and who invited him with such an old-fashioned gesture to be seated.

"I thought you would be surprised by my request, but I hope you can overlook my age. Just imagine that you have before you, shall we say, a six-year-old boy, who comes for the first time face to face with a tutor. May I offer you a glass of some refreshment, just to make the start easier." And he filled with trembling slowness a high-stemmed glass and handed it to the young man.

"Children mustn't drink," he said, indicating himself. The tutor did not find it at all easy to overlook the extreme age of his new charge, who, however, seemed to have learnt his part so admirably, that he even pitched his voice high and kept his hands dutifully on his knees, ready to shoot one up in the air when he knew the answer. The young man really didn't know whether he should take part in this game, which was, after all, going to bring him in, as had been agreed in writing, a good fee; nor did he know whether he was dealing with a lunatic, as the woman at the door had seemed to indicate. He was unsure of his ground and really felt quite uneasy, sitting there twiddling his glass around in his hand. "Well," he began hesitantly, "you must understand that I was not quite prepared for you. I want to make it quite clear that you have come as a complete surprise to me. There is so much that one has to take for granted with you that it is quite impossible for me to begin at the very beginning. You must admit that you know more than I do."

"Oh, that is only a polite assumption on your part," his pupil interrupted him. "You must on no account forget that I am probably in a position to pretend as if I know nothing, or at least very little. I can, if necessary, forget everything entirely," he confessed, beaming. "I shall take, with your help, the first tottering steps in the world of the mind. But let's stop this talk, let's get on to first principles, with the one times table and the Ten Commandments and our duty to the sovereign."

"There you are, you see," interjected the young tutor, "you know it all already; you're telling me what to do."

"Oh, I *am* sorry," said his pupil, "I don't want to confuse you. It is true I may know the beginning but I don't know how it goes on."

Still very sceptical, his hands still firmly clenched, trying to be dignified, but hardly daring to show it in front of this so adult pupil, the tutor answered: "Let's try it then, shall we?"

And, at first hesitatingly, then, under the spell of having made a start, he talked more confidently at his pupil, who was a model in his willingness and open-mouthed attentiveness, but was certainly anything but a model of childlike ignorance, so at least the tutor thought. He just could not pluck up courage to enlighten him about his beautifully written "i's", but philosophised extempore about the beginnings of brain work. He never noticed how openly his pupil yawned, poking about with his finger in the stitches of the table-cloth pattern, and made all sorts of other signs of boredom and a complete failure to understand what was being said to him, and finally interrupted this torrent of pedagogic advice with an angry shake of the head.

"No, no, *that's* not how I imagined it. You are philosophising about things which you have hitherto kept back from me. It's about time we got down to the 'i'."

"Have you got a slate?"

"You bet I have." He got up, disappeared for a minute from the room, and came back triumphantly with a slate, from which dangled a sponge and a slate pencil.

"You have thought of everything," sighed the tutor, drinking up his glass, hoping that it was not the only one he was going to be offered, for he could never, while completely sober, play the pedagogue with this old man, scrawling his "i", a thin, pointed, screechy "i", with all the proper loops and hooks, all ready for it to be joined by its neighbours in complete words. All this was quite ridiculous. He fidgeted about uncomfortably in his chair, watching his pupil, trying to discover some hitherto

hidden indication that there was something uncanny about all
this, even though his vis-à-vis looked quite reasonable, almost
worldly-wise, even if in an old-fashioned way. The generous cut
of his jacket was hardly sufficient to conceal his skinniness, while
his face, hollow and ascetic, reminded one of thought-provoking
photos of serious-looking people. No, there could be no doubt
about it, his pupil was deadly serious, from top to toe. His desire
to begin all over again as a learner, from the very beginning,
must have other reasons, quite serious reasons. Mad is a term of
abuse used only by the ignorant. So, without further ado, the
tutor took up the slate pencil and drew carefully with it a letter
"i". It was a squeaky beginning, but a damned good "i", so
much so that the pupil clapped his hands with delight and began
to copy it. He was so clumsy at this, skidded across the slate with
his pencil and used the sponge, so the tutor felt convinced that
this was the first letter "i" he had ever made, his very first.

So there was no question that the child would have to be
helped. When, after an hour, for he believed in being punctual
in these matters, when after an hour he finished the first lesson,
he was thoroughly exhausted—and not a little enraptured by his
pupil's ignorance. Here indeed was a case where help was badly
needed. Only at the door, whither his pupil had escorted him,
was he again reminded of his pupil's real age, when the latter
asked with some pride : "I was quite good for a child, wasn't I ?"

Good? He found it so difficult to manage even the alphabet,
persisted obstinately in improving his calligraphy of some letters,
showing in this a predilection for the "y", that the young tutor
saw himself forced to take sterner measures and gave him imposi-
tions. After the lessons they mostly chatted for a while, more
about childhood memories than about politics, and gradually
his pupil confided more and more in him. "You know," he said
after one particularly strenuous and stumbling lesson, "I hate
the world of the so-called grown-ups. Unhappily no children
were born to me in my marriage, although I really did try, oh,
no, no—it really did give me great pleasure. Just look at this
world."

Early on the tutor had a goodly number of arguments against
this glorification of childhood; he preferred to speak about the
advantages of maturity and tried his utmost to convert his pupil,
he tried to speed up the process of knowledge accumulation,

made his exercises more and more complicated and even sometimes found himself out of his own depth; doubts were raised
in his own mind, his thoughts grew confused, his arguments
dissolved in mere asseverations delivered with a stentorian voice:
"Well, that's all there is about it. Let us say it over again!"

The pupil repeated loudly, but in his mouth it sounded ridiculous and illogical. Once, when the tone of the lesson had
reached almost a roar, pupil and teacher declaiming loudly,
with fists clenched, the woman who had received the young man
at the door, rushed in shouting: "Max, listen to me, you are
driving me mad with all this childishness!"

"These are things which only men understand," answered
Max gruffly, forgetting for the moment his role of pupil, "we
don't want to be disturbed."

"You will see where all this leads to," wailed the woman,
weeping into her handkerchief.

"I know quite well where it will lead to," answered Max,
entirely unimpressed; and, turning to his tutor who was gazing
at the ceiling, he added: "I want it to lead to that."

This was not the only occasion on which the pupil's wife had
been encountered; she obviously listened at the door on every
occasion and witnessed, not without dismay, her husband's
infantile behaviour, a behaviour which removed him more and
more from her loving care. She fought this with all the strength
of her feminine nature, not shrinking back from even the most
drastic measures. Once she disconnected the door bell and on
another occasion she locked her husband in his room. All to no
avail. If she had been a younger woman, she would have packed
her bag; as it was she confined herself to desperate educational
measures, in order to try to preserve her husband as husband
and man.

The young tutor, too, still felt a strong temptation to put an
end to this ridiculous comedy, even if for no other reason that
his fee was doled out to him in a most niggardly fashion; Max
had even once tried to borrow money from him, to say nothing
of small errands he had been asked to run. On the other hand,
and this was the determining factor, he very soon found himself
succumbing to the fascination of a second childhood, and had,
to his horror, to admit that he, yes, even he was beginning to
derive some satisfaction from this game. He experienced great

difficulty in maintaining his role of tutor. If he had been a little more observant he would have noticed the look of triumph in his pupil's eyes. His uncertainty increased almost hourly; he often contradicted himself and, what was even worse, he no longer believed what he himself said. His pupil observed him, gloating openly, deliberately embarrassing him and smiling sphinxlike when he had caught his tutor in a trap. Then suddenly it happened.

One afternoon the tutor confessed to his pupil that he could teach him nothing more, because he himself—he would have found it very embarrassing to have to admit it—well, because he himself knew no more. He stopped and blushed.

"Call me Max," shouted the pupil enthusiastically, jumping up so suddenly that his cravat flopped out of his shirt; he seized his tutor by the hand and led him into the adjoining room which was crammed to the ceiling with toys: children's trumpets, drums, Red Indian feathers, balls, spears, tin armour, dented helmets, as well as flags, books of adventure, badly thumbed maps, a battered globe, a telescope, boxes, cases, top hats and a tricycle. By the window stood a rocking horse, worn to a disgraceful state through overuse.

"This is my kingdom," said the pupil proudly, making his way with difficulty into the middle of the room; and he began to sing, quite oblivious of the fact that his voice did not fit his dress; he skipped and pushed his treasures here and there, objects piled high in wild confusion and showing signs of careless treatment. The frustrated tutor stared around him open-mouthed and did not dare to take even a single step, for fear of getting lost in this labyrinth.

"To celebrate the birth of our friendship, I have thought up something grand," declared Max, rummaging about in a box and drawing out of it some cast-off clothing, holding it up at arm's length, examining it critically and then handing it on to his newly-acquired friend, who, at first hesitantly but gradually enthusiastically, tried on ragged shirts, jackets and trousers, until he managed to struggle into a motheaten sailor-suit. There was even a hat to match.

And with the manner in which he grew accustomed to this suit, however much it made him draw in his manly chest, to all these relics of children's fashions from an age when grandfathers all wore beards, there were associated at the same time long-forgotten aroma-memories of the coquettish strutting of Sunday walks, of days full of liquorice and honey buns, of a contentedly bilious stomach, of games of policemen and robbers ending in a carefree sleep of happy dreams. Max, too, had dressed himself up and had draped himself in threadbare velvet and had crammed a fluffy cap on his head.

Winking, he busied himself with a gigantic camera, resting there malevolently on its stand. He calculated the distance, raised his arm as though in magic rite, having previously set the trigger, and hurried as quickly as his tight trousers would allow, to the side of his quondam tutor, linked arms with him and whispered in a voice quivering with joy: "Now, come on, laugh!"

BIOGRAPHICAL NOTE

Herbert Heckmann. Born 1930 in Frankfurt. Grammar school. Studied literature and philosophy in Frankfurt. Now professor's assistant in Heidelberg. Prizes: Villa Massimo Scholarship, 1958; *Förderungspreis,* Federation of German Industry, 1959; City of Bremen, 1963.

Select Biblography

Das Porträt, 1958
Benjamin und seine Väter, 1962 *(Benjamin and His Fathers,* New York, 1964)

Max Frisch

Translated
by
R. P. Heller

MAX FRISCH

THE ANDORRAN JEW

THERE once lived a young man in Andorra who everybody thought was a Jew. Our story is about his supposed origin, his daily life among the Andorrans who see the Jew in him—it is about the ready-made image which awaits him everywhere. For example, the Andorrans mistrust his feelings, as even they know a Jew cannot have any. He has to rely on his sharp intellect which thereby becomes, of necessity, even more acute. Then there is his attitude towards money, which in Andorra also plays an important role. He knew, he could sense, what they were all thinking although they did not put it into words. He searched his mind to find out whether it was true that he was always thinking of money. He went on delving until he discovered that it was: he did, indeed, think about money, all the time. He admitted it and confirmed it. The Andorrans looked at one another. They said nothing and there was hardly a twitch at the corners of their mouths. As to the Fatherland, too, he knew exactly how their minds worked: whenever he had uttered this word they let it lie like a coin that had dropped in the mud. For to the Jew—and the Andorrans knew this, too—the Fatherland is a country he adopts or buys, not one into which he is born like the rest of us. And where Andorran affairs were concerned, no matter how well-meant his remarks, they would meet silence as if they had fallen on to cotton wool. Later, he realised that he was obviously being tactless. In fact once, when despairing of their attitude he got really heated, the Andorrans bluntly told him so. The Fatherland belonged to the others, and that was that. And they did not expect him to be able to love it. On the contrary, his persistent attempts and wooings merely opened a gulf of suspicion. They thought he was currying favour, seeking advantage, trying to ingratiate himself—doing something they felt to be a means to an end although they themselves could detect no possible purpose. And so it went on, until one day his restless, analytical intellect discovered that he really did not love the Fatherland and that he disliked the very word

191

which caused embarrassment every time he used it. Obviously, they were right. Obviously, he was incapable of love, in the Andorran sense. True, he had a passionate temperament. With it went a cold intellect in which they saw an ever-present secret weapon of his vindictiveness. He was heartless, one could not get through to him; unmistakably, he lacked the warmth of trust. Meeting him was stimulating, perhaps, but not pleasant; it did not make one feel at ease. He did not succeed in being like the others. And having tried in vain to be inconspicuous, he wore his "otherness" with a kind of defiance, pride and furtive hostility which, as it made him feel uneasy himself, he sugared with a fussy politeness. Even when he made a bow it was a kind of reproach as if the world around him ought to be blamed for his being a Jew.

The majority of the Andorrans did nothing to him.

That means nothing good, either.

On the other hand, there were some Andorrans of a more liberal and progressive spirit; a spirit, as they put it, that made them feel committed to humanity. They emphasised that they respected the Jew precisely for his Jewish qualities, his acute brain and so on. They stood by him until his cruel death; so cruel and loathsome was it that it horrified even those Andorrans who had been unmoved by the fact that the whole of life was cruel. Actually, they did not mourn him. And frankly, they did not miss him. They only felt outraged at those who had killed him and at the way in which they had done it—mainly at the way.

They talked about it for a long time.

Until one day something that even the deceased could not have known came to light: he had been a foundling whose parents were discovered much later—an Andorran, just like one of us.

They talked about it no more.

But whenever the Andorrans looked into a mirror they were horrified to see that each one of them bore the features of Judas.

BIOGRAPHICAL NOTE

Max Frisch. Born 1911 in Zurich. Began to study German philology in Zurich, but had to give it up after $3\frac{1}{2}$ years for economic reasons. Travelled as freelance journalist through the Balkans and Greece. At the age of twenty-five began course in architecture at Zurich Technical College. Architectural diploma, 1941. Won first prize in public examination, 1942, and began to practise as an architect. For the next ten years combined the professions of architect and writer. Made many journeys after the war through Germany, Czechoslovakia, Poland, France, Spain and Italy. Then worked as freelance writer in Uetikon, near Zurich. Visited USA and Mexico, 1951–2. Now lives in Zurich and Rome. Prizes: *C. F. Meyer*, 1938; *Wilhelm Raabe*, 1955; *Charles Veillon*, 1958; City of Zurich, 1958; *Georg Büchner*, 1958; Young Generation, 1962; *Nordrhein-Westfalen*, 1962.

Select Bibliography

Die Schwierigen, 1943
Tagebuch 1946–1949, 1950
Graf Oederland, 1951 (play) (*Three plays*, London, 1962)
Stiller, 1954 (*I'm not Stiller*, London, 1961)
Homo Faber, 1957 (*Homo Faber*, London, 1960)
Biedermann und die Brandstifter, 1959 (play) (see: *Graf Oederland; The Firebugs*, New York, 1963)
Andorra, 1961 (play) (see: *Graf Oederland; Andorra*, New York, 1964).
Mein Name sei Gantenbein, 1964 (*Wilderness of Mirrors*, London, 1965)

Hans Werner Richter

Translated
by
I. R. Gibbons

HANS WERNER RICHTER

FOOTSTEPS IN THE SAND

IT was during that spring that my mother tried to carry out her plans for my future career.

"You're going to be a shopkeeper," she said. "You're not exactly the brightest member of the family, but you'll manage that."

It was a lovely spring. I went for a walk with Meta nearly every evening and the number of kisses had risen from one to two. Her lips were still dry and unyielding when I kissed them, but I thought they were the loveliest lips in the world. We used to meet in the twilight at the Schloon Canal, a small canal linking Lake Schloon with the sea, and then we would walk arm in arm along the shore. If anyone came in our direction, we ran quickly in among the sand-dunes or drew back our arms and pretended we had just met by chance on the shore. Under the circumstances I had no desire whatsoever to become a shop-keeper and I told my mother so. She gave me a long, thoughtful look and began to laugh.

"Do you want to keep hanging on to my apron-strings for ever?" she said. "You're grown-up now and you'll have to go out into the world. It would just suit you down to the ground to carry on as you're doing—sledging and playing about and going for walks with Meta every day!"

"I'm going to marry Meta, Mother."

"You're going to do what?"

"Marry Meta."

"When? Right away?"

"Later on, Mother."

"Good gracious," she said, and there was laughter in her eyes, "you just put that idea right out of your head. You'll have forgotten her long before the time comes. You'll have to become a tradesman first and have a shop and be a rich man. How long will it take you to do all that?"

"Not long, if I can marry Meta, Mother."

"Well, if that's the way of it," she said, "we'll go to Wolgast tomorrow. There's a shopkeeper there who is looking for a boy to learn the trade. You ought to make a start right away and not lose any time."

"Yes," I said in a subdued voice and looked into my mother's laughing grey eyes.

"What are you laughing at, Mother? What are you laughing at all the time?"

"It's always a bit comical when somebody grows up," she said. "But don't let that worry you."

Next morning we both got up early and I put on my new Confirmation suit. Max was still in bed; he sat up as I was dressing.

"Well," he said, "so you're going to be a herring-tamer."

"What do you mean—a herring-tamer?"

"Don't you know what a herring-tamer is?"

"No."

"He struggles with herring all day long, from morning till night."

"*I'm* not going to be a herring-tamer!" I said.

"Well, take good care that you don't become one!" he said and crawled under the bedclothes again and turned round, so that I could only see his back and his hind-quarters.

It was still only half light and I began to feel numb with cold. My fate seemed bleak and absolutely hopeless, with the prospect of spending my whole life working with herring till I was a very old man—not even Meta could expect me to do that! I had a rooted aversion to herring because we had to eat them all through the war—boiled, smoked, pickled and salted. There had been a surfeit of herring. So I went over to Max and sat down on the edge of his bed. I was very depressed and began to sob violently.

"What are you crying for? Don't cry, there's a good fellow," said Max.

"What am I to do, Max?"

"How do you mean?"

"I don't want to be a herring-tamer.... They'll just have to deal with their herring alone, without me ... !"

"Well," said Max, "you'll grow ill, very ill. You're not very strong in any case."

"Ill?"

"With a pain in your stomach," said Max. "You'll go running

out to father's privy every five minutes, and every ten minutes you'll clutch your middle and cry out, 'Oh, oh,' and every fifteen minutes you'll turn pale and go as white as a sheet."

"But it's not all that easy, Max. How can I do it?"

"Act the part," said Max. "If you can't act, you'll never become anything at all . . . not even a herring-tamer."

My mother gave a shout from the hall and I rose and went out to her. We gathered our things together and my mother asked: "Have you been crying?"

"No, Mother."

"A big boy like you shouldn't cry. You're going to get married, remember." She looked at me and laughed, but I had the impression that she was laughing *at* me. We walked along under the chestnut-trees on which the buds were already bursting—up to the station. It was my first fairly long journey by train and I would have looked forward to it if I had not been so miserable. I saw my father with "Count Mons" and Wilhelm Voss hauling the herring-nets out of the water and into the boat and the herring, all silver and green, thronging the meshes of the nets in immense shoals. There were so many herring in the world and I felt as if even the train smelt of herring. My mother sat motionless beside me. She had put her arm round my shoulders.

"Where will all this lead to, I wonder," she said. "You never know at the start."

I thought to myself: I am going to be ill, very ill. And suddenly my stomach began rumbling and I was not quite sure if it was my imagination or if it really was my stomach.

"I'm not feeling well, Mother."

"That's a fine beginning, I must say. What's wrong with you?"

"It's my stomach, Mother. I've got a pain in my stomach."

"You can't be ill now—not just now! You'll have to stick it out till we get to Wolgast."

And she pulled me a little closer towards her and my stomach began to settle down again. It had only been a dress rehearsal and I was delighted to find that my stomach had reacted so quickly. When we got out at Wolgast the spring sun was shining and there was a smell of dried fish at the harbour. I sniffed the air, but there was only a faint smell of herring in the midst of all the other fishy smells. We walked over the high old-fashioned cobblestones with which the streets were paved and my mother asked everybody where Mr Hinzpeter the shop-keeper was to be found. Hinzpeter, I thought, how can anyone have a name like Hinzpeter? And my aversion to the whole idea of becoming a shopkeeper grew even stronger. We finally reached Hinzpeter's shop. A bell rang as we opened the shop-door and my mother said :

"Behave yourself properly now—and, if he asks you any-thing, just give him a pleasant nod, that's all. I'll do all the rest."

"Yes, Mother."

"By the way, he's an uncle of Meta's."

"An uncle of Meta's?"

"You're surprised to hear that, aren't you?" she said with a laugh. But I had no time to be surprised for Hinzpeter the shopkeeper was already standing there in front of us. He was fat and wore a grubby white overall and there was a smell in the shop, not of herring, but of paraffin. There was such a terrible smell of paraffin that I held my nose while my mother was speaking to Hinzpeter.

"Why is he holding his nose?" Hinzpeter broke off suddenly and looked at me and my mother turned round too and glared.

"It's only because there's a smell of paraffin," I said.

"There's no smell of paraffin here."

"And there's a smell of Harz Mountain cheese too."

"There could be a smell of cheese," said Hinzpeter and he turned round towards my mother again. They went on speaking for a while and I went on holding my nose. Hinzpeter gave a nod.

"Send him along in a week's time," he said. "He can live and sleep here and I'll attend to everything else."

I will never live and sleep here, I thought. Never! And I went out at the shop-door again behind my mother.

"What a way to behave!" said my mother. "Nobody behaves like that."

"No, Mother, but Hinzpeter really does stink of paraffin."

"You'll just have to get used to it. You'll be smelling it every day of the week from now on. You should be glad that he has taken you on, considering your bad school-report."

But I was not glad. The rumbling in my stomach started up again on the journey back. This time it was louder and more violent and from time to time I held my hands against my stomach and cried, "Oh, oh," as Max had told me to do.

"What *is* the matter with you—what's wrong?"

"It's the smell, Mother. I can't stand the Hinzpeter smell."

"Does it really make you feel ill?"

"Yes, Mother," I whimpered and, without going into the house, I ran straight to the privy as soon as we arrived, then scurried back into the house to my mother, clutched my stomach and ran back again to the privy. My brother Max was standing in the yard and I had to run past him every time.

"That's fine," he said. "And now you'll have to go as white as a sheet."

"Why don't you go white yourself!" I cried. I now felt as if I really was ill: Ill in body and soul, as it said in the song of the "Robber's Bride" that we used to sing in winter as we skated over the ice. I stopped in front of Max, clutched my stomach and cried, "Oh, oh," and Max said:

"You don't need to play a part in front of me, you know."

"But you told me to, didn't you?"

"Of course I did, but you're no good at it. You have to be good at it. Nobody will take you seriously."

Then I saw my mother standing at the open window. The late afternoon sun was shining right into her face. She must have heard everything—everything that Max and I had said. Her hair had been grey at the temples for a long time, but it looked white in the sunshine.

"It's because of the paraffin. He has breathed in too much paraffin, Max," she said, and then she shook her head and added: "And a boy like that wants to get married."

I left Max standing there and ran back into the house. My mother was sitting in the living-room and was folding her head-scarf on her knees. She looked tired. She was sitting on the flower-patterned plush sofa and nodded her head as I went in.

"What was all the acting for?" she said. "Why didn't you tell me straight out?"

"What acting, Mother?"

"You aren't ill at all. You're just pretending, aren't you?"

"Yes, Mother."

"That isn't necessary at all. You can say what you like to me—you know that."

"I don't want to go to Hinzpeter, Mother."

"Well, write to him then and tell him you're ill. Write and tell him yourself," she said and she gave me a smile. It was a gentle, kindly smile.

"But you're not really ill at all, are you?"

"Not really, Mother."

But she laid her work-worn hands on my shoulders and looked me up and down. I felt very small under her scrutiny and I was annoyed with Max.

"Well," she said, "you don't really seem quite yourself. You look quite pale—almost as white as a sheet. I'll put you to bed straight away."

"Yes, Mother," I said, "perhaps that would be best."

And I went to bed feeling fit and happy. My mother piled up a mound of bedclothes over me and I began to sweat terribly.

"You must sweat it out," she said. "That will help you. And I'll give you a little valerian essence as well. It will do you good."

So I lay there perspiring under the pile of blankets and all the herring in the world and all the smells coming from them suddenly did not matter any more. My mother came back out of the kitchen and gave me three spoonfuls of valerian essence. She had added in some castor oil.

"It tastes dreadful, Mother."

"It will do you good," she said. "Nearly everything that does people good tastes dreadful to begin with. And you're a grown man, after all, and you want to get married, don't you?"

"I don't want to get married, Mother. I'm never going to get married—never!"

"Well," she said, "that's a matter needing very careful thought."

During the night I had to go to the privy four or five times. Every time I got up my brother Max called out: "You confounded herring-tamer, you've gone and got dysentery too now."

"What is dysentery?"

"Herring-tamers call it dysentery. They've got a genteel way of expressing things. And you *are* going to be a herring-tamer, after all."

"No, never," I cried. "I'm never going to be a herring-tamer.

And I don't want to be genteel...genteel, oh." And then I had another bout of it and ran out to the privy once more. The next morning my stomach had settled down again and I was sitting, fit and well as ever, at the breakfast-table with my mother. My father had already gone down to the shore to haul in the herring-nets with "Count Mons", and my mother said:

"You went out five times last night. There really was something wrong with you, wasn't there?"

"Yes, Mother."

"You see," she said, "that's just what happens. Don't make believe you've got any illnesses again, or you'll really get them. And there's no need to tell me any more lies. It doesn't do any good."

And I realised then that my mother was more than a match for me. But I had escaped from Hinzpeter the shopkeeper. On my card to him I only put a short sentence which I tried to write in my best handwriting.

"I have become very ill," I wrote, "and am sorry that I canot come."

"Cannot is written with two 'n's'," said my mother when I showed her the card. "Didn't you learn that at school?"

And so I made a mark over the single "n", but a blob of ink fell from my pen and an oddly shaped blot appeared. I did not show my mother the card again, but ran down to the post-office and slipped it into the letter-box.

BIOGRAPHICAL NOTE

Hans Werner Richter. Born 1908 in Bansin, Pomerania. Primary school. Bookseller. In 1946–7, together with Alfred Andersch, edited *Der Ruf.* Founded *Gruppe 47* in September 1947. Lives in Munich.

Select Bibliography

Die Geschlagenen, 1949
Sie fielen aus Gottes Hand, 1951 (*They Fell from God's Hand,*
    London, 1956)
Spuren im Sand, 1953
Du sollst nicht töten, 1954
Bestandsaufnahme, 1962

Martin Walser

Translated
by
Richard Thonger

MARTIN WALSER

I WALKED BEHIND HER

I CHECKED at every step, groping for footholds like a young and inexperienced tight-rope walker, and came into the hall holding my breath, my arms dangling beside me, obedient to the general drift towards the rows of chairs. It was just like walking into the temple of some unfamiliar religion. Everyone present was an initiate as far as I was concerned, and I felt them watching me, perhaps resenting me because I was a new face in the club—or was it a religious splinter group, or a political party, or something worse? Already I was almost ready to be sorry for having the courage to go in at all.

Yes, but what else could I do to try to find the lady who had been walking in front of me along the pavement? My eyes had fastened on the back of her neck, in the cleft between the tendons, the place where her hair began and ran up on top of her head, and I cannot describe how her hair was arranged because I would not take my eyes off that hairline. And as I watched this neck it suddenly turned to the left.

I first truly realised all this when I reached the entrance to the hall and a steward asked me to leave my coat in the cloakroom. Wanting to keep close behind my lady, I said nothing and did as I was told. By now I should have liked to see her face, but when I got inside the hall I could not see her any more. I hoped I would, though, when everyone had sat down.

The sitting down took a long time.

At first no one seemed to want to be the first to sit down. Everyone trotted to and fro, shaking any hands he or she could find to shake, since many of those present seemed to be friends, or at least to be well enough acquainted to clap each other on the shoulder. I had of course not the slightest desire to be the first to sit down, so I trotted as diligently as the others (although far more anxiously) along the rows of chairs and up and down the gangways, still hopeful that I would find the lady on whose account I had ventured inside. Whenever I noticed a woman I slid quickly behind her to examine the back of her neck and her hairline, and every time I was disappointed at the sight of strange necks and unfamiliar hairlines. I saw necks as fat and round as pillars, which had long ago lost that delicate cleft, or indeed perhaps had never had one. And worse, thin and scrawny necks with knife-edge tendons all a-rustle with bristling hairs. Never the neck or the delicate cleft which had drawn me in here. And now the bell was ringing. Feet trotted faster, hands ceased to be shaken, groups broke up, and every person present selected a row of chairs and sank gingerly to a sitting position amid renewed bowing to right and left.

Once more I mustered the assembly, straining my eyes until they burned, then dropped into the nearest available chair and decided to go on looking during the meeting. I had no idea what the meeting was about, but I proposed to make particular use of the interval, if there was one, to carry on my search. Then my head was caught in a general wave of attention down the rows of chairs and towards the front part of the hall, where I noticed a curtained platform. The curtain moved, divided in two and released a gentleman.

The gentleman walked to a lectern at the edge of the platform : after which the proceedings no longer interested me, and I diverted my attention once more towards the rows of chairs.

I heard someone making a speech. It would be the gentleman who had just gone up to the lectern. I looked for the lady. The gentleman went on speaking, but I ran my eyes round the hall like searchlights, hardly moving my head at all to avoid betraying to those about me how very little the speaker occupied my attention.

Now and again I thought someone had noticed I was not listening : each time I froze completely for a few seconds, in a cold sweat for fear of a public reproof; and then resolved to stop looking and to wait for the interval, but immediately feared that there might not be an interval, so that I must do my looking now—and I went on looking. I do not know how long the speaker went on; I do not know how many speakers followed each other.

Once or twice the audience applauded, for which I was most grateful. It was an opportunity for me to look more quickly about me, to search more intensively. I clapped too, more than anyone else, looked eagerly about me, pretended I was trying to catch someone's eye and nod to him as though to say how pleased we were to have the privilege of hearing speeches like this. However, though the clapping often lasted some time and I even jumped up and gazed confidently about the hall as though encouraging all present to clap louder still, I simply could not discover that particular woman. By now, though, I was shackled to the back of that particular neck, and anyone who has had a similar experience will know that at the end of the meeting I was in no mood for the cold comfort, shall we say, of leaving it to chance whether I ever managed to come near the owner of the neck again. And if Chance doesn't want it to happen, I thought—no, no, I can't take such an easy way out. I asked a steward when another meeting would be taking place, and he said if the Association interested me he would see that I was invited to all its meetings.

I gave him my address and also a tip, much larger than my circumstances justified. I was immensely happy. Evidently this was a proper Association, and its meetings were nearly always attended by members only. So She was probably a member, and therefore I would very almost certainly come across her. I rejoiced several days later when the first invitation arrived, and with it, oh joy, an application form which I merely needed to fill in to become a member. I was not able to read the Association's articles, so strong was my emotion at the thought of belonging to an Association of which She was a member. I was a little depressed as I left the second meeting without having seen her, but reflected immediately that there was no reason for this. How could I ever have hoped that mere chance would have found me a chair from which I could have perceived the back of her neck? I must pursue my search systematically. The fact that the Association guaranteed an abundant programme of events stretching years ahead made my task all the simpler. I looked up all the women in the membership list. The first step was to procure an introduction to each of these lady members, which seemed a laborious task calling for great skill. It would not suffice just to murmur my name shamefacedly to the lady in question, nor to stare her in the face for so long as was proper and possible : I had to slide behind her only just after looking at her face in order to check her hairline and the cleft at the back of her neck. Up to this time I had been a man who spoke in single syllables; but the task of publicly staring at the backs of so many female necks and comparing them with the picture treasured in my memory—this task, which I had to accomplish evening after evening within the limits of good manners and propriety—changed me from a one-syllable man into a glib conversationalist.

Nevertheless, although I was thus busily scheming throughout numerous meetings, nothing could prevent the uninterrupted succession of speeches from penetrating into my ears, more or less collaterally and against my will, and settling and spreading in my subconscious mind. Without my ever having a clearminded grasp of my Association's aims and objects, after a few years I had quite a few details in my head. They were mere scraps out of many speeches, probably always the places where the speaker's voice was loudest, but if anyone asked me a question I was able to answer like an intelligently dedicated member, using the literal words of these fragments dredged out of my subconscious. Nor is there anything to prevent a reasonably intelligent person from establishing reasoned connections between this type of involuntarily recuperated fragments. I may safely say that I never consciously established any such connections, being far too preoccupied with the search for my lady.

True, even the search itself began, in time, to run on its own. Without needing to prompt myself I would procure introductions, evening after evening, to female members from the apparently inexhaustible supply, and without really knowing what I was doing I would immediately slip behind each lady in turn. Gradually I no longer felt disappointed when I failed to discover the hairline I was seeking. All that remained of any importance was the task of ticking off one more name on the list of lady members to indicate that this one had been checked. One or two members may perhaps have spotted my urge to be introduced to all the ladies, and may well have smiled at my mania for staring closely at the ladies' backs, but they left me to it, and that was enough to fill me with genuine gratitude towards the Association. And if anyone approaches me and goes so far as to ask me to make a speech or to read a paper, I will do so, even though I do not really care.

I might have considered resigning after years of work had substantially reduced the number of ladies still unchecked, but

I just could not do this. I slowed down the pace, using every
fifth meeting, and then only every tenth, for my research work.
I was filled with surprise at being able to get through meetings
without embarking on my own plans, and later I even resolved
to abstain from checking all the ladies and to shelve my own
research work completely. The lady I was seeking might well
have resigned, might have changed her hair-style or even the
colour of her hair, or the back of her neck might have fattened,
for all I cared: all this had been covered over by the speeches
of innumerable Association evenings, silted up beneath the tidal
sand of imperceptible words. And today I have advanced so far
that I need an effort to remember the times when I used Association evenings for intimate personal business. When I think
about it I feel ashamed, and a bad conscience brings a blush to
my temples.

I draw comfort from the thought that my lapses from grace
belong to a closely guarded past. Sometimes I catch myself slipping behind the shoulders of a lady to whom I have just been
introduced, dropping some gentle excuse from my lips to justify
the urge to get behind her during the conversation; but I always
check myself in time, murmur an apology and feign absent-
mindedness for a second before bracing myself into sharp attentiveness and staring her squarely in the face. These attacks disturb me no longer. They are gradually decreasing, and even when
they occur are easily overcome; they are comparatively pointless,
and only subsequent thought will reveal them to be scraps from
my former life.

The thing, however, which comforts me most about this
former life of mine is the benefit which I believe my experience
to have brought to the Association. Once, you see, we had to
vote on the question whether non-members should be admitted
to meetings or not. Several of our number spoke in favour of
strict controls at the entrances to the hall to prevent strangers
from enjoying the benefits of a meeting. I spoke against this
view, and on this occasion made the only speech of my career
in the Association. Our doors should stay wide open, I declared,
whoever might wander in from the street and whatever their
intentions might be. The Association, I said, should have
strength enough to absorb any such outsiders. I mentioned the
"strong encircling arms of our Association" and earned pro-

longed applause. As a result of my speech, the doors stayed open, and they will do so in future. May I not take pride in this? How else, indeed, would we ever get any new members?

BIOGRAPHICAL NOTE

Martin Walser. Born at Wasserburg, Lake Constance, in 1927. Joined the army in 1944. Studied history of literature, philology and history at Regensburg and Tübingen from 1946 to 1951, choosing Kafka as the subject of his doctorate thesis. His first publication appeared in 1949. Walser has been a radio and TV director, and since 1957 has worked as a freelance writer in Friedrichshafen. Prizes: *Gruppe 47*; *Hermann Hesse*, 1957; *Gerhart Hauptmann*, 1962.

Select Bibliography

Ehen in Philippsburg, 1957 (*The Gadarene Club*, London, 1960)
Halbzeit, 1960
Der Abstecher, 1961 (play) (*The Rabbit Race and the Detour*, London, 1963)
Eiche und Angora, 1962 (play) (see: *Der Abstecher*)
Lügengeschichten, 1964
Das Einhorn, 1966

Peter Weiss

Translated by
by
Christopher Middleton

MY PLACE

WHEN I started wondering what human habitation or what landscape would be best suited to be described as my place, many possibilities occurred to me. But, from the place where I was born, which is called Novaves and which according to the guidebooks lies next to Potsdam on the railway line to Berlin, and passing over the cities of Bremen and Berlin where I spent my childhood, to the cities of London, Prague, Zürich, Stockholm, Paris, to which I drifted later, all my stopping places have had something provisional about them, as well as all the shorter stops in between, little places I have not mentioned, Warnsdorf in Bohemia, or Montagnola in the Tessin, or Alingsas in West Sweden.

They were points of transit, they offered impressions whose essence could not be held steady, was always vanishing, and when I inquire what there is about them that can now be stressed and found valuable, to give a firm position in the topography of my life, I keep on coming up against what keeps retreating from me, all those cities become blurs, and only one place, where I spent only one day, remains constant.

The cities in which I lived, in whose houses I stayed, on whose streets I walked, with whose inhabitants I spoke, have no definite contours, they merge into one another, they are parts of a single perpetually changing earthly outside world, have a harbour to show in one place, a park in another, in one a work of art, in one a fair, a room in one, in another a gateway, they are available in the wandering design of my travels, they are reached and left again in a fraction of a second and their qualities have each time to be invented anew.

Only this one place, of which I had known for a long time, but which I saw so much later, is separate and special. It is a place for which I was destined but which I managed to avoid. I have had no experience of this place. I have no relation to it, except that my name was on the lists of the people who were supposed to be sent there for ever. Twenty years later, I saw this place. It is unchangeable. Its buildings cannot be mistaken for buildings anywhere else.

It, too, has a Polish name, like my birthplace which someone showed me once from the window of a moving train. It is located in a region where my father, just before I was born, fought for a fabulous imperial army. The place is dominated by the surviving barracks of this army.

It was given a German name so that people would better understand those who worked and lived there.

The goods trains are clanking by in Auschwitz railway station. Whistling of locomotives and smoke tumbling. Clashing sounds of buffers. The air full of the vapour of rain, the footpaths, softened, the trees leafless and wet. Soot-blackened factories, surrounded by barbed wire and walls. Wooden carts grind past, pulled by thin horses, the peasant who drives them heavily muffled, earth-colour. Old women on the footpaths, wrapped in blankets, carrying bundles. Farther off in the fields a few farms, bushes and poplars. Everything gloomy and worn. Ceaselessly the trains on the embankment slowly rolling back and forth, small wagon windows with gratings. Sidings lead away to the barracks and farther still across empty fields to the end of the world.

Outside the hut area, reoccupied since the evacuation and looking as if the war had only just ended, iron railings rise up in front of the building which is now called a museum. Cars and buses stand in the parking lot, a group of school children is just going through the gate, a troop of soldiers in wine-red caps is returning from a tour of inspection. To the left, a long wooden barrack. A little window for the sale of brochures and postcards. Over-heated attendants' rooms. Immediately behind the barrack, low concrete walls, over them a grassy slope, ascending to the flat roof with the short thick square chimney. My cap of the camp told me that I was already standing in front of the crematory, the small crematory, the first crematory, the crematory with the limited capacity. The barrack straight ahead—that was the barrack of the political section, there the registry was located, in which lists of arrivals and departures were drawn up, that is where the female clerks sat, that is where people wearing the death's-head emblem walked in and out.

I came here of my own free will. I was not unloaded from a train. I was not bludgeoned into this place. I have arrived twenty years too late.

Iron grids around the little windows of the crematory. To the side, a heavy decayed door, hanging crooked from its hinges, clammy cold inside. Crumbling stone floor. In a room immediately to the right, a large iron furnace. Rails in front of it, on these a metal vehicle shaped like a trough, the length of a human body. Inside the cellar two more furnaces, with the death-trucks on the rails, the furnace doors wide open, grey dust inside, on one of the trucks a bunch of dry flowers.

Thoughts, none. No impressions, except that I am alone here, that it is cold, that the furnaces are cold, the rigidity and rustiness of the trucks. Moisture drips from the black walls. Over there, an open doorway. It leads to the next room. A long room, I pace it out, twenty paces in length. Five paces wide. The walls whitewashed and peeling. The concrete floor worn, with hollows, many puddles; in the ceiling between the massive beams four square lidded apertures running like shafts through the thick stone casting. Cold. Breath at my mouth. Voices far off outside. Footsteps. I walk slowly through this grave. Feel nothing. See only this floor, these walls. Realise : through the apertures in the ceiling they threw the gritty preparation which in the damp air disseminated its gas. At the end of the room a door with iron fittings and a peephole, beyond it a narrow stairway, which leads into the open air. The open air.

There a gallows stands. A huge box of planks with openings that have collapsed inward, surmounted by the post with its beam protruding at a right angle. A notice says that the camp commandant was hanged here. As he stood on the box, the rope around his neck, he saw beyond the double fence of barbed wire the main street of the camp, with the poplars lining it. I walk up the slope on to the roof of the crematory. The wooden lids with the tar-board nailed over them can be lifted off the insertion holes. Down below is the dungeon. Medical orderlies with gas-masks opened the green cans, sprinkled the contents down on the faces as they gazed upward, quickly put the lids back on again.

On. I am still outside the camp, the gallows stands on the foundation walls of the interrogation barracks, in which there was a room containing a wooden frame with an iron tube above it. They used to hang from the iron tube and were swung back and forth and were beaten with the horsewhip.

The staff buildings stand close together, the administration, the commandant's building, the guard house. Tall windows overlook the crematory. Everywhere a view over the flat roof on to which the medical orderlies climbed. Very close, the barrack windows through which could be heard the beatings and screams from the swinging-room.

Everything close, tightly packed. Past the double row of concrete pillars which carry the barbed wire. Insulators on the wire; signs with the inscription VORSICHT HOCHSPANNUNG. To the right, sheds and buildings like stables, a few watch-towers; to the left, a booth with a sliding window and a shelf under the roof-overhang, for the stamping of documents, then suddenly a gate with the cast-iron curved strip of lettering in which the middle word MACHT tops the arch. A red and white striped barrier-pole is raised, I enter the square that is called the parent camp, *Stammlager*.

Have read and heard much about this. About the people who marched to work here in the early mornings, into the gravelpits, to road-construction sites, to the factories of the masters, and returned in the evenings carrying their dead, to the sound of an orchestra playing under the trees there. What does this mean, what do I know of it all? Now I only know how these paths look, lined with poplars, dead straight, with side-paths crossing them at right angles, between them the symmetrical 40-metres long two-storey blocks numbered 1 to 28. A small imprisoned town, with an order imposed by force, completely isolated. Here and there a visitor in the watery mist, looking up distantly at the houses. Far off, at a corner, the children passing by, led by their teacher.

Here are the kitchens on the main square, and in front of them a wooden sentry-box, with a high pointed roof and a weather-vane, with gaily painted stone dovetailing, like a tiny fort from a child's box of building bricks. It is the orderly officer's hut, from which the parades were supervised. I once knew about these parades, about these hours of standing in rain and snow. Now I only know about this deserted loamy square, at the centre of which three posts supporting an iron rail are

rammed into the ground. I know also how they stood here under
the rail on stools, and how the stools were then knocked away
from underneath them, and how the men with the death's-head
caps hung on to their legs, to break their necks. Hearing and
reading about it, I had seen it in front of me. Now I do not see
it any more.

Above all, the impression that everything is smaller than I
had imagined. From every point the boundary fence can be
seen, the light-grey wall of concrete blocks beyond the barbed
wire surround. At the outer right-hand corner of Blocks 10 and
11, connected by walls, the open wooden door in the centre,
leading to the courtyard with the Black Wall.

This Black Wall, at whose edges short bits of planking jut
forward to catch the bullets, is now disguised with cork slabs and
wreaths. Forty paces from the gate to the wall. Pieces of tiling
stamped into the sand floor. Along the damp-proofing of the
left-hand building, whose windows are boarded over, runs the
gutter where the blood gathered from the heaps of people who
had been shot. They came running, naked, turning right at the
doorway, down the six steps, two at a time, their arms held by
the corporals. And behind the nailed-up windows of the building
opposite, lay the women whose wombs were filled with a white
cement-like mass. This is where the Block 11 washroom is
located. Here the people who had to go to the wall took off their
pitiful blue-striped clothes, here in this small dirty room, its
lower half daubed with tar, its upper half with whitewash, full
of rusty and blackish marks and stains, with a metal washing
trough around it, run through with black pipes, crossed with the
tubing of a shower, here they stood, with their numbers inked
on to their ribs.

This is the washroom, this the stone corridor, divided up by
iron gratings, first the block-leader's room, with the desk, camp-
bed and cupboards, on the wall the motto EIN VOLK EIN REICH
EIN FUHRER, a wire grating over the doorway, like looking into
a display cabinet. A panopticon, too, the courtroom opposite,
with the long council-table, the minute-books on the grey cloth,
for now and then the sentences of death were also pronounced,
by men who now live honest lives and enjoy social respect.

Now the stairway leading to the bunkers. They have taken
the trouble to touch up the walls with a fringe of glimmering

marble. The centre corridor, and to the right and left the side-corridors with the cells, about 3 by 2½ metres, with a bucket in a wooden box and a tiny window. Some, too, without a window, with only an air-hole in a top corner. There were up to forty people in here, they fought for a space by the door, tore off their clothes, collapsed. There were some who were still alive after a week without food. There were some whose thighs bore the marks of teeth, whose fingers were bitten off by the time they were dragged out.

I look into these places, which I myself eluded, stand between the fossil walls, hear no stamping of bootsoles, no shouts of command, no groaning and whimpering.

Here, off this narrow hallway, are the four standing-cells. Over there, is the opening by the floor, a half-metre square, iron bars inside it still, they crawled in there and stood four together, in a shaft measuring 90 by 90 centimetres. Above, the air-hole, smaller than the palm of a hand. Stood there for five nights, ten nights, two weeks every night after the heavy toil of the day.

Against the outside wall of the block there are concrete boxes, each with a small perforated metal lid. From here the air passes through the long wall-shaft into the cells in which they stood, their backs, knees, pressing on stone. They died standing, had to be scraped out down below when the morning came.

I had been walking around in the camp for hours now. I know my way. I have stood in the courtyard by the Black Wall. I have seen the trees behind the wall and have not heard the small-arms shots fired point blank in the back of the head. I have seen the beam from which they were hung by the hands that were tied behind their backs, only a foot above the floor. I have seen the rooms with the covered windows, in which women had their ovaries burned away by X-rays. I have seen the corridor in which they all stood, tens of thousands, and slowly moved into the doctor's room, and were led, one after another, behind the grey-green curtain, where they were forced on to a stool and had to raise the left arm and take an injection into the heart, and through the window I saw the courtyard outside where the one hundred and nineteen children from Zamosc waited and went on playing ball until their turn came.

I have seen the drawing on the kitchen-building roof, on which were painted in big letters the words: There is a way to freedom—its milestones are OBEDIENCE, INDUSTRIOUSNESS, CLEANLINESS, HONESTY, SINCERITY, SOBRIETY, and LOVE OF THE FATHERLAND. I have seen the mountain of shorn-off hair in a display cabinet. I have seen the relics of children's clothes, the shoes, the toothbrushes, the dentures. It was all cold and dead.

There is constantly the clanking and rumbling of the goods trains, puffing from the locomotives' funnels, the long-drawn-out whistlings. Trains move towards Birkenau through the broad flat landscape. Here, where the loamy path ascends to the railway embankment, and crosses it, the masters stood with outstretched hands and pointed to the open fields and decided on the foundation of the place of banishment which is now subsiding again into the marshy ground.

A single track deviates from the main one. Runs across the grass, is broken here and there, to a faded long building far off, to a barn with a collapsed roof, a crumbling tower, and runs straight through the arched barn door.

Whereas in the other camp everything was narrow and close, here everything is endless expanse, cannot be surveyed.

To the right, as far as the strips of woodland, the countless chimneys of dismantled and burned-out barracks. Only a few rows of these sties for hundreds of thousands are still standing. To the left, in line and vanishing into the haze, the stone buildings for the women prisoners. In the middle, more than a kilometres in length, the ramp. The principle of order and symmetry is detectable even in decay. Beyond the barn door, at the points, the rail divides to right and left, grass is growing between the sleepers, grass is growing from the macadam of the ramp which hardly rises above the level of the rails. It was a considerable way up to the opened doors of the goods trucks. They had to jump one and a half metres down on to the sharp-edged stones, throwing down their luggage, and their dead. To the right went the men who were allowed to live a bit longer, to the left the women who were judged still fit for work, straight ahead for the old and the sick and the children lay the way that led to the two smoking chimneys.

The sun, near the horizon, breaks from the clouds and is reflected in the windows of the watch-towers. To right and left at the end of the ramp lie clumps of ruins among trees, the poplars by the fencing behind are motionless, far off in a farmyard some geese are cackling. To the right, that is the little birch forest. I see before me the women and children who are waiting there, a woman carries her baby at her breast, and in the background a group is moving towards the underground chambers. In the gigantic heap of stones, with its bent iron girders and collapsed concrete roof, one can still make out the architecture. Here a narrow staircase leads down into the hall-way which is about 40 metres long, where the benches were, and numbered hooks in the wall for hanging up shoes and clothes. Here they stood naked, men, women and children, and they were told to remember their numbers, so that they would find their clothes again after the shower.

These long stone trenches, through which millions of people were sluiced into the rooms going off at right angles, with the holed metal columns, and were then brought up to the furnaces, to be scattered across the surrounding landscape as brown sweetish reeking smoke. These stone trenches, to which steps descend, worn smooth by millions of feet, empty now, returning again to sand and earth, lying peacefully under the setting sun.

This is where they walked, in the slow procession, coming from all parts of Europe, this is the horizon which they still saw, these are the poplars, these the watch-towers, with the sun reflected in the window-panes, this is the door, through which they went into the rooms that were bathed in glaring light, and in which there were no showers, only these squared metal columns, these are the foundation walls between which they died in the sudden darkness, in the gas which streamed out of the holes. And these words, this knowledge, they tell nothing, explain nothing. Only heaps of stone remain, overgrown with grass. Ashes remain in the earth, ashes of those who died for nothing, who were torn from their homes, their shops, their workshops, away from their children, their wives, husbands, lovers, away from all everyday things, and flung into something incomprehensible. Nothing is left but the total meaningless of their death.

Voices. A bus has driven up, and children climb out of it. The class is now inspecting the ruins. For a while the children listen to the teacher, then they clamber around on the stones, some are already jumping down, they laugh and chase one another, a girl is running down a long cutting which passes beside the remnants of rails across a patch of concrete. This was the slide along which the dead bodies slid to the trucks. Looking back as I walk towards the women's camp, I can still see the children among the trees and hear the teacher clapping his hands to assemble them.

Just as the sun is setting, the ground-mists rise and coil around the low barracks. The doors are open. I walk in, somewhere. And now it is like this: here the breathing, the whispering and rustling is still not covered up by the stillness, these bunks, in three layers, along the side-walls and in the middle, not yet quite deserted, here is the straw, in the heavy shadows, the thousands of bodies can still be sensed, far down, at floor-level, on the planks, in the roofing bays, between the brick supporting walls, packed close together, six in each pit, here the outside world has not quite penetrated, here you can still expect some movement inside, the raising of a head, a hand stretching out.

Yet after a while everything is silent and unmoving even here. A living man has come and what happened here hides itself from him. The living man who comes here, from another world, has nothing but his knowledge of figures, written reports, statements by witnesses; it lies heavy upon him, but he can only grasp what he experiences himself. Only when he himself is dragged away from his table and manacled and kicked and beaten does he know what this is. Only when, beside him, they are herding people together and knocking them down, loading them into wagons, does he know how this is.

Now he is only standing in a vanished world. Here there is nothing more for him to do. For a while everything is utterly still.

Then he knows that it has not ended yet.

BIOGRAPHICAL NOTE

Peter Weiss. Born 1916 in Nowawes, near Berlin. Emigrated to England, 1934. Lived in Czechoslovakia, 1936–8; in Switzerland 1938–9. Has lived in Sweden since 1939—since 1945 as a Swedish citizen. *Charles Veillon* award, 1963.

Select Bibliography
Fluchtpunkt, 1962

Abschied von den Eltern, 1961

Die Ermittlung, 1965 (oratorio). (*The Investigation,* London, 1966)

Die Verfolgung und Ermordung Jean Paul Marats, 1964 (*The Persecution and Assassination of Marat, etc.,* London, 1965)